AF489865

10 "DERANGED" TALES...

of MYSTERY

HORROR & FANTASY

10 "DERANGED" TALES...

of MYSTERY

HORROR & FANTASY

Gianis Athanasiou Totonidis

*To those denounced by Life as Dwarves
but turned instead into **Giants**....*

Introduction (rather than prologue)

Ten is the basis of the decimal number system.

The digits of the number *Ten* (0,1) are the basis of the binary number system used in computer science.

Ten is the maximum number of electrons in d atomic orbitals.

There are *Ten* dimensions of space time, according to various superstring theories.

Ten is the number of commandments (Decalogue) given to Moses by God on Mount Sinai, according to the Bible.

Ten is the number of plagues sent by God to the Pharaoh of Egypt compelling him to liberate the Israelites from Egyptian rule.

Ten is the sum of two other divine numbers: Seven (the number of days taken to create the earth) and Three (Father, Son and Holy Spirit).

Ten is the number of human fingers and toes.

'10' is the title of the film by one of the greatest underrated directors, the American Blake Edwards, and *Ten* is the title of a documentary by the Iranian director Abbas Kiarostami.

Ten is the number of years it took to complete this work.

Ten, therefore, is the number of short stories I have chosen to introduce my collection of narratives in the Mystery, Horror and Fantasy genres for my debut as a writer.

CONTENTS

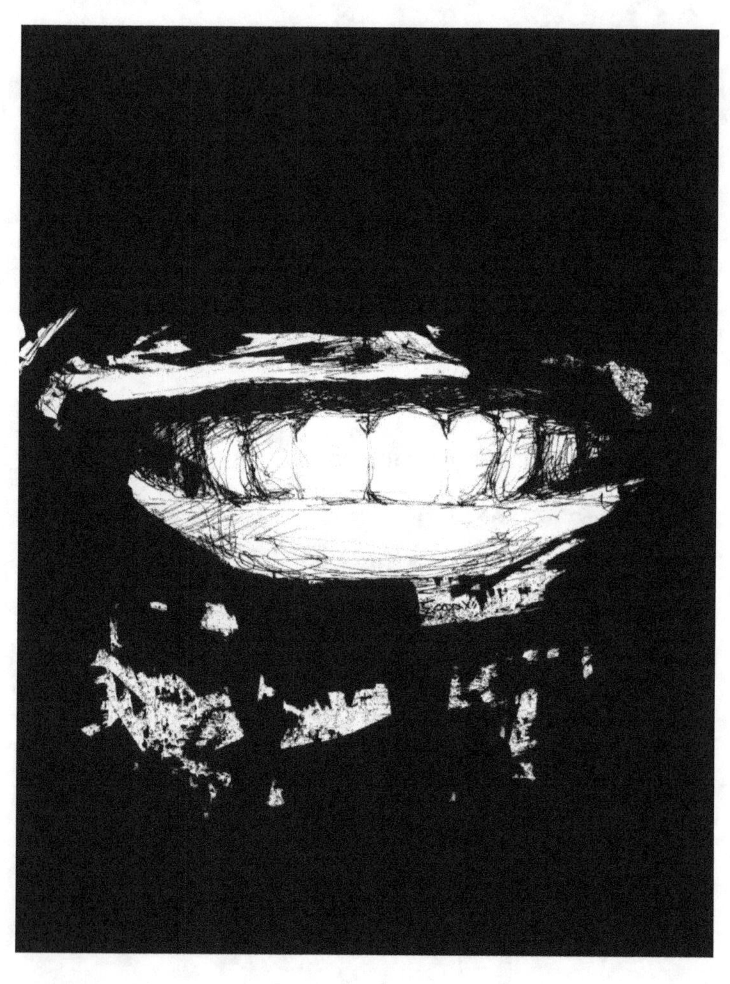

«Never trust a person who smiles at you!
Especially if he looks pleasant, polite, humorous,

1. CTHULHU FHTAGN

*'The oldest and strongest emotion of mankind is fear,
and the oldest and strongest kind of fear
is fear of the unknown.'*
H. P. Lovecraft

"Quick, Tommy, run!"

The shrillness of her voice cut through the casual silence of the night. A misty, damp, cold night. Street lamps and local premises cast vague shadows of the forgotten passers-by; any other light was distorted by the fog. The soles of his shoes rattled like machine-gun fire on the paved street as he frantically took off. A shot rang out, almost simultaneously. Without losing speed, he turned and saw his mother drop dead. It was like a dream. A man stood over her, glanced momentarily, then he and his comrade chased after him. He was much younger but they were much quicker and would easily catch up with him. They'd get him in no time.

He caught sight of a bus as he turned the corner of the street. Hope of salvation grew. He didn't care where it was heading. Without delay, he ran as fast as he could in the hope of catching it. Seconds before the doors closed, he jumped on, out of breath. Out of the back window he watched as the two men came to a halt, momentarily defeated, before running off in the opposite direction. There was no room for doubt. They would jump into a car and chase after him, more furious than ever. It would be impossible to escape them wherever he went. The bus would stop frequently and they'd follow close behind until it reached the terminal. Sooner or later, he'd fall victim to them. Unless…

A clever idea gave him renewed hope of escape. He calculated the time it would take the persecutors to reach their car, start the engine and drive off in pursuit of him. Meanwhile, the bus would be getting further and further away. If he got off at the first stop, they probably wouldn't be close enough behind to notice he was gone, and thinking he was still on the bus, would lose track of him. He looked out through the back window again. There were no cars in sight.

He jumped off the bus and hid in the first side street he came to. There was no point in running; it would give away he was being chased. He'd walked some distance when he noticed a car turning into the same side street. Had they anticipated his move? He looked around. Semi-darkness, rubbish and a wall. No door, no alcove where he could hide. He took off again intent on diving into the first alleyway he came to. Unexpectedly, after turning the corner, he found himself in a dead end street. He stared at the statuette in his hand.

"If what they say is true, and you've got the power, do something to save me," he said, fixing his eyes on it.

That was stupid, he thought and prepared for a fatal outcome. The sound of car tires grew louder. They were getting closer. Before long, it would all be over. Just then, out of the corner of his eye, he caught sight of a round, metal manhole. A sewer! Without a second thought, he hurriedly lifted it and jumped down the hole, replacing the manhole cover on top of him. Shortly afterwards, the front wheel of the car was directly overhead. He listened as the car doors opened, the men cursed and the doors closed again. The sound of the engine faded, signalling they had driven off. He stayed underground for five more minutes, and after making sure there was no one around, he lifted the manhole cover and carefully climbed out. He stood up and replaced the cover. A hand tapped him on the shoulder. His heart raced. He turned around, terrified. He was relieved to discover a drunk staggering about.

"Hey, you – hic – do you know where – hic – the *Green Parrot* is?" he asked. The stench of alcohol escaped from his mouth.

"The green parrot? I haven't seen any parrots around here, Mister," replied the boy, somewhat confused. He was still recovering from his ordeal.

"No – hic. It's not a patto…parro… - hic – bird. It's a pub."

"No, I don't know. I don't come from around here."

He walked on, giving him a wide berth. He suddenly got an overwhelming urge for a shot of brandy. Maybe the drunk was to blame. He was frozen to the bone and at times like this, his mother would give him a sip of brandy to warm him up.

He went into the first pub he came to, ordered a brandy and thought things through from the beginning. Fearing for his life overshadowed the sorrow of losing his mother. He looked at the statuette. He didn't know much about it, just that he had to protect it from the hands of the police. He was to deliver it to a house; he had learned the address by heart. His mother, perceptive of imminent danger, had made sure he was aware the object was sacred. It was meant for someone with supernatural powers, with whose help a soul, trapped in the depths of the earth or the ocean for thousands of years, would be released. For some, it might have been a very precious object. He, however, hated the sight of it. It had caused his mother's death and immediately threatened his own life.

The clock on the wall said six-thirty. The stores in town were still open. There would be little traffic on the streets and that would assist his getaway. He hastily paid the barman; he'd been giving him suspicious looks and was relieved to see him go – he knew he was underage. Police patrols were common and punishment for offenders strict. If he'd known the boy was just sixteen years old, he'd have thrown him out for sure.

He casually walked down a narrow street that led to the main road, confident he had managed to escape.

"That's him!" A voice cried out behind him. He turned around, saw the persecutors and fled in haste. This time, they looked well-organised and more resolute. As he reached the end of the street, just as he was about to turn onto the central avenue and get lost in the crowd, a shot was fired. The bullet got him in the back. It was a burning sensation, then pain seeped in and everything went black. He gritted his teeth and slowly walked on. As he turned onto the main road, he collapsed.

I bent over him, sad to see him that way. He looked me in the eye, stretched out the hand holding the statue and mumbled weakly. "Don't let them get hold of it… hide…they're coming…"

The young boy was dying at my feet, and whoever he was, whatever he had done, I felt sorry for him. A wave of compassion pooling inside me washed to the surface. It was weird. I offered to take him to the hospital. He stared at me, his eyes wide-open with fright.

"Hide…" he repeated loudly, in the throes of death.

I was baffled. The only thing that made sense was that I was to get away and hide as soon as possible. The statue had made me someone's target. There was no time to find out more. I closed his eyes with the palm of my hand and dived into a shop. It sold antiques. Strangely, something weird had driven me to that side of town. A voice insisted I go to an old curiosity shop and look for an unusual item. It would get me out of a rut, fire my imagination, heaving it towards inspiration. I hadn't written for a long time. My friends thought I was finished. On the contrary, I couldn't find anything suitable to write about. Occasional ideas seemed cheap, ridiculous. But yeah, maybe that would change now.

I pretended to browse at various objects and looked out through the store window. The two men had turned the dead boy onto his back and were searching for something – probably the statuette. Their search was fruitless. They questioned passers-by but no one knew or realised what had taken place. It had all happened so quickly. Thinking they had lost the game, they skulked off. I watched until they disappeared at the end of the road. Making sure no one saw me, I dashed home, desperate to get a better look at the mysterious object. When I got there, I locked all the doors and shone a light on the statuette.

The figure was between seven and eight inches in height, and of exquisitely artistic workmanship. It represented a monster of vaguely anthropoid outline, but with an octopus-like head whose face was a mass of feelers, a scaly, rubbery-looking body, prodigious claws on hind and fore feet, and long, narrow wings behind. This thing, which seemed instinct with a fearsome and unnatural malignancy, was of a somewhat bloated corpulence, and squatted evilly on a rectangular block or pedestal covered with undecipherable characters. The tips of the wings touched the back edge of the block, the seat occupied the centre, whilst the long, curved claws of the doubled-up, crouching hind legs gripped the front edge and extended a quarter of the way down toward the bottom of the pedestal.

The cephalopod head was bent forward, so that the ends of the facial feelers brushed the backs of huge fore paws which clasped the croucher's elevated knees. The aspect of the whole was abnormally life-like, and the more subtly fearful because its source was so totally unknown. Its vast, awesome, and incalculable age was unmistakable; yet not one link did it shew with any known type of art belonging to civilisation's youth —or indeed to any other time.

From that evening onward, I frantically searched for information that would enlighten me about the strange object that had fallen into my hands. I looked in the library, quizzed colleagues, without admitting the statue was in my possession – I told them I'd seen a picture of it – and talked to archaeologists, none of whom knew the slightest thing about it. All I got was suspicious looks. They probably assumed opium was to blame or thought I was on the verge of a nervous breakdown. Admittedly, opium had been a loyal friend in times of need. Everyone knew that. Tales of nights of frenzied revelry, where opium was more plentiful than the drink and the women, were not uncommon.

In the end, I was incredibly lucky. Someone introduced me to a Professor of Archaeology – Dr Howard Phillips Lovecraft. They said he specialised in ancient cultures and had travelled the world researching them. A tidal wave of enthusiasm came over me. Before long, I visited his home. From the start, I was able to convince him of my fiery interest in his branch of science. The Professor was a distinguished authority on ancient inscriptions, well-versed in Semitic languages and was often approached by curators of large museums in various parts of the world. An intelligent man, he soon recognised I was looking for specific, rare and inaccessible information, and from a particular standpoint. I wouldn't have bothered him otherwise.

I admitted he was right and explained my problem in short. He looked at me in an uncannily serious way and asked if I had any connections with global mystic or idol-worshipping affiliations. Once he was convinced that I was unaware of any form of worshipping or school of mysterious traditions, he asked me to follow him. He led me to his library where he took out some hand-written notes and, before he began to explain, asked me to swear I would never tell anyone about what I was about to learn and would never use his information for malicious intent. In exchange for his offer, I would have to let him take a close look at the statuette.

I gave him my word and he showed me a bas-relief he had made out of clay that was similar to the object. There were fewer hieroglyphs than on the original in my possession but he disclosed they were the only ones he had managed to copy from another statue in a New Orleans police operation on November 1st, 1907, after a frantic call from terrified locals. When I asked him what the hieroglyphics meant, he let out two intelligible sounds – Cthulhu and R'lyeh. I stared at him, questioning their meaning and he began to recount his adventure.

The squatters there, mostly primitive but good-natured descendants of Lafitte's men, were in the grip of stark terror from an unknown thing which had stolen upon them in the night. It was voodoo, apparently, but voodoo of a more terrible sort than they had ever known; and some of their women and children had disappeared since the malevolent tom-tom had begun its incessant beating far within the black haunted woods where no dweller ventured. There were insane shouts and harrowing screams, soul-chilling chants and dancing devil-flames; and, the frightened messenger added, the people could stand it no more.

Under the command of Chief Inspector Legrasse and alongside Professor Lovecraft, his long-time friend, a body of twenty police, *filling two carriages and an automobile, set out in the late afternoon with the shivering squatter as a guide. At the end of the passable road they alighted, and for miles splashed on in silence through the terrible cypress woods where day never came. Ugly roots and malignant hanging nooses of Spanish moss beset them, and now and then a pile of dank stones or fragment of a rotting wall intensified by its hint of morbid habitation a depression which every malformed tree and every fungous islet combined with the rotting flora of the forest created appalling instincts and awakened alien nightmares.*

At length the squatter settlement, a miserable huddle of huts, hove in sight; and hysterical dwellers ran out to cluster around the group of bobbing lanterns. The muffled beat of tom-toms was now faintly audible far, far ahead; and a curdling shriek came at infrequent intervals when the wind shifted. A reddish glare, too, seemed to filter through the pale undergrowth beyond endless avenues of forest night. Reluctant even to be left alone again, each one of the cowed squatters refused point-blank to advance another inch toward the scene of unholy worship, so Inspector Legrasse and his nineteen colleagues and Professor Lovecraft plunged on unguided into black arcades of horror that none of them had ever trod before.

The region now entered by the police was one of traditionally evil repute, substantially unknown and untraversed by white men. There were legends of a hidden lake unglimpsed by mortal sight, in which dwelt a huge, formless white polypous thing with luminous eyes; and squatters whispered that bat-winged devils flew up out of caverns in inner earth to worship it at midnight. They said it had been there before D'Iberville, before La Salle, before the Indians, and before even the wholesome beasts and birds of the woods. It was nightmare itself, and to see it was to die. But it made men dream, and so they knew enough to keep away. The present voodoo orgy was, indeed, on the merest fringe of this abhorred area, but that location was bad enough; hence perhaps the very place of the worship had terrified the squatters more than the shocking sounds and incidents.

Only poetry or madness could do justice to the noises heard by Legrasse's men as they ploughed on through the black morass toward the red glare and the muffled tom-toms. There are vocal qualities peculiar to men, and vocal qualities peculiar to beasts; and it is terrible to hear the one when the source should yield the other. Animal fury and orgiastic licence here whipped themselves to daemoniac heights by howls and squawking ecstasies that tore and reverberated through those nighted woods like pestilential tempests from the gulfs of hell. Now and then the less organised ululation would cease, and from what seemed a well-drilled chorus of hoarse voices would rise in sing-song chant that hideous phrase or ritual:

"Ph'nglui mglw'nafh Cthulhu R'lyeh wgah'nagl fhtagn."

Then the men, having reached a spot where the trees were thinner, came suddenly in sight of the spectacle itself. Four of them reeled, one fainted, and two were shaken into a frantic cry which the mad cacophony of the orgy fortunately deadened. Legrasse dashed swamp water on the face of the fainting man, and all stood trembling and nearly hypnotised with horror.

In a natural glade of the swamp stood a grassy island of perhaps an acre's extent, clear of trees and tolerably dry. On this now leaped and twisted a more indescribable horde of human abnormality than any but a Sime or an Angarola could paint. Void of clothing, this hybrid spawn were braying, bellowing, and writhing about a monstrous ring-shaped bonfire; in the centre of which, revealed by occasional rifts in the curtain of flame, stood a great granite monolith some eight feet in height; on top of which, incongruous with its diminutiveness, rested the noxious carven statuette. From a wide circle of ten scaffolds set up at regular intervals with the flame-girt monolith as a centre hung, head downward, the oddly marred bodies of the helpless squatters who had disappeared. It was inside this circle that the ring of worshippers jumped and roared, the general direction of the mass motion being from left to right in endless Bacchanal between the ring of bodies and the ring of fire.

It may have been only imagination and it may have been only echoes which induced one of the men, an excitable Spaniard, to fancy he heard antiphonal responses to the ritual from some far and unillumined spot deeper within the wood of ancient legendry and horror. This man went so far as to hint of the faint beating of great wings, and of a glimpse of shining eyes and a mountainous white bulk beyond the remotest trees.

Actually, the horrified pause of the men was of comparatively brief duration. Duty came first; and although there must have been nearly a hundred mongrel celebrants in the throng, the police relied on their firearms and plunged determinedly into the nauseous rout. For five minutes the resultant din and chaos were beyond description. Wild blows were struck, shots were fired, and escapes were made; but in the end Legrasse was able to count some forty-seven sullen prisoners, whom he forced to dress in haste and fall into line between two rows of policemen. Five of the worshippers lay dead, and two severely wounded ones were carried away on improvised stretchers by their fellow-prisoners. The image on the monolith, of course, was carefully removed and carried back by Legrasse.

Examined at headquarters in the presence of Professor Lovecraft after a trip of intense strain and weariness, the prisoners all proved to be men of a very low, mixed-blooded, and mentally aberrant type. Most were seamen, and a sprinkling of negroes and mulattoes, largely West Indians or Brava Portuguese from the Cape Verde Islands, gave a colouring of voodooism to the heterogeneous cult. But before many questions were asked, it became manifest that something far deeper and older than negro fetichism was involved. Degraded and ignorant as they were, the creatures held with surprising consistency to the central idea of their loathsome faith.

They worshipped, so they said, the Great Old Ones who lived ages before there were any men, and who came to the young world out of the sky. Those Old Ones were gone now, inside the earth and under the sea; but their dead bodies had told their secrets in dreams to the first men, who formed a cult which had never died. This was that cult, and the prisoners said it had always existed and always would exist, hidden in distant wastes and dark places all over the world until the time when the great priest Cthulhu, from his dark house in the mighty city of R'lyeh under the waters, should rise and bring the earth again beneath his sway. Some day he would call, when the stars were ready, and the secret cult would always be waiting to liberate him.

Meanwhile no more must be told. There was a secret which even torture could not extract. Mankind was not absolutely alone among the conscious things of earth, for shapes came out of the dark to visit the faithful few. But these were not the Great Old Ones. No man had ever seen the Old Ones. The carven idol that Legrasse had taken was great Cthulhu, but none might say whether or not the others were precisely like him. No one could read the old writing now, but things were told by word of mouth. The chanted ritual was not the secret that was never spoken aloud, only whispered. The chant meant only this: "In his house at R'lyeh dead Cthulhu waits dreaming."

Only two of the prisoners were found sane enough to be hanged, and the rest were committed to various institutions. All denied a part in the ritual murders, and averred that the killing had been done by Black Winged Ones which had come to them from their immemorial meeting-place in the haunted wood. But of those mysterious allies no coherent account could ever be gained. What the police did extract, came mainly from an immensely aged mestizo named Castro, who claimed to have sailed to strange ports and talked with undying leaders of the cult in the mountains of China.

Old Castro remembered bits of hideous legend that paled the speculations of theosophists and made man and the world seem recent and transient indeed. There had been aeons when other Things ruled on the earth, and They had had great cities. Remains of Them, he said the deathless Chinamen had told him, were still to be found as Cyclopean stones on islands in the Pacific. They all died vast epochs of time before men came, but there were arts which could revive them when the stars had come round again to the right positions in the cycle of eternity.

These Great Old Ones, Castro continued, were not composed altogether of flesh and blood. They had shape —for did not this star-fashioned image prove it?— but that shape was not made of matter. When the stars were right, They could plunge from world to world through the sky; but when the stars were wrong, They could not live. But although They no longer lived, They would never really die. They all lay in stone houses in Their great city of R'lyeh, preserved by the spells of mighty Cthulhu for a glorious resurrection when the stars and the earth might once more be ready for Them. But at that time some force from outside must serve to liberate Their bodies. The spells that preserved Them intact likewise prevented Them from making an initial move, and They could only lie awake in the dark and think whilst uncounted millions of years rolled by. They knew all that was occurring in the universe, but Their mode of speech was transmitted thought. Even now They talked in Their tombs. When, after infinities of chaos, the first men came, the Great Old Ones spoke to the sensitive among them by moulding their dreams; for only thus could Their language reach the fleshly minds of mammals.

Then, whispered Castro, those first men formed the cult around small idols which the Great Ones shewed them; idols brought in dim aeras from dark stars. That cult would never die till the stars came right again, and the secret priests would take great Cthulhu from His tomb to revive His subjects and resume His rule of earth. The time would be easy to know, for then mankind would have become as the Great Old Ones; free and wild and beyond good and evil, with laws and morals thrown aside and all men shouting and *killing and revelling in joy. Then the liberated Old Ones would teach them new ways to shout and kill and revel and enjoy themselves, and all the earth would flame with a holocaust of ecstasy and freedom. Meanwhile the cult, by appropriate rites, must keep alive the memory of those ancient ways and shadow forth the prophecy of their return.*

In the elder time chosen men had talked with the entombed Old Ones in dreams, but then something had happened. The great stone city R'lyeh, with its monoliths and sepulchres, had sunk beneath the waves; and the deep waters, full of the one primal mystery through which not even thought can pass, had cut off the spectral intercourse. But memory never died, and high-priests said that the city would rise again when the stars were right.

Then came out of the earth the black spirits of earth, mouldy and shadowy, and full of dim rumours picked up in caverns beneath forgotten sea-bottoms. But of them old Castro dared not speak much. He cut himself off hurriedly, and no amount of persuasion or subtlety could elicit more in this direction. The size of the Old Ones, too, he curiously declined to mention.

Of the Cthulhu cult, he said that he thought the centre lay amid the pathless deserts of Arabia, where Irem, the City of Pillars, dreams hidden and untouched. It was not allied to the European witch-cult, and was virtually unknown beyond its members. No book had ever really hinted of it, though the deathless Chinamen said that there were double meanings in the Necronomicon of the mad Arab Abdul Alhazred which the initiated might read as they chose, especially the much-discussed couplet:

"That is not dead which can eternal lie,
And with strange aeons even death may die."

Legrasse, deeply impressed and not a little bewildered, had inquired in vain concerning the historic affiliations of the cult. Indeed, all of this information was later confirmed by the internationally renowned Professor Dr Art Webb, *who had been engaged in a tour of Greenland and Iceland in search of some Runic inscriptions which he failed to unearth and whilst high up on the West Greenland coast had encountered a singular tribe or cult of degenerate Esquimaux, whose religion, a curious form of devil-worship, chilled the Professor with its deliberate bloodthirstiness and repulsiveness. It was a faith of which other Esquimaux knew little, and which they mentioned only with shudders.*

They said *that it had come down from horribly ancient aeons before ever the world was made. Besides nameless rites and human sacrifices there were certain queer hereditary rituals addressed to a supreme elder devil or tornasuk. Professor Webb had taken a careful phonetic copy from an aged angekok or wizard-priest, expressing the sounds in Roman letters as best he knew how. But just now of prime significance was the fetish which this cult had cherished, and around which they danced when the aurora leaped high over the ice cliffs. It was, the professor stated, a very crude bas-relief of stone, comprising a hideous picture and some cryptic writing. And so far as he could tell, it was a rough parallel in all essential features of the bestial thing* that we were talking about now lying before the meeting.

From all the narratives, it was clear that the *two hellish rituals so many worlds of distance apart* were virtually identical, as were *what both the Esquimau wizards and the swamp-priests had chanted:*

"Ph'nglui mglw'nafh Cthulhu R'lyeh wgah'nagl fhtagn."

Since childhood, I had always ridiculed stories of this nature and found them *quite entertaining,* but it was clear how terrified the professor was. Suffice it to say he was so descriptive, everything came to life.

Without being hostile, and full of incredible enthusiasm, Professor Lovecraft almost threw me out and sent me home to fetch the statuette. He escorted me to the front door and, still in conversation, we walked down the steps to the pavement outside his house. He looked rather gruesome. It was difficult to tell whether the strain of narrating the events or the anticipation of the coveted object he had sought for years with endless perseverance was to blame. On the other hand, poor lighting from the broken street lamp nearby distorted his features in the dark, which might have also have been to blame.

As I said goodbye, for the time being, a drunk staggered between us and tapped the professor on the shoulder. Caught in the moment, we paid no attention. I had only taken a few steps when I heard a thud and turned back to look. Returning to his front door, the professor had fallen to the ground, slid down the steps and landed on the pavement. I hurried back to investigate and was surprised to find when I turned him over that he was dead. The doctor who examined him later could find no pathological cause. What was it that had robbed him of his life from one minute to the next? A veil of mystery began to unfold. I realised I was possessed by an unknown threat.

Admittedly, the void left by Professor Lovecraft's unexpected death – or murder – was enormous. The only source of information about the extraordinary cult was gone for good, and it left me confused on a number of issues. I would have to continue the research alone. Fortunately, I now had a better picture of the object in my possession. Focusing on the facts, it would be best to find out more information. I went back to the Library.

My investigation was now specific. Books about similar subjects did not exist. Recalling the words of the late Professor, I looked up the work of the great mystic-researcher Charles Dexter Ward entitled *Worship of Mystic Gods*. The book was covered in thick dust, a sign it was unknown to most or that curiosity did not stretch that far. Browsing through its yellow pages, I couldn't help but admire the masterful images that enhanced the author's research. I came across a design that was similar to the statuette. A shriek of unbridled joy almost leapt from my throat, and with great difficulty, I managed to suppress it.

I carefully scrutinised the drawing and read the notes in detail. *"The material the idol of worship is made of is extremely remarkable and presents a mystery. The soapy, green-black stone with its golden or iridescent specks and ridges resembles no familiar rock in the science of mineralogy. The inscription engraved along its base is equally puzzling. The symbols, theme and material from which the idol is made represent something horrifyingly distant and distinct from mankind as we know it. There is no relevant information — despite thorough investigation of relevant literature in libraries the world over — to illustrate the slightest link to the most remote linguistic affinity. This in itself signifies the existence of ancient and godless circles of life, where our world and logic have no place."*

This observation convinced me I was in the possession of a rare, mystical, occult object of utmost interest, and shed much light on the reasons for the killings I accidentally witnessed. It amplified the voracious ambition of my persecutors and their measureless obsession to get their hands on the statuette.

Having gathered the information I needed, I put aside Charles Dexter Ward's book and began flicking through newspapers for the dates Professor Howard Lovecraft had mentioned – fortunately, I had not forgotten them. I came across a news story that sounded familiar. It occurred to me that if I had read it a few days earlier, it wouldn't have made the slightest impression on me. A banker on his way home one night suddenly died in a narrow side street after bumping into an old sailor. Despite much effort, the doctors were unable to justify the cause of his death. An eyewitness reported he heard the victim speak in an unrecognisable tongue shortly before he took his final breath. His mumblings were beyond comprehension.

If this was Voodoo magic, why weren't there any poisoned needles or mysterious death rituals, equally as inhumane and time-honoured as their sacrificial rituals and beliefs? The thought lodged itself in my mind and wouldn't go away. It soon became clear that searching through rare and expensive books in a stuffy, sterile library either in a public space or at the home of the person most enlightened on the subject was destined to be futile. What I needed to do now – and I was surprised it hadn't occurred to me sooner – was abandon everything and visit the places mentioned in the legends of Cthulhu for myself. It would bring me into direct contact with the initiated and I'd be able to unravel the mystery. I took off without delay.

My first stop was Haiti. I was disappointed by how dirty it was, but I would have to put up with it. My stay at the hotel, which was more like a pigsty, would not be long. It lasted a week. During this time, I managed to find a translator-guide and attend similar rituals as an observer.

There were no human sacrifices but the experience itself sufficed. Besides, initiation should be gradual. The excuse for my presence was that I intended to join the cult.

It seemed to impress the savage, indigenous people, who found it odd that an educated, white, well-to-do male wished to embrace their religion. Who knows what they'd have done to me if they'd known I was just hungry for adventure and all I wanted was insider information, seven-sealed in the social circles of Europe.

I must have put on a good show because an old man at the last ceremony, when informed about my interest, approached me and disclosed information few are aware of. Deep in the virgin forests of the Amazon is a tribe known to be the oldest initiated in the cult of Cthulhu. The tribal Witch Doctor is an expert in terrifying, untold rituals. He would be able to reveal some secrets. The old man sparked my interest in meeting him. I asked him for more information about the tribe, but he refused to elaborate. However, after handing over a few hundred-dollar bills, he took a pencil and a sheet of paper and drew me a map.

My next stop was Peru. The situation there was even worse. It took a lot of effort to find an interpreter-guide and when I eventually did and explained why I was there, he was terrified and took off. I had to find someone else, someone braver. I think the interpreter must have told his friends about me because wherever I went, people were watching me. Their inquisitive eyes restricted my movements and alert as I was, it felt like I was hallucinating.

At some point, a random person approached me and asked if it was true I needed a guide for the caves of the Amazon. There was something strange about him. He didn't look rough or violent but there was an intangible element that made my heart pound. But my ugly sense of foreboding didn't hold me back. I answered in the affirmative. In turn, I asked him how much he charged, but he declined every offer I made him. We arranged to meet at five that afternoon. He showed up exactly at the arranged time. He didn't say much and walked ahead without checking to see if I was following him. He seemed sure I was. We passed through places I would never have gone to alone or would otherwise never have noticed. Secret pathways apparently covered by dense vegetation were, in fact, accessible to the average hiker. I don't remember how long we walked. Extreme perspiration made it difficult to move.

Just before sunset, the guide paused for a moment and let out an animal-like call. Similar calls echoed back. His native tribesmen cautiously approached in increasing numbers along the way. Eventually, we arrived at the Chief's hut. According to the guide, on hearing the reason for my visit, the Chief summoned someone, who I guessed was the Witch Doctor. Dressed in a weird costume, his body was painted with colours I had never seen before and his face was covered by a mask symbolising the power of Cthulhu through his sole ambassador.

A long conversation began between the Witch Doctor and my guide. When it was over, the Witch Doctor was obsessed with me. I have no idea what they talked about but it was clear his intentions were not friendly. The guide explained that the Witch Doctor was angry that I had dared to disturb this mystical and isolated tribe for what he considered to be a sightseeing trip.

It was impossible to convince them, no matter how hard I tried, that I was genuinely interested in being initiated into the cult of Cthulhu and all I was asking was for them to share their untold secrets. For them, the mere fact that I had shamelessly and provocatively approached them by paying someone was sacrilege. It was Cthulhu himself who led the select few to the sacred location after appearing to them in a dream, they said.

I got the message that I was an intruder and was in an extremely dangerous position. I explained that I had been sent by a great Haitian Witch Doctor who had recognised my faith but all to no avail! They were adamant. Only those who had been chosen by the deity had a place amongst them. Those who appeared uninvited automatically condemned themselves to death. And for that reason, I would be sacrificed to Cthulhu for the sacrilege I had committed.

I complained, shouted, screamed, begged and beseeched like never before for them to listen to me and believe I was telling the truth. But it was all in vain! Their decision was irrevocable. Realising the end was nigh, I cursed the boy who had died in front of me, I cursed the moment I went into the junk shop, I cursed the statuette that had thrust me into this absurd affair, and I cursed Cthulhu, wherever and whatever it was.

It turned out I had been particularly brazen with this alien, mystical deity and had woken it from a deep sleep. The deity cursed me in return. Looking back, I should have sacrificed my life there and then and died ingloriously, because what followed turned me into a waste of a life surplus to requirements, a doomed, disgusting being, scum more putrefying than the Devil himself.

Seconds before my sacrifice came to an end, after spontaneously releasing a hideous, bloodcurdling scream from the depths of my existence, something inexplicable happened. Not a single expert has since been able to explain, speculate on, or analyse a situation similar to my phenomenal experience. Opium was considered to have been to blame. I, on the other hand, couldn't have been more certain about it.

The sky was clear and the golden-red sun was about to set when all of a sudden, lightning struck and thunder clapped. Strangely, not a drop of rain fell. The incident lasted about five minutes and stopped as suddenly as it had started. It was Cthulhu's response to my sacrifice. This was his message to the Witch Doctor.

Everyone bowed before me and began to chant. I made absolutely no attempt to understand what they were saying. Someone untied my hands and silence reigned. I was the one to break it, speaking in a language I had never been taught or heard others speak, a language I never knew existed. I had no idea what I was saying, but it must have been important because I was shown enormous respect. It took a long time to clarify if the event had actually taken place or was the result of my relentless turmoil. Looking back, I realise that this was the moment the revenge of Cthulhu began.

Subsequently, the Witch Doctor begged me not to kill him for his malicious behaviour. He blamed tradition, he was bound by the laws of the deity when he took part in such ceremonies. I agreed to forgive him in return for his knowledge of the secret that would give me Absolute Power to dominate and do whatever I liked. He was grateful for my generosity and, over the course of three days and three nights, he revealed how I would become the god's most powerful ambassador. I liked the idea of that, but if at the time, I'd had the slightest inkling of what was to come, I'd have fled the place, deleting every detail of the ordeal from my memory. Instead, I became the High Priest. Before I left, they asked me to bless them. I carried out their request, but couldn't help but laugh.

My next stop was Bolivia. According to the Witch Doctor, I would have to travel to a place on the map and locate the tomb of the previous High Priest. After much effort and without a guide, I found it. It didn't resemble anything that would normally spring to mind. Nothing signified that an important person, or any person, was buried there. I unearthed the skeleton of my predecessor. I was to take one bone, it didn't matter which.

I reburied the skeleton and left for Venezuela where, this time, I would have to retrieve a chalice, essential for the ceremonies performed by a High Priest. It was located in the basement of a mystic, ceremonial temple, which the Witch Doctor had also mapped out. The Sacred Chalice was stored in the temple until the High Priest came to power and took charge of it. Somehow the Chalice was returned to the temple as the end drew nigh for the High Priest, probably by means of a special mission by the faithful, who returned the sacred object to the purpose-built temple before it fell into foreign hands. This part of the plan was very easy.

Finally, I travelled to the Chilean Andes to seek out the tribe in possession of the Ouroborous Ring, another essential for High Priest rituals. And also a Cloak. The greatest difficulty I encountered with the final execution of the plan was that the specific tribe had no fixed abode, but moved on from time to time. I was given the location of their previous settlement and from there, it would be up to me to find them. It was like an exciting game and when difficulties arose, it charmed me all the more. I'd have quickly given up on it otherwise.

Anxiety as to how I would set about finding the tribe proved to be in vain. Luck was on my side and complications eliminated since the tribe had not yet moved on. So with the final essential items in my possession, I returned home eager to get on with the process of acquiring Absolute Power. All I needed to do now, and by comparison, this would be easy, was get hold of a goat.

I'd been gone for months and my friends were concerned – I had taken off without notice – and thought I'd had some kind of accident. Clearly, on the first night of my return, they were hungry for news of the events that led to my disappearance. I diplomatically explained how exhausted I was and they would have to give me at least two days to recover. Thus, I was able to temporarily avoid them and locked myself away at home.

I closed all the windows, locked the front door so no one would disturb me and began to prepare. According to legend, the ritual should take place at twelve midnight. There was plenty of time to do what was needed. I switched off the lights in the salon and lit some large candles. I cleared everything to the side, even the thick,

Persian rug, leaving a space in the middle of the room. I took the Chalice out of its case. It looked more impressive that way, or perhaps it was just more obvious. It was covered in multi-coloured rubies and diamonds. In the centre of its base was a large, black stone. I had never seen anything as black before; it was the colour of the abyss, the colour of a bottomless well, the colour of the centre of the earth.

Next, I took the bone I had taken from the High Priest's tomb and patiently pulverised it using a wooden pestle and mortar before placing it in the Chalice. Then, I went down to the cellar, slaughtered the goat and collected its blood in a small jar. I returned to the salon and with the goat's blood, I drew a circle around a pentagram in the middle of the room. I placed a huge burning candle and the statuette of the deity in the centre of it.

It was almost midnight. When the clock on the wall struck twelve drawn out chimes, I pricked my finger and dripped seven drops of blood into the Chalice. It was absurd! I still wonder if the phenomenon can be explained by the fundamental laws of Chemistry or if it would be possible to recreate the same reaction. Once the drops of blood came into contact with the pulverised bone, a strange concoction emerged. It changed colour continuously. I watched in amazement as the colours came and went and noticed how they matched the precious gems that adorned the Chalice.

When all the colours had emerged, the mixture began to foam. Now was the time to put on the blood-red Cloak and the Ouroborus Ring and drink the contents in one go. After swallowing the last drop, I was overcome by a weird sensation – impossible to describe, however hard I try. It was a burning sensation and I felt as if I was being catapulted into space at the speed of light. Then, I lost consciousness.

Two hours later, I awoke, thinking it was all a dream. Looking around the salon, it was obvious it had been for real. To my surprise, the special powers I had been so keen to acquire did not make me feel any different but would lead me to numerous adventures. To test it out, I experimented by wishing for something bad to happen to see if my wish came true.

A beautiful plant in my neighbour's garden came to mind. She was always boasting about it, which annoyed the hell out of me every time I was unfortunate enough to bump into her. It was time for revenge. I went into the garden, looked at the plant with all the hate I could muster and wished it to wither. Despite my effort, the plant stood proud. I had been taken for a ride. How ridiculous was that? How had I put my trust in uncivilised peasants, who idolise lightning and fire in this day and age? They had made an utter fool of me! With the bitter taste of disappointment and defeat in my mouth, I went to bed.

The following morning, I opened the window to take in the sunlight and feel its rays caress my skin. I stretched my arms and legs but was soon distracted by something different in the garden. I struggled to suppress the urge to scream with sheer delight. My neighbour's plant looked as if it had been struck by lightning! I possessed those mystic powers, after all! I wondered how I could put them to use.

Before I came to any conclusion, the doorbell rang. It was my good friend Elizabeth, who I had lost touch with due to recent events. Pleased to see her, I let her in and gave her a hug. I had really missed her. She didn't seem to be in a very good mood. Elizabeth was the only person I shared my innermost feelings with. She knew everything about me and all my woes, just as I knew everything about her. Her companionship was invaluable. Whenever I tried to open up to other people there was always something missing. My peculiar temperament was probably to blame.

Her hang-ups and quirks were different to mine but she knew how to listen and showed genuine interest when I was mentally worn down. She was clever, patient, gracious and kind. Spiritual well-being was seeded inside her, but her insecurities would not allow it to bear fruit. It was because of this that we were closely connected and I knowingly allowed myself to become dependent on her. She was aware of my weakness for her, and I knew she would open up only to me.

I very much wanted to tell her about what had happened but held back because I knew she was afraid of the occult. Her pretty face struggled to force a smile. I asked her what was wrong and she confided that, for some reason, she had had a lot of bad luck, which had led to a mental breakdown. We talked it through and explored the reasons but couldn't come up with a logical explanation. I promised her I'd find a solution, which she seemed relieved to hear. She trusted my intuition, expertise and competence. Often in the past, when she found herself at a dead-end, I helped her focus on the problem and find a solution. When she left, it seemed like a good opportunity to use my newly acquired power.

The same evening, I followed another kind of ritual. On a purple table cloth, I placed the statue of the deity, a few lighted candles and some herbs, which gave off a strange, intoxicating smell when burned. Wearing the Ouroborus Ring and the Cloak, I called on Cthulhu, with a couplet in an old Celtic dialect. Roughly translated, it went like this: *"Animals are silent, the dead are silent, I seek your spirit to increase my power."*

It was a very laborious and tedious ritual but successful in the end. The whole household shook as if in the throes of an earthquake. Doors opened and shut, poisonous snakes wove themselves around the table and my feet, the wind howled as if possessed, eerie shadows fluttered around the room and a voice from the depths of the earth gave answers to the questions that tormented me. Finally, I asked for assistance on behalf of my friend Elizabeth.

He revealed that her misfortune was caused by powerful evil spirits that ambushed her undertakings and those of the people around her. For some reason, he tried to explain the mutation of Love into Hate which get mixed up in the emotional world. Sometimes Hate brings Love and vice versa. Pathological, toxic Love turns into Hate. I was aware of that, but couldn't understand why he mentioned it.

He continued by stating it was impossible to get rid of these forces with the usual methods such as spells, consecration and exorcism. It seemed there was little hope my friend would be relieved of her unhappiness and her situation would gradually decline. Taking the initiative, I asked him personally to drive the evil spirits out of her home. His laughter made my hair stand on end. What thief would steal from another thief? What kind of demon would harm another demon? It was beyond belief.

I asked if he had done anything similar before. He declared that there had been times in the past, but only in exchange for the most alluring offer of all. I challenged him to reveal what would be appealing enough for him to change his mind. It was clear he had anticipated my question. His answer was serious, direct and rather hurried. He would help me out in exchange for my soul. I would be owned by him entirely, an eternal slave to assist him with his scheming plans.

There was no hesitation on my part. My admiration and sheer weakness for Elizabeth forced me to agree. But it was my turn to set the terms. She and her family would be rid of the evil forces but he would also protect them in the future. No one would ever be able to do her harm again. With enormous satisfaction, he accepted to honour our agreement.

In the following months, the smile began to return to Elizabeth's face. Every now and then, she dropped by to see me and tell me how happy and how much stronger she felt. She knew I had done something but had no idea what. Then, she disappeared. Her troubles were forgotten and so was I. Being a friend to others in their times of need was my destiny, it seemed. I could have used similar methods to bring her back, even make her mine. But for me, that would have been going against the grain. I could handle the contempt of others, but not my own.

Contrary to my friend, I was getting weaker and weaker every day. Cthulhu was taking absolute control of me. I cursed myself repeatedly for craving for more and considering it all a game, even after my return. I should have let them sacrifice me for the ritual I performed to Cthulhu instead of being allowed to live.

I hid myself away. I lost my appetite and avoided company. I couldn't sleep. And since I didn't venture out in daylight, I looked like something out of a nightmare. Forced by basic necessities to go out and get things done, I couldn't help but notice the look of horror on people's faces when they clapped eyes on me.

Suddenly, out of the depths of my darkest despair came a shining light. An idea came to mind. What if I tried to fool Cthulhu? What if I refused to obey him, what if I broke my promise? What if I left him there, lost and forgotten for so many years, what would happen? It was time to figure out how to strike the final blow.

It didn't take long. It was a cold, sunny day in February. I flung the windows wide open to let the light and fresh air into the room which had become a Voodoo ritual parlour. I scrubbed the floors, got rid of all the ceremonial stuff and anxiously waited for noon. When the clock struck twelve, I burned the Cloak, crushed the Ouroborous Ring with a hammer and destroyed every last precious stone on the Chalice with such malice it was unrecognisable. If it wasn't for the fact that it was made of gold, it would have been no more than a useless piece of metal.

Satisfied with the result, I scornfully howled with laughter into the raging wind and thunderclaps of a spontaneous deluge. The weight was lifted from my shoulders and carried away by the wind; it was a mighty sense of relief. As the ecstasy wore off, the sound of my laughter returned to normal. It reminded me of something, but I was so overjoyed it didn't matter what.

The months passed by. Almost a year later, and my life had changed with arithmetic progression. Everything was going my way; I couldn't believe my luck. One day, I came across a sheet of newspaper wrapped around an item I had borrowed from a friend.

There was news from Haiti. *"According to a local police report, a mass suicide of Voodoo worshipers has come to light. An elderly man from a neighbouring tribe claimed an organised renunciation of life on earth in accordance with a certain aspect of succession certifies the incarnation of the deity they worship, the great Cthulhu. Tribal legend has it, that when the soul of the divine Cthulhu enthrones itself in the body of a chosen one — the indication of which will be made clear — a number of believers from this world must sacrifice their souls in exchange. The greater the number of souls sacrificed, the more powerfully the spirit of Cthulhu will be established in his chosen host."*

The same article referred to similar acts of mass suicide in other locations — Peru, Bolivia, Chile, New Orleans, China and Arabia. It blatantly satirised similar superstitions and came to the ironic conclusion that Cthulhu is among us in flesh and blood. Referring to the passion of this Cthulhu tradition, the author concluded the article with the final words of the elderly man, who claimed he knew about the secret worship of his neighbouring tribe. According to legend, the incarnation of Cthulhu takes place in the most sacrilegious way when the High Priest sacrifices the objects that afforded him Absolute Power, those being a Ring, a Cloak and a Chalice. *"Life,"* he concluded, *"hinges on a sheet of cloth and a few grams of gold."*

"Whatever rises must fall. But whatever falls may rise again." I rose to the heights on the unruly steed of Mystery, from the sterile world of Contemplation to the orgasmic world of Inspiration, but was plunged into the selfish Erebus of Ignorance. I rose, embracing blasphemous Manichaeism, from the barren world of Apraxia to the fertile world of Adventure, but plunged into the Darkness of harrowing abomination. I rose to unlock the mysterious troves of the Intangible, from the human Subconscious to the gloomy Universe of the Mind, but drowned in the chaotic terror of mirrored Reality. On this journey, I was transformed into a staunch warrior defending the Gate of Infinity, fighting in an eternal battle against those who seek to extinguish the flame of Understanding.

Never trust a person who smiles at you! Especially if he looks the pleasant, polite type, humorous, communicative and charismatic, with superior literary, political, philosophical and religious traits, or if he believes in the selectivity and superiority of his descent, and declares himself a materialist and an atheist. Much more if he is enigmatic, contradictory or quirky. This is the most dangerous type of person on Earth.

And as strange, absurd or idiotic as it may seem, I am that person. You may even consider me to be fit for a mental institution or in need of psychiatric medication. However much you might like to deny it, I am the most dangerous person on earth, and that's the truth! The incarnation of Cthulhu, risen from a dark abode in the magnificent, sunken city of R'lyeh, with its monoliths and mausoleums, to summon the Great Old Ones, exiled (beyond the stars) by the Elder Gods, back to earth because it was they who practiced black magic on the forbidden face of the Earth. Do not mock but embrace

Reality. Look closer at the blemished, dilapidated, black and brown stained reflection of the distorted image of the World.

Deceit, violence, corruption, wars, profit, exploitation, trivialisation of souls, debauchery, contempt, selfishness, moral shame and decline hover above fragile human dwellings as atrocity awakens in the blackness of the abyss. This vile universe, where terror sprawls in concentric circles until the revelation of unmentionable one. The universe, that will inevitably crush and devour you, is your spiritual universe. The stars waited patiently for centuries to take up the right position, to release you from your prison. The time has come for me to unlock the sealed Dimension Gate for the return of the Old Gods, and I call on all believers to follow me. The time has come, let there be no denial. There is no time for prayer, not the faintest hope of survival and neither you nor your heirs have the wisdom or the courage to resist.

The Elder Gods are omnipresent their features carved into the craggy cliffs of memory, their faded signatures intertwined with the Gematria of Paranoia and the fractal waves of the distorted musings of the human mind, their word echoing in the shattering equation of time. Yes! I am Cthulhu, High Priest of the Outer Gods, of Azathoth, Yog Sothoth, Nyarlathotep and other gods of cosmic scale and colossal power, doomed to roam among you for two hundred years, from country to country, speaking every tongue, era after era, devoid of tranquillity until their heinous plans have been fulfilled.[1]

---

1. *This short story is inspired by "The Call of Cthulhu", 1926, by the American Horror and Fantasy author Howard Philips Lovecraft.*

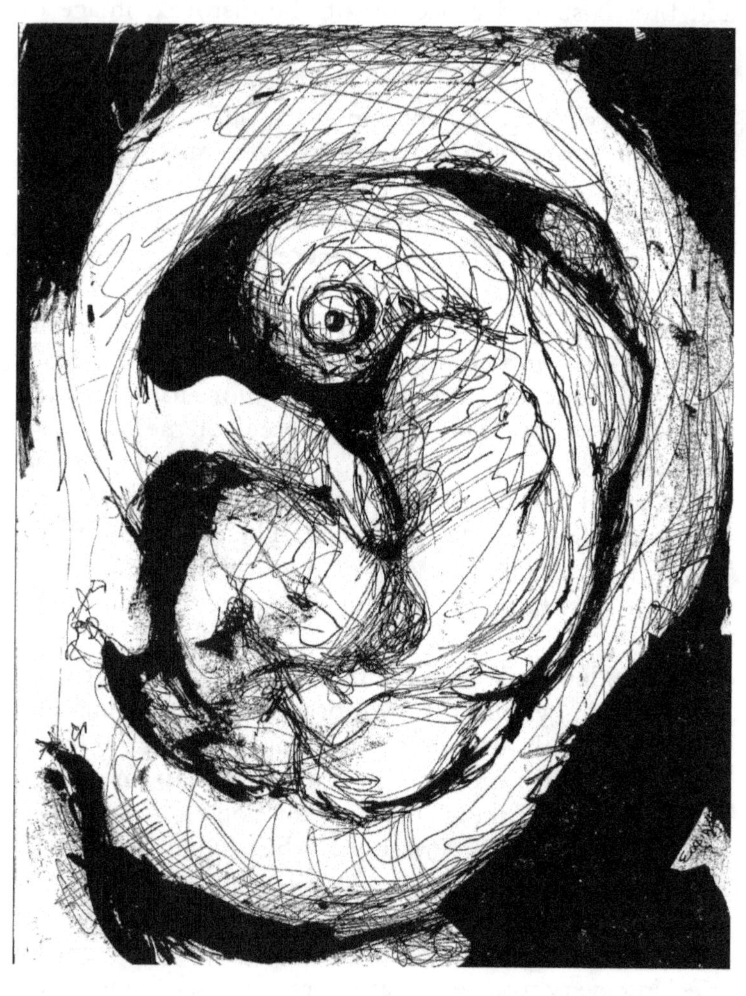

«...young Daniel had an unbelievably acute sense of hearing»

2. DANIEL

The human being is, without doubt, a mysterious creature and sociable by nature. Teams of psychologists and researchers have repeatedly tried to explain man's methods of behaviour, thought and reaction. Albert Bandura stated that mental processes play a fundamental role in the shaping of behaviour. John Watson, the father of behaviourism, claimed that humans are born with innate behaviours which are activated and occur automatically when exposed to certain triggers. Sigmund Freud was convinced that human behaviour is determined by unconscious processes such as desire, fear and conviction, and man is unaware that they even exist. The theories of psychoanalysis, social learning, cognitive psychology, reciprocal determinism, behaviourism or individual psychology, however, have not been able to clearly explain human individuality.

In general, behavioural and psychoanalytic theorists accept that human behaviour is influenced by many factors which are either innate or environmental. They conclude that Personality accounts for individuality, and is defined as a result of the way we think, feel and behave and therefore differentiate from other people. Personality develops gradually based on experiences from the childhood years onwards and into later life. However, despite outstanding scientific implications, serious deviations do occur.

Another attempt to explain human behaviour cites geographical location as an important factor. Indeed, careful observation of the behaviour of individuals and populations in a variety of countries reveals enormous differences in their ways of thinking, personalities, and even levels of intelligence. Populations can be categorised based on certain attributes and characteristics. Examination of the climate of specific areas confirms the significant effect it has on the character and personality of its population and certain attributes are noteworthy. As far back as the fifth century, the Greek historian Thucydides was able to identify and analyse the differences between the Spartans, who were disciplined and had better self-control, and the more liberal and indulgent Athenians. But what happens in the case of two characters from the same place? Do they behave in the same way? Do they think the same way? Of course not!

Furthermore, individuality is held up by Astrology, which advocates that a person's life, for some as yet unknown reason, is directly influenced by the position of various planets at his or her time of birth. According to Newton, all planets exert a gravitational pull above the planet Earth which influences Life on Earth. The effect of the gravitational pull of the Moon on the Natural environment (tides, for example) and on human behaviour (at full moon the workload in hospital emergency rooms is particularly high) confirms his theory. Astrologists study the planets in the zodiac to create the familiar horoscopes. In doing so, they account for the uniqueness of individual character based on the signs of the zodiac. But unanswered questions remain. Are all Taureans, for example, the same? What about Scorpios? Surely there are good and bad Librans. Are there good and bad signs of the zodiac? Of course not!

Whatever the case, no one can dispute that man is a peculiar species and how nature denies one person the unique, differential, superhuman characteristics it generously gifts to another remains, for now, in the realms of the unknown. This applies to children often characterised as intelligent, genius, gifted, talented. Their parents are admired, because such children will go far in life, they'll succeed, as is often heard. But is that actually the case? On the other hand, what happens if a certain individual wants to rid himself of this natural genius and longs to be normal?

"But why would he want to do that?" you may ask. Surely it's an advantage to be gifted. Well, there are occasions when being gifted proves fatal. This probably sounds very

strange, but to demonstrate my point, I'll tell you a story about a wonder child I once knew.

He was born in a small mountain village in the Macedonian region of Greece, in a particularly unfortunate year. It was a leap year. To be precise, on the twenty-ninth of February, and as the superstitious would say, a day of great misfortune. The moment he was born, his father, a quarry miner, was killed in an explosion. From then on, rumour had it that young Daniel – that was his name – was cursed.

At the request of his mother, a superstitious person herself, elderly women dressed in black would go to the house from the day he was born and pray for deliverance from the evil eye and envious gossip and tell tales of exorcism. This would rid him of evil spirits which, according to them, would otherwise commit him to a life of sorrow and hardship. The woman performing the ritual to rid him of the evil eye would first spit on her chest, and then Daniel's, put some water in a cup, say a prayer and then add a few drops of olive oil. Next, she would dip a piece of cotton wool into the cup and dab the oil on the boy's forehead. The rest was thrown to the ground or poured into a flowerpot. In desperation, Frosso, Daniel's mother, would pin charms on his clothes and hang them in his crib and all around the house – blue beads to ward off the evil eye, horseshoes, crucifixes, cloves of garlic, and the like. She took him to godly people and priests for their blessing and to all-night vigils to miracle-performing saints.

From the start, Daniel was different from children his age. He was easily disturbed by noise and spoke more quietly than normal. While playing with his peers he would often put his fingers in his ears. His mother found it strange and it caused her to worry. She feared he suffered from epilepsy or something similar, and took him to countless doctors. They all came to the same conclusion: young Daniel had an unbelievably acute sense of hearing. He could clearly hear conversations behind closed doors, even if they weren't very loud. Indeed, he was beaten on numerous occasions for that very reason, having been accused of eavesdropping. What's more, he could identify the origin of certain sounds, even if they were masked by others. His mother never needed to call more than once for him to hear her, even if he was in another neighbourhood.

He learned the alphabet very quickly at school but was not very impressed with writing. Numbers, on the other hand, were far more captivating and an enormous, magical world opened up to him: the World of Mathematics. His teacher was impressed by his intelligence. She noticed he was able to retain large amounts of information, understood concepts meant for older children, had a richer vocabulary and was more articulate than the rest of the children in the school (she had thoroughly researched the subject). He was a quick and flexible thinker, had original ideas and solutions to problems, preferred complicated assignments and anything that provided a challenge. He liked to work alone. On the other hand, he took a negative stance to education when it came to learning about things he was not interested in, got bored when the teacher taught the rest of the class things he already knew and always strived for perfection.

The teacher – an educated woman of culture – quickly and easily realised he was a gifted and talented child. She remembered from her studies that gifted children had been familiar to society since ancient times. The Chinese and ancient Greeks had their own ways of dealing with them. In more recent times, however, despite being characterised as wonder kids and worshipped by those around them, they are known to progress only if circumstances allow them to develop their talent and special capabilities. The teacher was aware that if this generous gift of Nature was not recognised in Daniel's childhood years, it was in danger of being wasted and he would probably lead an unhappy life.

To be absolutely certain and ensure this was not simply a superficial surge of enthusiasm on her part, she began to take note of the signs that indicated he was a gifted child. She created a personal account of Daniel's behaviour. In it, she recorded his achievements and commented on them, his stage of development and behaviour both in and out of school. Based on this account, she was able to form an opinion on what the child knew, what he was capable of doing with appropriate guidance and what he was mature enough to achieve. By coincidence, she noticed the young boy learned to read music very quickly in his music lessons and easily remembered a variety of tunes. She swiftly concluded that, for Daniel, there was an unequivocal connection between Mathematics and Music.

Referring to the scientific resources available, she confirmed that such a relationship exists. The idea of the connection between Mathematics and Music was conceived centuries ago in ancient Greece by Pythagoras. According to Pythagoreans, the immediate and close connection between mathematics, music and the sensation of joy was the ultimate proof that truth at its highest level can be expressed in mathematical terms. They believed the soul was transported by Mathematics and Music, connecting it with the Universe. Later other mathematicians such as Aristoxenus, Euclid, Keppler and Fourier believed in the same relationship.

She fastidiously observed the young boy's talent for music and, convinced he was a gifted child, went to see his mother. She explained with enthusiasm how extremely talented he was at music, and after singing his praises, ended the discussion by recommending, with some hesitation, he attended music school. Financial circumstances, however, would not allow Daniel's mother to give it any further consideration. There was no doubt about that. How would he survive? Where would he stay? Who would take care of him?

When Daniel reached the age of nine, a music competition happened to be taking place in Thessaloniki, where children of his age from primary and secondary schools in the province of Macedonia would be taking part. The winner would be rewarded with a full scholarship to the Franz Schubert Music Conservatory, the oldest private music school in Vienna. It offered music lessons to very young children, allowing scholarship beneficiaries to gain a diploma in music. Food, accommodation and studies would all be paid for. Founded in 1867, the music school was internationally renowned and previous scholars had become world-famous musicians.

It was an opportunity not to be missed for young Daniel. His teacher immediately suggested to his mother that he took part in the competition. Frosso – like every other mother in the world – was hesitant at first, fearing she would lose her child. Pressure from friends and the words of the headmaster…, *"madam, your son's future and a distinguished career are at stake,"* persuaded Frosso otherwise, and she gave her approval. But Daniel didn't have a musical instrument to play. His teacher suggested the school started a collection and enough money was raised to buy an ordinary guitar good enough for Daniel to practise on until the day of the competition. It was only a month away and he would have to try his hardest.

Contestants would be tested in three areas. Firstly, they would have to play an unknown piece of classical music from a musical score. This would enable them to demonstrate their ability to read music both quickly and correctly as well as give an excellent performance. Secondly, they would have to perform a piece they had composed themselves as an example of their creativity and inner sensitivity. Finally – and most difficult of all – they would have to identify precisely each note played to them on the piano and the octave to which it belonged to demonstrate their musical proficiency.

One Sunday morning, in the presence of music school directors and a large audience, the process began. Young Daniel was up against children from wealthy families, whose parents had been able to pay for music lessons from the age of three in some cases, as well as extra lessons before the competition. There were forty-seven competitors in all and Daniel would be the thirteenth child to take part. Remembering what had been said about her son the past, Daniel's mother was sceptical and somewhat nervous. The competitors were dressed in their finest outfits, in bow ties and shiny, polished shoes. Poorer children dressed in borrowed clothes and looking rather neglected were also taking part. Rosy-red cheeks and chubby necks joining heads to chubby stomachs were a common sight among the participants.

One by one, the competitors were examined. The judges were dazzled by Daniel's talent by the end of the competition. He was awarded perfect marks for his performance of a piece by Schubert, a perfect score for his personal composition and, finally, nine out of ten for the recognition of musical notes. Of course, other competitors also scored perfect marks in parts one and two of the contest, but in the third part, the participant who came second to Daniel scored just six out of ten, and that was put down to luck. So it was Daniel who won the scholarship to the Franz Schubert Music Conservatory in Vienna.

He lived in a boarding school in the middle of town. He found it difficult to adjust to big city life. The noise from the motor scooters, beeping horns, cars and the general hum of the city disturbed him immensely. Early on, his skill, imagination, sensitivity and personal attitude revealed an enormous talent and he was chosen to continue his studies in America. Initially, he moved to San Francisco, where he studied the piano and violin with a scholarship at the local Music School. Soon afterwards, he completed his post-graduate education at the Manhattan School of Music, which is considered to be the greatest music school on the east coast of the United States of America. The competition at these famous educational institutions was extremely fierce but Daniel always came out on top. Everywhere he went, however, he found it impossible to adapt to the irritating noises around him.

The years when by and Daniel entered adulthood. Loyal to his specialism, he became a professor of music and taught at the Manhattan School of Music. He often took part in international competitions, winning the adulation of the audience and songs of praise from the judges. His friends and acquaintances were dazzled by his continuing successful career. As the years went by and his excellent career progressed, everyone forgot about the troublesome circumstances under which he had been born or the prejudice that had grown around him.

I met him when I was nineteen years old. I was a student at the school of music and he was my tutor. He wasn't much older than me and we soon became friends, probably since we were neighbours in Astoria, located in the north-west corner of the state of New York, at Queens, near Long Island City. He enjoyed, as much as I did, a daily walk in the park of the same name, which was situated opposite East River and had an amazing view of Manhattan. It was an escape from the pressure of it all and we talked for hours on end, calmly and free of stress, about various common interests. He often advised me on how to improve my technique, sometimes we joked about, and gradually, he began to confide in me about the personal issues he faced.

In the end, I wasn't able to complete my studies in music. Like most other people, I had to toe the line and find a job which would give me a steady income. But we didn't stop seeing each other and I would probably say I was his best friend, or the closest person to him in his world, shall we say. That's probably the reason both he and I remained single, unlike all our other friends. Neither of us liked the idea of marriage; we were sure it would make our lives difficult. Judging by our friends' lives once they'd got married, it seemed like an example not to be followed! Besides, Daniel had a more important reason not to marry: he could never commit to a woman as much as he could to his music.

Apart from that, he was a particularly awkward person. He never stayed in the same apartment for very long because of the torturous noise made by his neighbours – children, shouting, arguments, pets – it all infuriated him. He often moved on, until eventually, he bought a house of his own in an isolated location, and took extra care to soundproof it because he hated noise. His home was the only place he could relax. There was nowhere else. He avoided social gatherings because the music was always too loud and it made him feel uncomfortable. He didn't go to the cinema because, for him, the volume was unbearable. But it wasn't just that. He couldn't stand the noise of people unwrapping and enjoying the snacks on sale there, either. He even avoided engagement parties and weddings, however close he was to the people who'd invited him.

One time, I remember, we went to the wedding of a very good friend. As usual on such occasions, a band had been invited to play. Our table was very close to the band and he insisted on leaving. We managed to persuade him to stay; I still feel guilty about it. Ten minutes after the band struck up, blood began to drip from his ears. The pain was intolerable and we took him to the hospital. It was feared he might never hear again and that his eardrums had been destroyed. The doctors later revealed the problem was to do with the anatomy of his inner ears. As soon as a noise disturbed him, his ears began to bleed, forewarning of danger. It was a kind of self-defence mechanism to prevent fatality, and in this case, had saved his life.

Daniel's many international awards did not inflate his ego. On the contrary, he was down to earth and easy going with his friends. He didn't speak very much in company and he had a strange habit. When he heard a sound he didn't like, he grasped his right ear and pulled it down. Nevertheless, the advantage of fine-tuned hearing enabled him to pick out talented musicians and he promoted many who later became famous opera singers.

Some years later, however, Daniel changed. He was sombre, sceptical and lost in a world of his own. I thought his loneliness was to blame. I invited him out with me and my friends and tried to introduce him to women with similar interests. He always refused even my most innocent proposals. I asked him about his baffling behaviour. Why was he so stubbornly negative? Persistence paid off and eventually, he confessed he still had a problem with his ears and couldn't sleep at night. True enough, his eyes stuck out, red and veined and had dark shadows underneath them; a clear sign of insomnia. But I knew his house was well sound-proofed to keep out the noise, the telephone was always set to ring as quietly as possible, and the doorbell was stuffed with cotton wool and could hardly be heard. So what was it that disturbed him so much and kept him awake? Initially, I assumed the trauma of the bleeding ears episode that awful night at our friend's wedding was to blame, but then I discovered, with much regret, the tragedy of his situation.

I was horrified to hear him reveal that his problem was not external but internal. However strange it may sound, it was the noise of his heartbeat that disturbed him so terribly! At first, I thought he was joking, but I knew he wasn't like that. Besides, the look in his eyes left no room for doubt. So that was it! The sound of his heartbeat was too loud for his sensitive ears to take and it drove him to despair. He never got any peace.

I recommended a doctor I knew; an excellent physician. He was fearful of any kind of surgical procedure which, instead of reducing the intensity of his hearing, could possibly leave him deaf for the rest of his life. The idea that he would never be able to listen to music again and be confined to deafness, just like Beethoven, caused Daniel to panic. The only remaining solution to the problem was sleeping tablets. Since there was no alternative, he began to take them. The problem was solved and he got the sleep he so desperately needed. His face lit up, he smiled again and was much more cheerful.

Until not long afterwards when he became addicted to the sleeping tablets and again, had trouble sleeping.

"If only there was a way to make the noise stop," he muttered to himself all the time.

He took ever-increasing doses of the tablets but the human body becomes accustomed to long-term therapy. So it was back to square one. He tossed and turned all night waiting for sleep to come. He drank warm milk, as recommended by friends, and took hot baths to relax.

Overcome with disappointment, he revealed he'd tried other methods too. It made him want to cry, scream, and rip his clothes to shreds. It was a horrendous situation. He was beginning to lose control.

No one knew his terrible secret but me. Others took offence. His behaviour was erratic, he ignored his friends, locked in his world of scepticism and indifference. He was fired from his position at the music school for hitting a student who hadn't done his homework, but the real reason was that he couldn't control his anger. One by one, his friends abandoned him. Much was said about Daniel, most of it hideously false. I was the only one who knew the truth and the only one to visit him. He wasn't human anymore, but an unrecognisable stooge. His hair was ruffled and unkempt, his face unshaven and his hands clasped tightly over his ears as he tried to block out the sound of his heartbeat. But the noise didn't stop. It was a living hell. The genius that had given him an outstanding career was now a debilitating infliction, greedily sucking the life out of him from the blood down to the marrow.

I begged him to go ahead with the surgery, time and time again, even if it robbed him of his hearing. Surely it was better than suffering. But he would rather suffer than never hear music again. I did everything I could and talked to doctors, university professors, hospital managers and nurses to see if there was a pioneering solution to my friend Daniel's problem. But all in vain. This was beyond humane.

As time went by, we saw less of each other, on the one hand, because he never left the house, and on the other, I was working and had no time to visit. I also went down with a virus. He didn't use the telephone, so we couldn't talk anymore either. Daniel was dismissed from my mind.

I went to visit him as soon as I could to see if there was anything he needed or required help. It was on a dusky evening in January. Light but steady drizzle pierced the biting cold. I put on my warmest clothes and took a taxi. When I arrived, I rang the doorbell and while waiting for an answer, a foul odour filled the air. There was deadly silence. I knocked hard on the door, rang the bell again, but to no avail. Absolute silence. I approached the window and knocked, maybe he would hear me. I leaned my ear against the wooden blinds, but there was no indication of movement or life inside. For a moment, I thought he might have gone out. But where would he have gone? He had no one. And I knew he didn't like going out, anyway. After much fear and trepidation, I decided to break in through the window.

It was securely locked and barred and difficult to open. I looked around in the garden for some kind of object to make the job easier. I found a sharp, iron rod and made my way to the lowest window holding it tight. At that moment, a car drove by with headlamps blaring my way. Exposed by the ray of light, the driver caught sight of my ruffled appearance and the sharp rod in my hand. He stopped and asked if there was anything wrong or if I needed help.

"No thank you," I said.

He looked at me again, obviously suspicious. Then he left. I took a large stone and banged the end of the rod and eventually, after much effort, the wooden shutters opened. It was exhausting. I broke the window, slipped my hand inside and turned the latch. Without resistance, the window opened wide. A suffocating stench from the sealed house leaked out and hit me in the face. Daniel never opened the windows and the house was never aired. The atmosphere inside was repressive.

Twilight filled the room. The moon was almost full. I rummaged around for the light switch and turned on the light. It was like a scene from a horror film. The room was turned upside down. Clothes strewn everywhere, drawers full of linen and towels emptied onto the floor, pillows ripped apart and the door to the room destroyed by persistent thrashing. Total disarray! And there on the bed, Daniel lay dead with a knife driven through his heart. A red river stained the bed sheet and drops of blood dripped rhythmically to the floor. It was clear it had only just happened. If I'd got there earlier, minutes earlier, he'd still have been alive. Suddenly, there was a snort from the deathbed and his body shook spasmodically one last time. My friend had just taken his final breath.

To me, who knew his terrible secret, it was blatantly obvious. Unable to bear the shrillness of the beat of his heart, there was one desperate thing left to do. He had to put a stop to it. It sounds crazy, but tragically, it was true.

I sat down in the chair next to him, elbows on my knees and sank my head between my hands. Combing my fingers through my hair, I remembered the time we met, the friendship we had, how it all began and how it had come to this. I still couldn't believe it. What a horrific end!

Deep in thought, I failed to notice the voices and the blue light that circled the room. I don't know what happened afterwards, and the next thing I realised, I was on the back seat of a car between two men in uniform, who said they were taking me to the police station. I tried, in vain, to explain to the inspector at the police station, and later to the judge during my trial, that it was suicide, and it wasn't me who killed Daniel, as I had been accused. But everything went against me. It was an intrigue of Destiny.

The driver, whose car headlights exposed me, neighbours who saw me break in through the window, foolishly grabbing the murder weapon by the handle which then bore my fingerprints as I tried, in vain, to remove it from Daniel's heart; it had been driven with such malice. And last but not least, my clothes were covered in blood. The time of death was estimated by the coroner to be the time I arrived on the scene. And that was not all. My explanation of his death, to them, was nothing short of ridiculous. Unable to bear the sound of his heartbeat any longer, my friend had killed himself to stop it, I had tried to explain. Ultimately, I was convicted as an extremely dangerous and ugly murderer.

So here I am, nervously pacing up and down behind the bars of my prison cell, anxious and distressed, the sweat rolling down my grief-stricken face. But it's not the injustice that's killing me. It's the sound of the footsteps of the prison guards on their way to collect me. I forgot to mention, by the way, I was sentenced to death by electric chair for premeditated murder.

As for those who blame me, don't believe a word they say! Guilty by association as a result of my final move, they claim. Unable to tolerate the thunderous booming of my demonically beating heart, and with the guards approaching to take me to my death, I grabbed a spoon, the handle of which I'd sharpened on the stone wall of my cell and secretly hidden beneath the mattress of my iron-framed bed, and stabbed myself with equal malice, equal desperation, with the same hand, and in the same manner as my friend Daniel. The irrefutable similarity branded me his assassin!

«In Africa, with its jungles, wild animals and native tribes, I lived a nightmare so unpredictable, so bizarre, it drove me to the depths of despair»

3. THE CURSE OF ZENTAR

The combination of primaeval and twentieth-century culture on the African continent is fascinating and creates a veil of mystery, myth and fantasy. This marriage of diametrically opposed cultures captures the attention of the press now and again and has indeed been widely publicised. The depths of its vast, unexplored, virgin forests nurture native tribes, untouched by civilisation and oblivious to borders beyond their jungle kingdom. Stories of conflict with native tribesmen, even cannibals, have often been reported by explorers.

For anyone thirsty for adventure, the continent provides an enormous challenge. The familiar *safari* is often organised for the purpose of killing animals, whether dangerous (tigers, hyenas, lions) or harmless (monkeys, zebras, elephants) to man. On some occasions, purely for personal reasons (an outlet, a change of environment, a status symbol). On others, for commercial reasons and the exploitation of dead animals: crocodile skin for leather goods or elephant tusk for the precious ivory used to create *objet d'art*. Sometimes even for the purpose of capturing and encaging certain animals, destined for the zoos of civilised countries.

The first category includes trophy hunters. They like to be photographed with their prey, mount animal heads on the walls of their homes, or decorate its floors with animal hide, or are lovers of taxidermy. These individuals have one thing in common – financial euphoria. They usually hail from wealthy families. Understandable, given the amount of paraphernalia and equipment required, not to mention the burden of native guide hire, living and travel expenses. The typical wage-earner is unlikely to set off on safari, after all.

Another feature of financial euphoria is that the rich become bored and frustrated with life very easily. So they seek out new adventures, new horizons, or whatever else is left to do that they haven't already done. Wealth inflicted apathy is unfamiliar to the man on the street, however. His idea of a new adventure is archaic for his wealthy opponent.

So it was in Africa, with its jungles, wild animals and native tribes, where, compared to the *civilised* world, superstition and prejudice abound, that I came to be. But no one in their wildest dreams, their worst-ever nightmare, could possibly have imagined what lay in store for me. A nightmare so unpredictable, so bizarre, it drove me to the depths of despair.

This poses the question of how I came to be there in the first place. I'm by no means rich, but I don't need an extra job to get by either. So how does a lover of cocktails, late nights out and endless philosophising, a loafer, who hates organisation, social order and private ownership, have the means to travel to Africa?

It's quite simple. Bar hoppers like me are very knowledgeable about alcohol, have excellent taste and know how to make the most exquisite cocktails. *Chemists* who specialise in liquor, you might say. We make friends easily too, especially with the upper classes, since they're usually the ones who take care of our welfare. Wealthy people lose interest easily, and when life has lost all meaning, they take to the bottle. Specialists in the field, suitably qualified to guide them through the world of alcohol consumption, appear on the scene offering exclusive, incomparable delights, promising nothing short of ecstasy. The least they can do in return is compensate the provider of such delights. And because for the rich, the easiest, most practical way of returning the favour is with money – invitations to banquets, cruises, parties and the like – I, too, was compensated accordingly.

My last acquaintance with a rich person was on a cruise in the Pacific. He was fascinated by my cocktails and impressed by the dozens of combinations I came up with, depending on his mood, the weather, the place or the time of the day. He took a great liking to me and invited me to his London mansion where he went to unwind. He gave me his address, a ticket for a one-way flight and some cash for my expenses.

When I got to London, it seemed like a good idea to get to know the local bartenders. Before long, I'd met numerous people in the trade and completely forgot about my acquaintance. Time went by and money began to run out, but I was ashamed to visit him after such a long time, reluctant to reveal my desperation. Always the optimist, however, I didn't worry or panic, even when times were extremely hard. Destiny would soon send another *saviour* to my rescue, there was no doubt about that.

I had been in a similar situation before, this time further north, in Denmark. Destiny sent me an Italian businessman and we hung out together for about a year. He took care of my wardrobe, my meals, gave me a place to sleep, and thanks to his contacts, I had some amazing experiences with women from all over the world, experts in the art of making love. They introduced me to exotic secrets most people have never heard of. In return, I shared what I knew about alcohol, divulging the secrets I never shared, like the spirits I use as a base for my cocktails. Scotch whiskey, gin, vodka, then there's brandy, Kahlua, black and white rum, red and dry martini, and Bourbon too. Clear spirits like gin and vodka can be mixed with any type of fruit juice. Some, however, can never be used for cocktails – ouzo, for example. Whiskey doesn't mix with juice, but mixed with Drambuie you get a *Rusty Nail.* Wine is superb and much tastier with Crème de Cassis, a blackcurrant liqueur, but no more than two drops. The famous Five Whites, of course, are often underestimated, but here's a tip: use small shots each of vodka, rum, tequila, gin and Cointreau and top up with cola. Serve in a long glass.

In the famous *Whisky Bar* in London, where a lot of the rich hang out, I drank away the last of my money, hoping a worthwhile opportunity would come along. On the verge of despair, thinking Destiny had given up on me for good this time, a guy walked into the bar. He must have been around thirty-five. He sat down on a revolving stool two seats to my left. A well-built, athletic-looking type. My attention was drawn to his face. He was clean-shaven and had red, wavy hair. He had the look of an *aristocrat* about him. There was a sullen expression on his face; something was troubling him. He looked pensive, as if he was pondering over a decision he'd made. It was plain to see; his gloomy face wasn't the only giveaway. He was staring permanently into the glass in his hand. It was then I realised that Destiny hadn't forgotten me after all.

We soon got talking. It was easy enough. I'd learned from experience how to strike up a conversation and take it exactly where I wanted. We began with the subject of alcohol. I made an effort not to mention the worried look on his face. *'Keep the serious stuff till last'.* Start with a cheerful and friendly atmosphere. One of my basic principles.

I shared a few tricks of the trade to gain his attention and help him relax. There are two types of cocktail shaker, I said: the American and the European. They differ in the number of parts, the material they are made of and the price. He listened intently as I explained in more detail how the European shaker consists of three parts: the tumbler, a strainer for the ice, and a small cup-like lid, all made of metal. Shaking the ingredients is done with one hand. The American shaker consists of two parts, which fit into each other, one made of glass, the other metal, and is shaken with two hands. The American version is more expensive. A chopping board and a knife to cut the *accessories* (slices of lemon, orange peel garnishes, slices of banana and pineapple, strips of carrot and cucumber ribbons) are also essential for making cocktails, as well as a small champagne bucket for the ice, a scoop, some tongs, a special strainer exclusively for ice, and finally, a long-handled spoon.

Then he started talking about various things. He gave me the impression he was magnetised by the new and unknown. Just as he was about to order *"the same again"*, I held him off by recommending another place that served more delectable drinks. He agreed to give it a try, so I paid for our orders, we got into a taxi and set off for the *Long Glass*.

On the way, I managed to impress him with stories about life in general, travelling and my personal experiences, to prove I wasn't inferior. I wanted him to regard me as his equal, not some *crazy alcoholic*. And I got away with it, because wealthy people are easily impressed, especially when you claim to lead a life that's similar to theirs, even if you aren't as well off.

By the time we got to the *Long Glass*, my ice-breaker had worked. I was the best friend he'd ever had. I ordered a *Whiskey Squirt*, to begin with, a lavish, mysterious cocktail – one and a half parts Cutty Sark, a teaspoon of icing sugar, a teaspoon of Grenadine topped up with soda water and garnished with a strawberry or a chunk of pineapple. Obviously, I had no intention of introducing him to the weird and wonderful drinks all at once. Besides, it wasn't necessary; the starter was impressive enough, not that he knew any different. And if I introduced him to my best cocktails now, what was left for later? How would I continue to impress him? How else would I maintain his interest so he didn't get bored with me?

The next drink I recommended was the *Summer Dream*. I explained to the barman how to make it, since it was one he didn't know. One part Pisang Ambon, half a part Batida de Coco, one part vodka and two parts pineapple juice. Shake it all up and serve on ice in a long glass. He seemed to like it a lot, which meant he'd be ordering it all the time for the next few weeks until he got fed up of the taste. I recommended drink after drink until it was time to be on my way and find another *saviour*. I also knew the liquor was strong enough for him to open up to me. And that's precisely what he did.

He said he lived in a castle outside London, inherited from his great-great-grandfather. That his family had a glorious history complete with titles and honours. He was a Knight of the Order of the Garter, an honorary English title, like a Spanish Don, or a French de whatever. He told me of the excellent relationship they had with the Queen of England – they were often invited to events at the palace – and that he enjoyed sport, especially hunting, a sport exclusive to the *upper classes*. He told me a lot of things and now it was my turn to be impressed. Finally, he revealed what had been troubling him so badly. It was a decision he'd made recently to go to Africa on safari. Mostly for a change of environment, because he was fed up with England and in desperate need of something new. The only thing holding him back was that he had no one to go with, and for that reason, he was still unsure.

After several more drinks, William Hammersmith – that was his name – was in a much better mood. The booze might have been partly to blame, but it was more to do with the fact that I was a *good listener*. I came across as the most trustworthy person he'd ever met, someone who would listen to his problems. An invitation to his castle for a few days came soon after. At first, I said I'd have to think about it, though I'd never been to a castle before, but I knew all along I'd say *yes*. The bar closed and we set off for Hammersmith Castle.

It was a pleasant drive culminating in a woodland pass with a view of the castle high on a hill, regally dominating the surrounding area. As we approached, I discovered it stood on the edge of a cliff about eighty meters tall, with the ocean unfolding below. Fear swept over me as I gazed at the chilling landscape in the distance. The familiar sense of foreboding would later return brought on by the sight of the foaming rocks, the savage waves crashing against them, *exposed* to the elements, and the magnitude of the ocean that churned in endless turmoil, unrelenting until the time I left.

The landscape reminded me of stories I'd heard in a Transylvanian bar about blood-thirsty vampires and the isolated castles they chose to haunt. I must admit, this castle was much more harrowing than I any other I'd imagined. Fortunately, it would only be for a few days.

During my stay with the Hammersmiths, William gave me a guided tour of the castle. It was enormous and you'd easily get lost if unfamiliar with the layout. It was built many years ago in the typical rambling architectural style of the era with countless spacious rooms. Underground corridors were lit by torches, exposing visibly dank walls. There were lots of cells, where his forefathers would hold their enemies captive. There couldn't have been a more suitable place for the kingdom of the devil.

In a large hall with a glistening chandelier — a resplendent centrepiece — I was introduced to the Hammersmith ancestry, featured in paintings on the walls. Each with its own story to tell of brave conquests and heroic feats. The family tree went as far back as the seventeenth century. William was able to recite the intricate details of each of his ancestor's lives by heart.

The Hammersmith family was not particularly large. His mother, Ellen Hammersmith, had died six weeks before I met him. His father, Sir Thomson Hammersmith, had a strange, long, white moustache and was continually smoking a pipe. I assumed he was about sixty-five. He was fond of horse-riding, golf, archery and hunting especially. The love of both father and son for hunting would explain the enormous stables with plenty of horses, ponies and dogs.

The person who impressed me most, however, was Lady Mary-Ann Morris (Morris was her husband's surname), who was visiting home at the time. She was twenty-seven years of age, but looked much younger. Her face was surrounded by a mass of pretty, blonde curls and her skin was soft, smooth and white. She was stunningly beautiful and I was captivated by her from the very first moment we met. She pleaded with me on several occasions to persuade her brother to abandon his trip to Africa. How could I possibly refuse? But hard as I tried, William was adamant. Mary-Ann and I set off unaccompanied on many walks together and shared details of each other's lives. I'm not ashamed to admit that I fell in love with her, but out of respect for my friend, and her brother, I was determined not to let my feelings show.

I hadn't yet decided whether or not to accompany William on his trip. Yes, I wanted to try out new adventures, and no, I couldn't let him go alone. So we packed our bags, tickets and everything else we needed and set off on the journey to Africa. The weather was dreadful and the plane was forced to land in several cities, where we waited for hours until there were signs of significant improvement. In the end, it took us a whole day to arrive at our final destination. The first thing we did was seek out some locals to carry our belongings. One of them promised to bring seven people and would also act as our interpreter. We arranged to depart at dawn the next morning *in search of big game.*

To be honest, I had never been keen on hunting. I didn't like killing animals either, however wild they were, or even watch them being killed for that matter. But I was already in over my head and there was no going back now. I had no idea how to handle a gun. I was a gate-crasher on this mission. The exquisite flavours of the liquor extracted from fruits of the earth unknown to Europe was a comforting thought, nonetheless.

And true enough, at sunrise, around twenty people stood waiting to load the mission essentials onto their ample, muscular, black shoulders. It was easy enough, to begin with, but became increasingly difficult along the way to cut through the bush with our long, sword-like knives. We had no idea what lay before us, and were exposed to any number of risks. There were two things I feared most. One, the snakes that would invariably be hanging from the branches of random trees, undetectable, thanks to nature's gift of camouflage. Snakes that were extremely dangerous and venomous. One bite would mean instant death. And two, the plant life, either poisonous or carnivorous, and impossible to tell whether it was dangerous or not. Nature, once again, had endowed a deadly species with the ability to appear innocent.

After the first three days, I was feeling uneasy, missing civilisation, the noise, late nights out on the town, comforted by alcohol and loud music. I longed for the groaning of mechanical city beasts fuelled by petrol, rather than the fear of being eaten alive by jungle beasts fuelled by flesh and blood. Oh, how I hated the stillness, the insidious silence, the anxious beating of my heart, dreading every moment what the next might bring.

The first kill was a tiger that had threatened one of our guides, luckily without ripping him apart. He would, however, be indelibly scarred for the rest of his life. Trophy hunting was gruelling, but we rarely came across any prey, as if they had anticipated the threat. And even when we did, we lost them again easily; they knew the jungle much better than we did. William was furious. I begged him to turn back, but to no avail, for to return empty-handed would mean serious ridicule.

At the end of the first week, on the seventh day to be precise, the situation changed. Instead of predators, we became prey. It was midday. We had stopped for a while to take a break. Several of us took the opportunity to eat, since there was no fixed schedule for meals. It depended on how the hunt was progressing. I was drinking from a bottle I carried in the back pocket of my trousers, an exotic drink I particularly liked and was able to get hold of before we set off. The squawking birds went unnoticed when a band of tribesmen with painted faces jumped out of the bush, wielding canes. One of our escorts grabbed his weapon in self-defence but before he had the chance to act, a sharpened arrow glided through the rushes and struck his arm. He dropped dead instantly. It was a poisoned arrow. And now, they had taken us captive. However much our interpreter tried to reason with them, it was useless. They didn't speak any of the dialects he knew, and neither did he recognise the tribe they belonged to.

We surrendered and were herded to their village, directly to the Chief himself. Next, they put us in what looked like a livestock enclosure. Before long, they began to sing and dance to the accompanying rhythmic beat of the tam-tam. It appeared to be a celebration. Little did we know what they wanted from us or what was about to follow.

Discovering that the tribe with painted faces were cannibals freaked us out. And it was me they singled out initially, along with one of the escorts from our mission. It was obvious from their conversation, that some were asking for white flesh, while others preferred to save it for later. Dark flesh was tried and tested. Maybe our white flesh wasn't as tasty. To settle the argument they drew lots. Then, three of them came over and seized our escort. He screamed desperately with fright.

I had heard stories about man-eating tribes from African-American seamen, including the methods they used to kill their victims. Each tribe had a different method and the most gruesome of all was imprinted in my memory with indelible ink. The victim is tied, hand and foot, to stakes in the ground. A gooey substance, a delicacy it seems, for a certain species of ant, is pasted on just above the wrists. As soon as the ants catch scent of it, they crawl up the victim's arms. Dining on the substance as well as flesh, the victim's veins are severed. Once the blood starts to flow, the ants disappear; they hate the taste of it. The human is left to bleed to death, then dismembered and eaten.

As it happened, my personal experience easily surpassed the blood-curdling tales I'd been told. I was reminded of ancient Greek mythology, one of Theseus's feats, to be precise. The cannibals pulled on the bendable trunk of a tree and tied it to the ground with rope. The same was done with a nearby tree, bringing the tops of both trees together. The screeching native's feet were fastened in turn, one foot to one tree, one to the other. Then, they cut the ropes and the trees sprung back to their original positions, ripping the native in two. The sound of his body being wrenched apart and the, piercing shriek he let out sent shivers down my spine. I'd been saved by the luck of the draw. It could have been me, and the very thought of it brought me out in a sweat. The unbearably torturous heat was much less to blame. For an instant, my heart skipped a beat.

Cheering with victory, the cannibals dashed forward in two groups. Tugging on the trees, they ripped the dismembered body apart with their bare hands and the meat was divided up. Some obviously preferred the plentiful, gushing blood and drank their fill, grabbing chunks of meat from the unfortunate native's body now and then, like a decent, civilised person enjoying a hot-dog with a beer. Gastronomic bliss beamed on their ecstatic faces as they gorged themselves full. Naturally, the Chief was awarded the lion's share, getting the heart and the liver, and the genitals were given to his wife. The head, eyes wide-open in sheer terror, mouth agape in agony and fear, was reserved for the Witch Doctor.

The meal was over much quicker than I imagined and it looked as if they were still hungry. Now it was my turn. I was marched towards the trees. The Chief came up to me and scrutinised my clothes. He seemed puzzled, probably because I was fully dressed and they were all but naked, except for a leather thong strapped around their waists. He said something to the others and they began undressing me. Before they got to my tunic, I made a desperate attempt to distract their attention by gesturing to the Chief. I tried to convince him we weren't enemies. No such luck! All my hopes were now set on the trunk of ammunition close-by. If I could get to it, I'd teach them a lesson or two. Impossible. They had a tight grip on me, and anyway, as soon as I made a move, I knew they'd shoot me down with their poisoned arrows.

I pulled a mirror from my pocket and held it out to the Chief. He took it for further scrutiny and smiled at his reflection. It made him laugh and he started pulling faces like a baby. Obviously, I was killing time, but more critically, I had to win him over. When he'd finished playing with the mirror, he remembered he was hungry and focussed his attention on me again. Reading his mind, and before he could act any further, I whipped a cigarette lighter out of my pocket. History reminded me of how man had struggled over time to discover fire and how useful it had turned out to be. So I ignited it. Startled at the sight of the flame, they stood back, terrified. I flicked it on and off again and again until eventually, they realised that fire was controllable. The Chief approached me again, his hand outstretched, asking me to hand it over. So I did. Curiosity had got the better of him as it had with mirror. He tried but failed, to ignite it, so I showed him how it worked. From the satisfied smile on his face, I could tell my trick had worked. I'd been able to preoccupy him for the moment, at least. If only I had lighters for all of them! If I could somehow distract their attention, maybe we'd get a chance to escape.

But worse was soon to come. As I was planning our getaway, the Chief flicked the lighter one more time, but much too close to his face and it set fire to his beard. It was badly singed by the time they put it out. I'd achieved precisely the opposite of my original intention and he was furious. Roaring like a savage beast, he ordered the others to strip me naked. Bare and defenceless, they pulled and pinched me, comparing the colour of my skin to theirs. They had a good look at my genitals, too. Baffled, they exposed their own, switching glances between mine and theirs, hooting with laughter. The women hooted louder. One of the "braver ones" came up for a closer inspection. Suddenly, she pulled on them hard, I don't know why. Then another tribesman, probably her partner, pulled her away abruptly and slapped her face. Before I knew it, three of them grabbed me and dragged me off towards the trees. Thinking my life was over and how stupid I'd been to come on this wretched journey, but before they began to strap my feet, there was a torrential downpour. These spontaneous, torrential rainstorms – the *monsoons* – are a common phenomenon in Africa. They last for hours and can flood a whole village in fifteen minutes. The rain was heaven-sent. We'd been granted salvation.

The cannibals dropped everything and ran to take cover from the sudden deluge. Beneath the foliage, in hollow tree trunks, under branches. They'd abandoned us! In a flash, I ran over to the ammunition trunk. An arrow shot in my direction failed to strike its target due to the torrential rain and strong wind. I grabbed the gun, pointed it in their direction and pulled the trigger. One of the tribesmen fell dead. I set my companions free and handed them weapons. An unequal battle began with nature and better ammunition on our side. There was no other way. If we'd tried to escape with our heavy load, and clueless about the jungle, they'd soon have caught up with us. We'd have suffered a similar fate.

Slaughter ensued. Unable to retaliate or outstep the bullets, the cannibals dropped like flies, one by one. Dead. Men and women alike. Gruesome as it was, there was no alternative. I wept with nervous tension. I'd just annihilated a bunch of defenceless humans, or maybe it was because I'd been spared the most horrifying death, the victim of wild beasts, and all because of the rain. William came over, gave me a friendly pat on the back and a shot of brandy to calm my nerves.

When the rain stopped, we decided to return. It would have been foolish to continue the hunt after all we'd been through. Our lives had been saved, that was the main thing. We were sure we were going to die. We searched for the track we'd cleared earlier but to no avail. It had disappeared in the deluge and we'd have to start again from scratch. We continued in the direction of the township of Manaoue, deep in thought and silence. About half an hour into the trek, we came face to face a strange animal that none of us – *civilised* people – recognised. Similar to a young deer, it had an elongated head with upright ears like a guard dog, where other animals might have horns. Its eyes were a bluish shade of green, the colour of the exotic Fijian ocean. Its snout was black and wet, its body rather slight, brown in colour with two white, wing-shaped patches on either side. Its forelegs were also white, just above the hooves. Our interpreter explained that this was a holy species, protected by Zentar, the god of Serenity, and we should leave it well alone. If it came to any harm, Zentar would punish the perpetrator.

William, raised as an aristocrat, dismissed all such preconceptions. To him, it was a load of *nonsense*. At the same time, he was determined not to return empty-handed, and with more than his own precious life. Without further ado, he ignored the interpreter, pointed his weapon at the impartial creature looking down the barrel of his gun and pulled the trigger. The gun went off, the animal staggered and fell to the ground. Blood spurted from between its eyes. Smug with achievement, he pondered how best to stuff the creature and where it should hang in the castle. It was a beast unlike any other, a legend, with a story to tell, and had earned a space worthy of that.

Our native guides, offended by his actions, began to lament. As the interpreter explained, they were calling on their god, Zentar, blaming the white man, who committed the abuse to rid himself of anger, and at their expense. William grinned sarcastically. I don't believe in such nonsense either. Polytheism and idolism are obsolete as far as Europeans are concerned, but I have learned, at least, to respect the opinions of others.

Our adventure appeared to be over, there'd be no more surprises. Then, about ten minutes from the township, William clumsily fell into a stinging bush. The almighty reaction numbed his entire body. Within seconds, the pain was unbearable. It was highly likely the bush was poisonous, and getting him to the township to be given first aid as soon as possible was my new priority. The natives, however, refused to cooperate. They believed William's fate was Zentar's revenge for the slaying of the holy animal, and if they helped a heretic, they'd be equally as guilty.

In a flash, I lifted him onto my back, using what little strength I had left, and set off in the direction of Manaoue, hopefully in time to save him. Any later would have been too late, the doctor explained. The injection he gave him ensured he was out of danger. He promised to do whatever he could to improve his condition, which wasn't particularly serious. But he would have to be kept under strict observation.

I took him to a place they called a hotel. The room wasn't particularly spacious, but comfortable enough for our needs. There was no furniture and no bedside tables, just two beds, a chair and a picture on the wall beside the empty bed. A picture of a desert landscape with animal carcasses and human skeletons scattered here and there. Black birds fluttered about on high. The ugliest of them all was sitting on top of a cactus, ready to tear into the nearest available flesh. It was easily recognisable as the carnivorous desert vulture.

When William opened his eyes, he looked lost, oblivious to his environment. He didn't recognise me. He mumbled incessantly but I couldn't understand a word he was saying. He was gripped with fear at the sight of the vulture. *'Get rid of the picture,'* he appeared to mumble. I consoled him as best I could, and assured him it was just a painting. The vulture was not for real. It couldn't do him any harm. There was nothing to fear as long as I was by his side. Then he lost consciousness, so I don't know if he understood.

Before long, the doctor appeared and gave him another injection. His fever was still high. I recounted what had happened including my friend's fears. He explained that high fever causes hallucinations and loss of the ability to distinguish between reality and fantasy. Everything is taken for real. Fears from as far back as childhood are easily recollected creating a sense of panic and immediate threat. Before he left, he promised to pass by again at midnight to follow up on this strange condition.

I remained at his bedside and mopped his brow with cold compresses doused with a local potion to help the fever subside. Now and then he woke with a start, terrified and soaked with sweat, his eyes fixed on the painting and babbling absurdities. Hard as I tried, it was impossible to understand what he was saying. I assumed it was to do with the vulture. It was amazing how the stinging bush had messed with his brain, enough to blot out the line between reality and fantasy.

After all that had happened, I was dog-tired. I'd had nothing to eat and the thought of alcohol never entered my mind. Though desperate for sleep, the idea that my friend might need me kept me wide awake.

Just before midnight, the doctor returned. He was encouraged by a notable slight improvement. He gave him another injection and advised me to rest since the medication would send him to sleep for several hours. I said I would rather stay awake to keep an eye on him. I wanted to make sure his situation was improving before getting any sleep myself. Before wishing me goodnight, he said he'd be back again at dawn.

Not long after the doctor left, William suffered a critical attack. He bolted half upright in a bath of sweat, shouting he must kill the vulture. *'It's going to eat me'* he repeated, time and time again. He was still confused between fantasy was reality. I spoke to him gently, hoping to infiltrate the labyrinthine corridors of his mind and persuade him otherwise. It took superhuman effort to lay him back down on the bed. Once he was calm again, he drifted off into his own little world and stayed quiet for quite some time. Soporific silence filled the room and my eyelids drooped with exhaustion. As fatigue got the better of me, I remembered the doctor's words, and with my conscience clear, sat in the chair and allowed myself to nod off into a deep and wondrous sleep.

Before sunrise, I awoke from an ugly nightmare brought on by the events on safari. I opened my eyes to an even more hideous scene. William was dead, drowned in a pool of blood. His half-eaten heart had been ripped apart, as if he'd been savaged by a man-eating beast. Black feathers lay scattered on the bed. My mind turned upside down. I recalled his fears, the jumbled words he screamed each time he clapped eyes on the desert painting. Instinctively, I turned my head.

Horror of all horrors! Even now, after all these years, I fail to find words to describe it. The vulture was no longer sitting on the cactus. The feathered creature had disappeared for some inexplicable reason, though the rest of the painting was unchanged. I don't know what came over me, something weird inside took over, and with all my remaining strength, I yelled uncontrollably. I can't remember how long it lasted or what happened next. Just vaguely, that some people came into the room, saying things, doing things. Suddenly, I was flying above the clouds, as free as a bird, and angels in white dresses bore my weightless body. Two doors opened, I seem to recall. The gates to Heaven or Hell?

Several days passed before I realised they were the doors of the ambulance that took me to the psychiatric hospital to be examined by a panel of specialists. I described the whole story to them in perfect detail. I was diagnosed with *schizophrenia* and accused of murder but acquitted by the courts, citing a *"neuropsychiatric condition"*. It was my decision, however, to be sectioned and cured.

I've been in the same institution for years now and it's from there that I'm telling my story, shut off from the outside world, forgotten by all – friends and acquaintances alike, never having received a single visitor. My only companions through the endless, dark nights are the recurring nightmares of the events that unfolded in Africa. Nightmares that pass by as shadows on the sound-proofed walls of my cell, meticulously re-enacting, minute by minute, my unbelievable peril.

You'd be entitled to think the story I have told is pure fiction, a part of my sick ego, a flight of fancy, not something I actually experienced. And if that is the case, you have honoured me with an award the world's greatest minds might easily envy. Recognition of my vivid imagination and the ability to concoct such preposterous stories.

*«The human tissue gradually rematerialized
in a similar cubicle keeping transit time
between one location and another to a minimum.»*

4. THE FOURTH DIMENSION

The siren blared reminding him it was time to call it a day. He pressed a button to set his chair in motion. A buzz signalled his command had been obeyed. The chair was more a kind of vehicle. Its flat base was about a metre wide but had no wheels. It hovered above the ground driven by an electromagnetic field operated by a touch-screen in front of him.

The hover carrier turned one hundred and eighty degrees and headed towards the laboratory exit. *Research Time* was finished for the day and it was time to go home. Doors automatically opened and closed before and after him as he made his way along the corridor leaving the lab behind. When he arrived at the exit, he pressed another button, the hover carrier lowered to the ground and he climbed out. Similar hover vehicles were parked in designated spaces.

He stared into the retinal scanner and waited for verification of his code number and identification brief.

The scanner registered his retina, various coloured lights flashed and the familiar dull, metallic buzz confirmed that identification was complete. The giant automatic gateway opened and he headed out. The walk to the *Teleportation Terminal* was one of the few occasions when he needed to go on foot.

The *Work Station* towered majestically behind him as he walked down the steps. It was enormous, both in length and breadth, and around seventy metres tall. Buildings of this kind were common on Mars. The *Ministry for Urban Development* approved of massive multi-populated superstructures firstly, because transit time between the State employees' workplaces was greatly reduced and secondly, they allowed for more efficient supervision of the workforce.

He didn't have to wait long for a free cubicle at the *Teleportation Terminal*. He stepped into the first empty one that came along, programmed his destination, fastened himself in with the metallic safety belts, put on a metal helmet and pressed a black button. Within seconds, he began to dematerialise.

The metal helmet and safety belts were connected to a complex mechanism fitted with multiple microchips, a VS-4 generator, a transformer and a molecular resonator which converted human biological material into molecular radiation. The device transmitted the radioactive material to the programmed destination where a similar mechanism with opposite poles acted as a receiver. The human tissue gradually rematerialised in a similar cubicle keeping transit time between one location and another to a minimum.

Initially, telephone booth-like cubicles were deployed for the general public at strategically placed teleportation terminals around the planet but as time went by, unforeseen problems arose due to ever-increasing use and the gradual abolishment of aircraft. When two people from different departure points were scheduled to travel to the same location at the same time, they often rematerialised in the reception cubicle with various limbs conjoined. The solution came at a later date with the creation of *Healthcare Clinics* where both travellers were removed from the cubicle, transformed into molecular radiation using a programme specially designed to separate their frequencies and were returned to their original shape and form.

He headed for the *Residential Block*. Along the route, video clips of the Empire's achievements played on gigantic screens located on central squares. This year marked the centenary of the colonization of Mars. Since the beginning of the year, much effort had gone into promoting the *Empire's* accomplishments from its inception until the present day. Short clips were projected on loop on the sides of various high-rise buildings for all to see. Audio content was transmitted to the masses by a wireless network of megaphones normally used to broadcast the daily news.

The videos depicted the most significant events leading up to the final colonization of the planet.

"Missions to Mars first began approximately halfway through the twenty-first century, once Scientists had solved outstanding transportation issues. A mission to the moon including the safe return of the astronauts took one week. A mission to Mars required a total of two and a half years: approximately seven months to get there, a year spent on the planet until Mars re-entered the Earth's atmosphere and around another seven months to return.

"As soon as electrolysis in Space (once the rocket entered orbit, water electrolysis produced hydrogen to fuel the spacecraft and oxygen for life-support within it) was safely established, the first volunteers were able to travel to Mars and mission costs were significantly reduced. This had previously been deemed impossible. Colonization followed in the middle of the 22nd century. Cities were enclosed in huge semi-circular domes made of synthetic material highly resistant to pressure and heat. Astro-insulation allowed for visibility of the crimson-coloured upper atmosphere. Automatic artificial lighting was fitted throughout the planet as needed and none of the cities came into direct contact with the Universe. Enormous transparent tubes were used for inter-city communication. Oxygen was provided by special tanks strategically located in the ceilings of the domes."

The *Residential Block* didn't look much different from the Work Station on the outside. Apartments were built for single inhabitants only. No one shared a home. It was forbidden. The simple procedure required when a man and a woman wished to make physical contact deemed permanent relationships absurd. All you had to do was select the partner of your choice from the multi-page *Screening Guide*, enter their code into your computer and provide some details about yourself. The request was transferred to the *Central Computer*, forwarded to the person of choice and the searcher notified. The selected male or female candidate thereby discovered whom he or she was required to call on. All inhabitants were potential candidates and obliged to obey orders. There was one limitation, however. Calling on the same person more than twice a month was forbidden to avoid any foolish romance.

Conception, motherhood, sterility, breastfeeding, love and *pain* were unfamiliar concepts. The Molecular Biologists and Geneticists responsible for *Genetic Reproduction* suspended the reproduction cycle by epigenetic intervention, thereby ruling out the possibility of deliberate conception. The process was greeted with much enthusiasm. Previous scientists had discovered a way for men to give birth but it created serious problems. Women were side-lined and their mental health affected. It also had a direct impact on their work. Men were giving birth to children and focusing their attention on them and began to neglect their jobs. The number of births rapidly declined. Mars was still in its infancy and there was still much work to be done.

Research was needed into the permanent suspension of conception and when this was finally achieved, both men and women were forbidden from getting pregnant. The new method allowed interested participants to voluntarily donate sperm or eggs to the *Bio-Regeneration Centre*. Again, couples did not need to cohabit. The eggs and sperm were tested to see if they were healthy and divided into categories for the creation of citizens who would hold leading positions in society and those who would carry out the more menial and hazardous tasks.

From the beginning, it was considered necessary to change the way time was measured to provide sufficient opportunity for work. Time had previously been divided into units which proved minimal in relation to the enormous amount of work to be done. A *New Time System* was therefore conceived. A year on Mars was equivalent to 687 Earth-based days. Due to its orbital inclination (~ 25°), its seasons were almost twice as long as those on Earth. The year was divided into twelve months, similar to those on Earth. Each month consisted of fifty-seven Earth-based days. A day was added every four months to give a total number of 687 days. A week was the equivalent of ten Earth-based days and was called a *"tenday"*. The *New Time System* correlated to the old system as follows:

• 1 *"new"* year = 12 *"new"* months = 687 Earth-based days

• 1 *"new"* month = 57 Earth-based days (plus 1 extra day every 4 months) = 57 days X 12 months = 684 + 3 (every 4 months) = 687 Earth-based days

• 1 *"new"* month ≈ (approximately equal to) 6 *"tendays"* = 57 Earth-based days

• 1 *"tenday"* ≈ (approximately equal to) 10 Earth-based days

• The 3 extra Martian days were called *"sol"*

The second was kept as the basic unit of time while all other chronometric subdivisions (minute, hour, day, etc.) retained their names and concepts. The *"New"* working day consisted of ten Earth-based hours and one day off was given every four days. In brief, a *"tenday"* was made up of eight working Earth-based days of ten-hour shifts and included two days off.

He usually carried on working at home. But today, he was much too tired and couldn't be bothered. He lay down on his comfortable bed, contemplating. It had been a while since he'd invited a woman to his apartment. He remembered the pretty colleague he'd seen in the corridor of the *Work Station* a couple of days ago. She was rather impressive so he looked her up in the *Screening Guide*. From her figure alone, which was not easy to forget, she wasn't difficult to find. He discovered she was called EBN 3715. He followed the required procedure and waited. *DEFERRED* flashed up on his screen, which meant someone else had got there first.

'Probably for the best,' he thought. *'I'm not really in the mood today, anyway. I'll go and visit PKA 274 instead. Haven't seen him for a while.'*

He checked on his computer to see if he was home and in next to no time, he arrived at his apartment.

"Hello, PKA 274," he said.

"Hello, PNO 968," his friend replied.

The introduction of letters and numbers to replace original names was another change that had been made. Healthy males' names began with the letter P and healthy females' names with the letter E. The letters that followed indicated where on the planet they were born, their social status, day of birth, time, and place of residence. For example, PKA 274 indicated that he was a healthy male, born in the K region of the planet, was a musician (A), born on the second day of the *tenday* (2), the seventh year after the completion of Mars (7) and lived in the 4th section of the *Residential Block*. The more letters a name consisted of, the higher the social status of the person concerned. Equally, a person in a minor position had fewer letters in their name.

"You look tired, exhausted, more like," said PKA 274.

"Absolutely," his friend replied. "Time flies by so quickly at work these days; it's unbelievable. I'm determined to get my latest project done as soon as possible, though. Not that I have to or anything; I just want to."

"Is it that exciting?" he asked.

"As a matter of fact, it is. I'm not supposed to talk about it but I'm going to tell you anyway, and for two reasons."

Their eyes met and he began to explain.

"First of all, because you're my friend, and secondly, because I'd like you to come with me when it takes shape."

"What's it about?" he asked with interest. It sounded pretty unique.

"It's a theory that, so far, no one has been able to put into practice," he continued. "Recently, I discovered a way to make it work and it's almost complete. It has to do with travelling in the *Fourth Dimension*."

"*Fourth Dimension?*" he repeated. "Could you explain that, please? Only if you want to, of course."

It would take time and patience to explain the theory. He took a deep breath and carried on.

"As you know, there are three dimensions: length, breadth and height. The *Fourth Dimension* has to do with Time. Theoretically speaking, the quadrilateral system allows you to align the *Bio-intersection* with the fourth axis and break away from the present. Depending on how much you increase or decrease the alignment, you find yourself in either the past or the future. At the moment, I'm trying to work out the correlation between time measured in years and dimensional coordinates in degrees. There's always the possibility of getting lost in eternity, of course; it's the first time it's been attempted, after all. I've thought it through hundreds of times though, and verified it all on my computer, right down to the very last detail. There can be no mistake."

"Listen, PNO 968," he interrupted, "I wasn't much good in *Primary Education* as you probably remember. I still can't recite the Theory of Relativity – the easiest of the theories they taught us in the second year. I had no idea what micro-chip computers were all about in Year 5 either. Luckily, the goddamn machines were programmed according to individual skills. Now, if it's music you're talking about, I'm your man! But as far as your explanation is concerned, I'm sorry, I have no idea what you're talking about."

He paused for a while.

"But however it works, you're going to be the first person to try it out, right?"

PNO 968 nodded his head.

"Which period in time are you planning to visit?"

"The end of the twentieth century," he replied.

"So why did you chose the past?"

"There's something I haven't told you yet," he confessed, "something that happened on one of those interplanetary trips the *People's Further Education and Entertainment Bureau* organises from time to time."

He leaned back in his triangular, metallic swivel chair and explained.

"We were on our way to the planet Earth. We only got as far as the exosphere because radiation was detected in the upper layers of the stratosphere. Using the *Telelens*, we observed the surface of the Earth. It consisted of nothing but water and vast deserts of dry land. Despite that, it had a weird charm, I must admit. We stopped to refuel in Oasis – 3. I got out of the spacecraft and walked around to stretch my legs. At some point, one of the propellers caught my eye. There was a metal box attached to it. As you know, *'any unknown object must be handed over to the authorities'*, but I broke the rule. Making sure no one was looking, I dismounted it and hid it inside my spacesuit. I examined it thoroughly as soon as I got back to my room. It wasn't difficult to open. It was secured with an ancient padlock which was no trouble for my laser cutter.

"Slowly and with much trepidation, I opened the lid and was surprised to find it contained an object abolished on Mars many years ago – numbered sheets of paper bound together inside a hard outer cover. I remember learning about such objects in *History*. They were called *books*. The title and name of the person who wrote the book were usually written on the front. They were called *authors*. Authors were some of the people the first occupants of Mars decided to get rid of. They were considered lazy, useless and worthless to society, but above all, dangerous. It was the same with *poets, artists, composers* and *lyricists* – they didn't conform. They were on a mission to stimulate the imaginations of the masses and were capable of influencing people's thoughts and turning them against those in power.

"The book in question was written before the *Second Nuclear War*. It contains pictures and descriptions of life on Earth before the *First Nuclear War* and tells of the circumstances leading up to it as well as the kind of life that followed. Do you remember the stories they told us in *Pre-Education* about shipwrecked Earthlings sending messages in bottles they cast into the sea? I think the metal box was something similar. It was fitted with a magnet so it could attach itself to passing vessels."

"And what did the anonymous message say?" asked PKA 274, clearly intrigued.

"As I said, it was written before the *Second Nuclear War*. At the time, the planet Earth was inhabited by humanoid beings whose bodies were saturated with radioactive matter. Having learned from the mistakes of the people who destroyed their world, they tried to reboot it and start again from scratch. An amazing culture evolved but despite that, and as far as the rest of the Universe was concerned, they were outcasts. Nobody wanted to have anything to do with them for fear of the radiation they emitted. Other planets sought conflict with them, believing that if the humanoid race became extinct, radioactive matter would eventually disappear. Otherwise, it would be passed down from generation to generation for as long as they lived, making the planet Earth impossible to exploit. The *author* was clearly very perceptive and anticipated the inevitable destruction of the planet he lived on. He conveniently attached the box containing the book to the propeller to remind future settlers of their origin, *our* origin. He wanted them to know the planet Earth was once a beautiful place and could return to its former glory and they MUST seek to achieve this. Only then would man become aware of his natural environment and discover the true meaning of life. Only then would he experience emotions that have ceased to exist and which undoubtedly led to the destruction of the human race."

"I still don't understand why anyone would want to go back to that era, I'm afraid." Just the thought of it made him feel sick.

"I've seen pictures and read about the planet Earth in those times," said PNO 968. He knew what he was talking about and seemed very enthusiastic. "Have you any idea what clouds, sky, grass, soil look like? Have you ever felt *rain, snow, wind* or *sun* on your skin? Do you know what *trees, waterfalls, birds, rocks, animals* are? There are so many things we have never seen or experienced. Over time, our *History* has conveniently been deleted. What more can I say? Life on Mars might have come a long way since those days, but there is so much stuff we can't even begin to imagine."

The old-fashioned world obviously appealed to him. PKA 274's disdain for it was equally as evident.

"I don't agree," he said, raising his voice. "Everything here is organised and perfectly planned, right down to the very last detail. We are all treated equally and given the same opportunities and the same rewards. We are fortunate not to believe in such selfish ideals. We have one Leader who always has our best interests at heart. If I remember rightly, everyone wanted to be a leader in those days, History lessons taught us that. There were thousands of *political parties, organisations* and *committees* everywhere. And what did they achieve? Nothing but the spread of injustice. The planet was divided up into sections – *countries*, with *borders, guards* and *armies*. In those days, some people were rich while others were dying of starvation. Even the Climate was unfair. It was freezing in some places and unbearably hot in others. Nowadays, we have done away with *crime, fear, cruelty* and *inequality*, too.

"Are you sure about that?" said PNO 968.

It was his turn to disagree, to defend and justify his case.

"Are we really all equal? Aren't you forgetting about the short-named people? The Z–5s, the I–12s, the X–2s, the B–9s in our society? The ones that do the menial work. The ones that aren't entitled to the *Rejuvenation Pill.* Why shouldn't they be allowed to retain their youthful appearance and live to the age of a hundred and sixty without suffering? Why don't they have access to it? They have no choice but to grow old, suffer pain and die at the age of seventy. What about the people with the sanitation tanks and magnetic sweepers who clean your home, your workplace, the corridors in all the buildings, the streets in the cities? Those that expose themselves to cosmic radiation to maintain the supplies of oxides and hydrogen, and those who work in the mines on this planet? Surely, that's a crime. It's cruelty, isn't it? If you break the rules, you're punished and deprived of the *Regeneration Pill*, medical assistance, your work, your home and all the comforts you enjoy. Surely that's unfair. How can you possibly believe we're better off than people in those days?"

"Even if what you say is true," he said eager to end their disagreement, "I can't accept the offer to come with you. It's alright for you; you have the right knowledge and skills and would easily be able to find work on planet Earth. But what about me? All I know about is music. Remember the old-fashioned instruments they used to play in those days? We learned about them in *History*. *Trumpets, violins, guitars, pianos, saxophones, drums, clarinets,* and so on, and they played them with their hands or mouths or feet. These days, it's much easier. All I have to do is enter my choice of instruments into my computer, add the details about the type of sound I would like to create, the rhythm, meter and scale, etc. and it will come up with a solution for me. From then on, it's a matter of personal taste. Even if I did get used to the way they did things in those days, the raw sound of those ancient instruments would drive me crazy. I'd never stick it out. It took hundreds of years to phase out those archaic sounds and fine-tune the music we listen to today. No, no way!" he said finally. "Forget it!"

"Very well." He was clearly sad. "If you don't want to come with me, I'll have to go alone."

He got up to leave. His friend went after him.

"Wait, have you discovered a way to get back? I mean, if you get fed up with it or if you don't like what you see, will you be able to return?"

"No." He was quite categorical. "At the moment, that's impossible. In a generation or so, I'm sure it'll be doable, though. You should be able to go wherever you like and return safely by then."

"Aren't you worried about that? You'll be just like the people with low-number names, destined to grow old, suffer pain, die a torturous death!"

"No, I don't mind at all," he answered calmly. There was a sweetness in his voice. "Besides, the same will apply to me here, if they discover what I'm up to. That's why I haven't told anyone, except you."

"You really want to do this, don't you?" he said.

"Yes, I do. And knowing my *History*, I hope to convince people to change their way of thinking, the way they behave, the way they perceive things. I'm determined to warn them about the catastrophe their world is heading for."

He made his way to the exit.

"When do you think you'll be ready?" he said, looking him in the eye.

"It shouldn't take much longer." He was unspecific. "As soon as I've discovered the correlation between the geographical coordinates and time scale, basically, and am absolutely sure it will work, of course. And as far as the others are concerned," he added shrewdly, "I've managed to convince them a number of problems are yet to be solved."

They reached the door. Seconds before the photoelectric cell detected them, they stopped and looked at each other.

"I'll miss you, PNO 968," he said, sadly. "I hope it works out! And as soon as it becomes possible to travel in time and return safely, I'll enter the era you've chosen into my computer and come and visit you. You can be sure of that."

"I'd like that very much, PKA 274," added PNO 968. He was rather upset. "I look forward to seeing you."

They hugged each other tightly. Knowing they probably wouldn't meet again anytime soon, it was their last opportunity to say goodbye. PNO 968 couldn't have been more certain of it. He was leaving the very next day; that was the truth of the matter. He had lied about the issues with the geographical coordinates and time scale as an extra precaution. He was only going to tell the truth if his friend had agreed to go with him.

He returned to his apartment and was comforted by the thought of leaving. EBN 3715 came to mind so he sent her an invitation. *DEFERRED* showed up on his screen. She was indeed a beautiful woman and obviously in great demand. He suddenly realised he didn't know anything about relationships between men and women in times gone by. Choosing a partner as they did nowadays probably wasn't an option in those days. He continued to search through the Screening Guide.

'Might as well carry on where I left off,' he thought. *'It doesn't look as if I'll be able to try them all out now, anyway.'*

He typed in EXN 475. He smiled when *AVAILABLE* beamed up on his screen. A few minutes later, a tall, slim, green-haired woman with purple eyes knocked on his door.

He didn't sleep a wink that night. The escape plan went round and round inside his head. Night had fallen by the flick of a switch for the last time. Soon, there would be real nights and real days. He tried to imagine life in the historical era he had chosen to visit. Soon enough, he was taken back to the time the idea had originally taken shape.

Admittedly, he had thoroughly planned every last detail and it had been wise to keep the extent of his progress to himself in the initial stages. No one could ever have imagined what he had in mind and none of his colleagues would have had the faintest idea how to make it work. He was convinced however, that someone else would arrive at the same conclusion in the years to come and the experiment would be complete. They might even justify his actions. Or maybe they wouldn't. What did it matter anyway? At least he would be happy. *"Happy"*… What was that supposed to mean? Why did happiness come to mind in the first place? He must have read about it in the illegal *book* he had secretly acquired.

His personal computer buzzed reminding him it was time to be getting on. Justifiably nervous, he sprang into action. His luck was in at the *Teleportation Terminal*; there were no transit delays. Soon, he was walking up the steps inside the *Work Station*. He approached the entrance, fixed his eye on the retinal scanner and waited to be recognised. He got into his hover carrier and slowly proceeded along the corridor looking at the surroundings for the last time. Doors automatically opened and closed before and after him.

He entered the laboratory. It was exactly as he had left it and awaited his next move. He trembled nervously. The time had come. He fiercely tapped on the keyboard of his computer for final confirmation. His heart beat like a drum when he was given the all-clear. All he had to do now was start the engines, enter his destination, align the *Bio-intersection* with the fourth axis and press the button. But the engines wouldn't start. He tried again, taking extra care this time. Nothing. He broke out into a sweat. Now? Right at the end? He gave it one last try. No luck.

Before he had the chance to think about what to do next, the door of the laboratory opened and in barged his Director accompanied by three armed men.

Overcome with fear, PNO 968 lost his cool.

"What's going on?" he stammered. "Nobody was supposed to know about this."

"Precisely," the Director replied. "Though I must admit," he continued, "you planned everything perfectly. Extremely admirable work! But you forgot two important details which proved disastrous for your escape plan. Firstly, your computer is under our control and programmed to pass on real-time information to our files. Every calculation you made was stored in its memory and then relayed to us. We would never allow precious long hours of research to go to waste. What if something happened to one of our subjects? It's a test of your obedience, that's all. Secondly, the aim of the *Establishment* is to instil absolute obedience in all its subjects."

"Absolute terror, more like," he added sarcastically.

"Yes, maybe so," the Director replied. "Your friend PKA 274 informed us of your intentions when he realised what would happen to him if we discovered he knew. And we would have found out one way or another, you can be sure of that. Besides, why do think we provide you with so many luxuries? Out of love? Make no mistake, you would sorely miss them if they were taken away from you. And in return, we demand absolute obedience. Although it hasn't worked with everyone, I must admit. There are others like you, indifferent to the consequences. Allow me to tell you a secret. And however strange it might seem, it's true. Indeed, fear exists. But not only the kind of fear you mentioned; we also live in fear of you. One day, maybe one of your kind will get away with it. And do you know that would mean? A precedent would be set for disobedience, revolution. It would only take one person to destroy our entire civilisation. In your case, however, there were other reasons to fear. What if you managed to convince the people of planet Earth to prevent the *Nuclear Wars* once you got there? If you succeeded, we would automatically disappear. If the *Nuclear Wars* hadn't taken place, our ancestors would never have settled on Mars. We would be non-existent. Enormous effort was required to create our civilisation and it would be gone in a single moment. And for that reason, giving you a second chance would be far too dangerous a thing to do. Clearly, we can't trust you anymore. In your case, there is only one penalty."

He signalled to the three armed men who turned their weapons on him and fired. Lethal rays from their laser pistols spewed all over his body. Within seconds, PNO 968 was reduced to a handful of dust.

"Hello PNO 968," called a friendly voice from afar. He slowly opened his eyes. It was a familiar figure.

"Hello I–12," he hoarsely replied. He was yet to recover from his ordeal.

"You're one of our most regular customers, PNO 968, surely you know that by now! Tell me this," he continued, shutting down the machine, "what did you dream about this time?"

"The usual," he replied. He slowly got up and removed the electrodes from his head.

"The Fourth Dimension with the Scientist and the Time Machine?" He smiled facetiously.

"You've guessed it. But at least the protagonist was more exciting this time," he joked. "The *Virtual Reality Developers* did a great job."

"Look, the machines are programmed to keep our dreams strictly in line with the *Establishment*," he reminded him. "Isn't that obvious now?"

"That's exactly my point, I–12," he stubbornly replied. "They are just machines. And no machine is perfect. One day, they'll make a mistake and I can't wait for that to happen. I want to discover the true meaning *"happiness"*, and if it is as I imagine it to be, I will die happy. Until then, I'll just have to be patient."

He got up and made his way towards the door. He stopped in front of a mirror and looked at his reflection. He was around forty-five if the lines on his face were anything to go by. I–12 was ninety-seven and looked much younger, thanks to the *Rejuvenation Pill* provided by the *Welfare State*.

He stepped away from the mirror with bitterness and pain in his heart and returned to his vacuum-powered and magnetic sweeper.

«*He grabbed the handle of the iron poker, the tip of which had been*

5. INEXPLICABLE

"To be honest, I'd forgotten you existed."

He nodded his head in agreement.

"That's quite understandable," he said. "It's been twenty-seven years since you've heard from me… you probably thought I was dead."

"It's a long time not to hear from someone, and of course, unpleasant thoughts like that do cross your mind.

He lit his pipe and drew on it several times to char the tobacco. He took the crystal, stemmed glass half-full of wine in his right hand and raised it to propose a toast.

"To our family reunion!" he said.

The man raised his glass in return, approving of the tribute.

"Exquisite," he said, taking a sip. "It's probably an old one, though I don't know much about wine."

"You're right," the host answered proudly. "It's a hundred years old. There are only a few bottles left in the cellar. To be used on special occasions only. As you know, you are my only relative," he replied, justifying his choice. "Probably a distant relative, but the only one, nevertheless. I have no parents, wife or children. I did get lonely over the years, I must admit. Not that I don't have friends and acquaintances, of course, but that's different to someone who shares the same blood. I used to look at those yellowing old photographs of us and it made me sad. I yearned for you, the only remaining link to my heritage, to be alive. But Edward," he reproved, "you disappeared so suddenly and without a trace."

Edward leaned towards one of the lighted candles on the four-pronged candelabra on the grand oak table before him. He carefully lit the cigar between his lips.

"I must confess, Jason," he began to explain, puffing clouds of smoke, "I was forced to disappear suddenly and without a trace, because of an unfortunate entanglement with a woman. I left for Algeria one rainy night, on a merchant ship, having given the captain the last of my money."

He took another sip of his wine and drew deeply on his cigar. Ash fell onto the white, porcelain plate with a light blue design in front of him.

"Not even a letter or a telegram!" Jason persisted. "Was it too much trouble? Why? What happened?"

"When I got there, things were very difficult," Edward began to tell. "I had no friends or acquaintances and just two dollars left to my name. I had to find a job as quickly as possible. My employers took advantage of my desperate situation, whatever work I found. I worked sixteen hours a day for next to nothing, and by the time I'd finished, all I wanted to do was get a good night's sleep. As time went by, I became more active, saved some money and began to live a better life. That's when I tried to contact you, but I was told you'd moved. This must be the new house. I didn't know your address."

"Yes, that's right," Jason confirmed. "After graduating from the University of Ohio, I received a very good offer to pursue a doctorate in Illinois."

The tobacco in his pipe ran out. He emptied its contents into the ashtray, tapping it lightly.

"As soon as I had completed my doctoral thesis," he continued, "they offered me a job as assistant professor. I've been living here permanently ever since. After several years, I was promoted to professor."

"Indeed? What did you study?" he asked with interest.

"Parapsychology," he replied.

"And what was the subject of your thesis, if I may ask?"

"I was researching a strange phenomenon known as time travel."

Edward looked perplexed.

"Time travel?" he questioned.

The professor knew there would be a lot of explaining to do.

"Yes, time travel, also known as a time vacuum," he said. "It concerns the phenomenon where time appears to lose its linearity and doubles back on itself, permitting a glimpse into the past. Scientists researching the subject are unable to accurately determine the nature of the phenomenon, despite having recorded tens of reports from people of varying social classes and with various levels of education. In most cases, the people in the past were not aware of the presence of visitors from other eras. Nevertheless, there are cases where two-way eye contact was observed, or where animals were involved, their presence was felt.

"Time travel occurs when a person is suddenly transported from the present to a specific moment in the past. Both timescapes function simultaneously and the person experiencing the phenomenon discovers he is living in the past and the present at the same time. The most likely explanation is that for some, as yet inexplicable, reason, the time barrier is broken and one experiences a few minutes – or even seconds – in another era, quite involuntarily and unaware of it at the same time. It's also possible to be transported to another place and continuum of time in a parallel world, which has a lot in common with one's current timescape. There are also recorded incidents of time travel that lasted much longer than a few seconds. What's more, contact between the people of both eras has also been recorded.

"Now a classic case of time travel would play out something like this. At first, the person concerned realises he is lost. The surrounding environment becomes blurred and unrecognisable, but only slightly different, and is usually accompanied by a strange silence. He knows something is wrong, subtle differences are detectable, and he becomes disorientated, as far as his location and the messages he receives from the world around him are concerned. Before he has time to adapt to the changes, he realises he is back in his familiar environment. Later, when he recalls the scene, especially if his memory is good, he can probably identify some unusual detail that stood out: a passer-by wearing out-moded clothes, a side street that previously didn't exist, a shop that is nowhere to be seen, however hard he looks for it, a landscape… Then, it suddenly occurs to him that, somehow, he'd been transported into the past, if only for a few seconds or minutes!

"Simply said, since the beginning of time, man has always used the concept of time – the hour of the day, day of the week, season of the year, and so on, to organise his life and classify the chaos of time. Chronology, however, is shaped by our definition of it and may be conventional to us, but unrelated to the actual passage of time. In the same way, it's quite possible the

Universe has a completely different concept of time to that of our own. The clash between these two time concepts – one universal, one man-made – could be the cause of time travel."

He stopped for a moment to relight his pipe. He was passionate about the subject and, by this stage, had become quite animated.

"When we've finished our meal," he continued, "we can go to the library, and I'll read you some excerpts from the book I'm reading at the moment. It's extremely interesting, but only if you would like to, of course."

"By all means," urged Edward.

They got up from the magnificent oak table. The dining room wasn't particularly large but was comfortable enough and special attention had been given to its décor. It was obvious the designer charged with furnishing the house had an elevated sense of charm. Soon, the butler came, and as ordered by his master, restored both order and cleanliness.

They walked through a hall of paintings, though Edward had no idea how to interpret them. But he was certain they had something to do with his cousin's scientific interest. Jason stopped at a painting which evoked both awe and melancholy.

"I commissioned this one. It's not an original. It depicts a scene from a 1562 oil painting by the Flemish artist, Pieter Bruegel the Elder, titled *The Triumph of*

Death. It hangs in the Prado Art Museum in Madrid. A piece that stimulates the imagination, a precursor to early Baroque, and a work restored by the romanticists two hundred and fifty years later, and the surrealists almost four hundred years after that. As you can see, the painting depicts a panoramic scene of an army of skeletons wreaking havoc across a blackened, desolate landscape. Fires burn in the distance and the sea is littered with shipwrecks. Also visible is the *scorched barren earth, devoid of any life as far as the eye can see.* A few leafless trees on hills otherwise bare of vegetation, fish lie rotting on the banks of a corpse-filled pond. Legions of skeletons advance on the living, who either flee in terror or try, in vain, to fight back.

"In this work, Bruegel depicts the relentless course of time and the inevitability of death. Fate in the form of a death cart crushes material human desires — treasure chests, crowns, musical instruments — and the Grim Reaper follows close behind. "For dust you are and to dust you shall return." There, where we are all equal, where there are no social or spiritual differences or segregation. There, we are oblivious to feelings of pain, joy, ingratitude, or sadness. Time is a meaningless dot compared to the eternity of the soul. Paintings like these are known as *memento mori* (a reminder of death), which applies to everyone, however mighty or humble. While life is miserable and often cruel, time is a tyranny that drives its victims to their day of judgement."

Edward was fascinated by the description, transcended from this world to another far away.

"Follow me," said Jason.

The library was amazing. Jason must have been the only person in the world with so many books, all shelved accurately in order. There were tens of bookcases, both large and small with hundreds of books. Most impressive of all, the walls were invisible. Beyond the double sliding doors stood cases crammed with books from end to end and from top to bottom on all sides of the room. Dazed by the spectacle, he hovered at the entrance.

"Please come in, Edward," he said with pride.

Jason was like a goldsmith displaying his most exquisite and valuable jewellery made from rare, precious stones. Edward stepped inside, hypnotised by the spectacle before him.

"Have you read them all?" he inquired.

"Not all of them, but most of them, yes!"

He went over to the armchair and took a book from the table beside it. A bookmark was placed about halfway through. He sat down and suggested his cousin do the same. Then, he continued.

"I'll read you an extract from a strange experience of time travel from the past. A middle-aged seamstress by the name of Mrs Brown went to Norwich in England to buy some fabric. She had been told of a shop on the outskirts of the town that sold good quality products at attractive prices. She decided to pay them a visit. Though she knew the district reasonably well, she had never been to the specific retailer before. On the way, it began to rain and to save getting wet, she took a short cut through some old side streets. The cobblestoned streets in the area and the traditional appearance of the shop front were no surprise to her at the time.

"Inside, she noticed there were a number of vintage items – pictures on the wall, a desk, an umbrella stand, a small table and the vase that stood on it. Before she had the opportunity to see what else was on display, a shop assistant appeared, dressed in a formal gown. Without paying too much attention, Mrs Brown asked to see some rolls of cloth to choose which fabric to buy. Willing to help, the shop assistant placed them on the counter and when she had measured and cut the fabric the seamstress had selected, she wrapped it neatly for her customer. While doing so, she happened to mention that some of her regular customers were seamstresses to the ladies of high society.

"Mrs Brown was taken by surprise but said nothing. She took the fabric and asked to pay. The young woman politely told her it would be nineteen pounds, a sum that wouldn't usually have paid for half the material she'd chosen. Though certain the girl had made a mistake, Mrs Brown eventually paid the sum that was asked of her without further ado. She was more concerned about whether the rain had stopped and was in a hurry to leave. She threw the change into her bag without counting it and asked for directions for the quickest route to the station. The strange silence throughout the exchange made her feel somewhat uneasy, however. And there was no noise from the traffic outside either, which also seemed peculiar. The girl's directions were rather confusing and Mrs Brown was obliged to ask passers-by to get to the station on time.

"Three weeks later, she decided to buy more fabric. She and her customers were very satisfied with their purchases. So she paid another visit to the familiar store in Norwich for more quality fabric at reasonable prices. When she got there, she couldn't believe her eyes. Compared to three weeks earlier, this was another world! The cobblestoned streets were now paved, the shop, both inside and out, looked drab and dark with age, and the décor was very unfamiliar. What's more, the shop assistant who came to serve her was a middle-aged woman and did not know the girl who had been there three weeks before. Most extraordinary of all, when she asked for the fabric, she was informed by the assistant that it was not available and that they had never stocked anything similar. The owner of the shop confirmed the information. The only evidence of her previous visit were some offcuts of the fabric she had in her sewing room and a handful of old coins with the bust of King Edward VII. The cobblestoned street, the sales assistant dressed in the fashions of Edwardian times and the old stock of material had ceased to exist. It might just as well have never happened at all.

"A later investigation into the origin of the fabric, known as worsted, revealed it had been manufactured by Flemish and Wallonia weavers who had settled in the town during the Renaissance. It came from the large weaving mills in the village of Worstead to the north of Norwich. Undoubtedly, it was a very strange case of time travel, where the past defied the concept of time and entered the present.

"There are other cases of time travel, too. A couple of Italian journalists were reporting from the Belfast shipyard in Ireland. Thick fog they encountered made them lose their way, and after returning through a labyrinth of side streets, they claimed to have come across a monstrous vessel, two hundred and fifty metres long and fifty metres tall. It was state-of-the-art in design, and, as they discovered on board, had been fitted with all kinds of innovative features. An elevator, a hammam, a gymnasium, a swimming pool, a post office and endless extravagant luxury. Being double-sided, it was certain never to sink. They inquired after the name of the impressive iron vessel and discovered it was called *Titanic*. A ship that went by that name, however, proved impossible to trace. Only the future would tell if they had travelled in time travel or it was just an illusion.

"According to the accounts of two women of their visit to the Gardens of Versailles some years ago, they lost their way and found themselves in a strange kingdom with even stranger people dressed in the fashions of another era. Among the crowd was Marie Antoinette, in a supernatural world of spirits and ghosts. The ladies concluded they had been teleported to eighteenth-century France.

"An American lawyer claimed to have journeyed into the past on many occasions and attended notable events, such as the murder of President Lincoln. Every time he went back into the past the situation was slightly different, as if he was travelling in a parallel universe, and sometimes he even bumped into himself in a universal mix of space and time continuum!

"A British Royal Air Force pilot claimed that while flying over a disused aerodrome near Edinburgh, he encountered an unusual thunderstorm. Having escaped disaster, he was amazed to find that the ruined aerodrome had undergone a miraculous transformation. The buildings had been restored, the aeroplanes were a strange aerodynamic shape he had never seen before and the ground technicians were wearing blue, instead of brown, uniforms. He was certain he had travelled through time, that this was what future aerodromes would look like, that the RAF would soon begin to fly the kind of aircraft he had seen, and that airmen would wear blue uniforms instead of brown. He made an official report to ensure his experience was recorded. Whether this was an incident of time travel or simply an illusion would be confirmed in the decades to come. I could give you tens of other examples," he said, closing the book, "but I fear I am boring you without reason. And anyway, I think I've said enough to prove my point."

Edward had been listening intently throughout, unable to say a word.

"That's amazing!" he whispered.

Jason was as proud as a peacock, like a missionary who had managed to convert a crowd of wild, indigenous heathens!

"My love of science is infinite," he added. "And that's the reason I never had a family. I've devoted my entire *self* to the study of a life-long passion."

"I understand completely," said Edward, impressed. "But I think you could have combined the two. What I mean to say is, if a woman really loved you, she'd understand…"

"Go no further," Jason interrupted. "I have a confession to make, and very few people know about it. When I took up the position of assistant professor, I got to know a beautiful, intelligent girl. We shared the same interests. She was a student of mine. I was very fond of her but put off by the difference in age between us. She was thirteen years younger than me."

"There are plenty of couples with a bigger age difference, you know." It was Edwards turn to interrupt.

"That's true, and well, eventually, I began to get to know her better. We kept our relationship secret so her fellow students and my fellow professors wouldn't find out. I could have been accused of favouritism."

"So what happened?"

Edward waited, full of curiosity and impatient to learn what happened next. He rose from his comfortable position and leaned forward. Jason sighed, and laden with melancholy, he continued in a heavy, slow voice.

"Unfortunately, my happiness didn't last long. She got to know other students, male and female, with whom she had things in common. She thought they were much better friends than they turned out to be, though. It was then that she began to neglect me. The change affected me deeply; I felt left out. I'd become dependent on her. I anxiously waited for her to come home or for her to call. It happened less and less as time went by.

"It was a nightmare. If it was just me, I'd have known what to do. But I never knew if we were still together or not. She came – but not very often I admit – and it was as if nothing had changed; it was just like the beginning. I couldn't go on like that, so one day, I'd had enough and said we needed to talk. She said she hadn't realised she'd done anything wrong. She heard me out but reacted as if this was the first time. When I had finished, she bowed her head. *You're right, it's my fault,*' she whispered.

"I would have forgiven her, but she didn't want us to go back to the way we were. She said she needed time to think and decide what she really wanted. Time went by, and I couldn't concentrate on anything else, feeling neither joy nor sadness. I thought about our situation all the time and felt very bitter. I tried to meet up with friends and acquaintances to forget all about her, but just when I needed them most, they'd all disappeared.

"I walked the streets in a daze, thinking about her having fun with her friends while I was suffering. I began to neglect my work. I was irritable with my students. I almost lost the job I had fought so hard to get. At some stage, and feeling stronger, I told her we had to talk. She was still confused and unsure of what she wanted to do. I took the initiative and said we should break up. I remember the pain in my heart and feeling like I'd been kicked in the stomach. I started to smoke like a chimney. She seemed neither happy nor sad. One thing I'll never forget, though, was that she cried.

"After that, we didn't see each other again. She celebrated her birthday a few days later with friends. I didn't even get an invitation, out of politeness, if nothing else. A colleague took over my class she'd been attending. I went back to work at full pace. It was hard, but I kept it up and soon pulled myself together again. After that, I promised myself I would never make the same mistake again."

"Initially, I put your success down to good luck," said Edward, when the story ended. "But now I realise you deserved it as well. Your career could have been ruined. It takes a lot of strength to get over something like that, forget it all, and move on. I very much admire you!"

The clock in the lounge struck eleven times.

"It's getting late," said Edward, looking at his watch.

"Sorry for babbling on." Jason excused himself. "I'm sure you must be tired after such a long journey. I'll ask Simon to prepare your room."

"I wouldn't want you to go to any trouble," he responded politely. "I can stay at a hotel."

"Don't be ridiculous!" he retorted. "You come and visit me after all these years and I'd allow you to stay in any old hotel room? It's out of the question! Don't give it a second thought!"

Resolute, he pulled the bell cord hanging next to the curtains that dressed the window of the lounge. Before long, the butler appeared.

"Simon," he said, "we have a visitor tonight. Please make up the guest room."

"Yes, sir."

Simon bowed and left to carry out his master's orders.

"Thank you kindly, dear cousin. I hope I can return the favour one day."

Jason smiled.

"I'd like that very much," he replied.

Soon, Simon returned.

"Follow me, if you would, sir. Your room is ready."

"Thank you, Simon, after you."

Then he turned to Jason.

"Goodnight, cousin. Or rather, farewell. I'll be gone before you rise tomorrow. I have some errands to attend to. I'm afraid I won't see you in the morning, but I hope to return by evening."

"Goodnight," repeated Jason. "Oh, and if there's anything you need, please don't hesitate to make yourself at home. I sleep rather heavily and after all this wine, I'll probably snore. I hope it won't disturb you."

Edward smiled and followed Simon. A short time later, he put on his pyjamas, set his alarm clock for six o'clock and switched off the light. He was so tired, he fell asleep immediately.

(A FEW DAYS LATER)

"So you claim, Mr Marlow, that when you left the house that morning, you hadn't seen your cousin. And you returned somewhat later?"

"Precisely. If necessary, I can tell you the name of the restaurant I ate at, or you could ask Simon, of course. I had a lot of things to do, you see, and it wasn't convenient to return."

At that moment, a man entered the lounge and referred respectfully to the gentleman who had asked the question.

"Jason Marlow's butler has confirmed Edward Marlow's statement, Inspector, sir. They were speaking loudly enough for everything to be heard."

"Okay, Ted," said the Inspector. "You can go now."

He turned to Edward.

"Your cousin was murdered around seven-thirty in the morning while eating breakfast, just before he would have left for work. To be precise, there are four suspects. You are the first. Your reappearance was as sudden as the death of Jason Marlow himself. What's more, you are now the only heir to his large estate. He had managed to change his will."

Edward interrupted. "I'd hardly have been stupid enough to do it that quickly! Surely it wouldn't have mattered if I'd waited a couple of weeks or even months to get my hands on his fortune."

"Of course!" The inspector agreed. But by doing so, you'd have had the perfect alibi. Only an astute, devious person would have acted that way."

"Yes, but just one detail. You have no evidence against me," Edward reminded him.

"Patience, Mr Marlow." The inspector smiled. "Before long, we'll have all the personal information we need.

Until then, I have to inform you that you are forbidden to leave the area."

"Whatever you say," answered Edward, condescendingly. "Besides, I'm innocent, so I have nothing to fear as far as your investigation is concerned."

He got up and walked over to the bar.

"Do you mind if I fix myself a drink?" he asked.

"By all means. Besides, from now on, you are the owner and host of this house."

"Yes, that's right," he admitted awkwardly. "It's rather difficult to adjust to the idea. I didn't know Jason very well, but from the conversation we had the other day, I admit I took a liking to him. I admired him as a person. I am truly sorry about his death."

He went about making his drink.

"But tell me this. Who are the other suspects? There are another three if I'm not mistaken."

"The second suspect is the butler," the inspector explained. "At the time of death, your cousin had eaten a piece of toast, a hard-boiled egg and had drunk half a glass of milk. He was reading the newspaper and smoking his pipe. But not for very long, because his life was forcibly cut short. Our investigations lead us to believe he could have been poisoned. There were no external injuries and he wasn't strangled either. He could also have been smothered with a pillow and died of suffocation.

The post-mortem is underway and the results are expected within the next few days."

"Maybe he had a heart attack or something like that," said Edward.

"No." The inspector was quite categorical. "His personal physician assured us that he was in the best of health."

"By the way," he continued, "why exactly do you consider him to be a suspect? If he poisoned him, it must have been for a reason."

"Very true." The inspector agreed. "Our investigation shows that Simon assisted Jason Marlow with his research."

"A butler assisted a genius? But how?" Stunned by the revelation he was eager to find out more.

"I think you should know, Mr Marlow," the inspector smiled, "that things are never what they seem to be. Your cousin was by no means a saint."

In turn, the inspector asked a question.

"Did he talk to you about his latest research?"

"No, but he did mention parapsychology as his field of interest."

"That's correct. You didn't spend very much time with him, did you? You see, your cousin was researching the theory of reincarnation; whether a person comes back to life after death in another body."

"But how could he prove such a thing?" he asked. Curious as ever, he longed to find out more.

"By using hypnotism," the inspector explained. "From books I've read, reincarnation, or metempsychosis, as it is sometimes called, has its roots in the distant past. The dogma occurs in primitive religions, such as Indian Assam, Nagas and Lushai. Later, Buddhist and Hindu theory claims that the body dies, but the soul is eternal and indestructible. The cycle of Birth and Death evolves the soul. The course and circumstances of each reincarnation are determined by the law of karma."

"The law of karma?" he asked. He did not understand.

"Yes. It's one of the Seven Universal Laws, otherwise called the Law of Karma," the inspector added. "The word *kar* means action, and the word *ma* means consequence. In Hinduism and Buddhism, karma refers to the relationship between cause and effect. If a person's actions in his present incarnation are generally bad or negative, he accumulates bad karma, and in his next incarnation, he'll be faced with the negative forces he created for himself. So he becomes the victim and not the perpetrator."

"And what happens next?" asked Edward, full of interest.

"According to the Hindu religion, if his soul has accumulated a lot of negative karma, he could return as a cactus, a frog, a lizard or poison ivy."

"And what do the Buddhists say?"

"Buddhists believe the elements which make up a person – body, sensation, perception, emotion, impulse and awareness – leave after death. A person is no longer a person as such, and a new individual life begins, according to the quality of his previous life."

"And what about the soul?"

"After the death of the body, the soul enters another body and continues to evolve according to the good or bad karma accumulated in previous incarnations until only good karma is left. The cycle of reincarnation stops when the soul, having gone through multiple incarnations, reaches nirvana."

There was a short silence. Edward was trying to process what the detective had said. He asked another question.

"You have only referred to eastern religions. What do we believe about the subject in question?"

"In western civilisation, the idea was first developed by the Orphics in the sixth century B.C. and then by Plato. Accordingly, human souls started out as spirits that dwelled in the heavens, but then fell back down to earth and were enveloped by a material body. As a result, physical indulgence by material beings is considered sinful and unclean. The physical body is taken captive by the soul from which it must be released in order to return to *life after death* in the heavens."

"So.... i... i... if it's true we've lived a previous life, why don't we remember it?" he stuttered.

The inspector continued his explanation. "The brain has a natural tendency to reject scenes or matters that caused pain or sadness, so it's quite natural that someone would want to forget a previous unpleasant life. Hypnotism reawakens memories of events that caused physical and mental pain."

"Can I assume you know how hypnotism works?" Edward was unsure.

"I will try to clarify it in the simplest possible terms." The inspector began his explanation.

"The human brain is divided into two semi-circular sections. The left side is responsible for logic and consciousness and the right for emotions, artistic expression and instinct. Under hypnosis, the logic of the left side ceases to exist and the right side creates a reality in the form of visions not controlled by the left side. The patient is aware of external noise, but it does not disturb his concentration. His experiences are recalled from memory and the brain thinks what he sees is reality.

"Nowadays, most people who believe in reincarnation, like your cousin, for example, claim than when someone is returned to a former life under hypnosis, it proves the concept of reincarnation. The search for actual, irrefutable proof has even progressed to hypnotising people who have been blind from birth."

"Blind from birth?" he repeated. He wasn't sure if he had heard properly.

"Yes, blind from birth. Just think, if a blind person is hypnotised and can accurately describe what a sighted person can see, how is that possible, unless he has seen it in a previous life?"

Edward stared at him, speechless, and waited for him to continue.

"In a recent study where three blind people were hypnotised," the inspector continued, " – that is to say blind from birth – they were taken back to previous lives and described events exactly as they had seen them. Of course, when a blind person says *I see*, it might just be a turn of phrase that means *I understand*. But listen to these descriptions… *'green leaves floating on the water', 'the man's unshaven face concealed a mole', 'the flickering flame in the hearth wrapped itself around the logs, giving off thick, black smoke'*. Do those sound like the descriptions of a person blind from birth?" he asked. His explanation was complete.

Edward was dumbfounded.

"I can see that you are very well informed," he said, full of admiration.

"On the one, hand, that's the nature of my job," he reasoned, "I need to be well-informed about anything that might be related to the case. It's the only way to get a clear perspective of the situation and be able to judge, not with my own common sense, my own mind, but according to the protagonist's point of view. On the other hand," he said with a satisfied grin, "I'm fascinated by science, and am passionate about reading up on it!"

The inspector got up from his seat and paced the floor, looking at his watch. Edward, who had been sitting opposite him since their discussion began, took a sip of wine.

"And Simon," he continued after a short pause, returning to the subject, "was the guinea pig for those experiments. He hypnotised him regularly, sending him psycho-spiritually back to previous lives. Jason made hand-written notes of the things he said. Close scrutiny of the text revealed that Simon had suffered a great deal. I can't really say whether I believe in reincarnation or not, but from the notes, it's easy to conclude he relived – or thought he relived – scenes from previous lives, which caused him insurmountable psychological pain. As a result, he felt awful when he came out of hypnosis. It is obvious his problems began as a result of the hypnosis, so the possibility exists, I suppose, that he decided to put an end to the torture he was unable to refuse from his master."

He went over to the window and gazed into the distance. He turned to Edward again.

"On the other hand," he went on, "it's impossible that he is the murderer. And why do I say that? First of all, he would surely have realised that everyone would be suspicious of him. He was the prime suspect. Secondly, he would have tried to lead us astray instead of assuring us of your innocence. Thirdly, if it had been an act of revenge, he would have confessed immediately, because if, as far as he was concerned, it was right to murder him for the torture he had suffered, it would also have been right to confess to it. It would have taken the weight off his shoulders, and obviously, he wouldn't want to torture himself with the burden of more guilt."

"But if, as far as he was concerned, it was right to commit murder, surely he wouldn't have felt guilty about it."

"Maybe so. That is why I am not entirely convinced of his innocence. Similar cases in the past, however, were based on what I have told you."

The wall clock chimed six times. They mulled over the details.

"There are two more suspects," said Edward, breaking the silence.

"That's correct," the inspector said. "There are two more suspects, and the next is a woman."

Edward was taken aback.

"But Jason told me he hadn't been in any relationships with women recently, though he had been badly hurt by someone in the past."

"So he told you about her, did he?" The inspector was taken by surprise. "Tell me, what exactly did he say?"

He recounted his cousin's adventure as briefly as he could but without omitting important details of the pain she had caused him, as a result of which, he had lost interest in women.

"Is that all?" the inspector asked, once he had finished.

"Is there anything else he should have told me?" he asked.

"A child was conceived from that relationship, an adorable little boy."

Edward raised his glass and drank the remains of his wine in a single gulp. He couldn't believe it.

"Did Jason know?" he asked, blandly.

"Of course he knew. But to be honest, he had no idea that Alice – that was her name – had become pregnant. She didn't tell him, not even when they went their separate ways; there were enough problems already. He was completely unaware of it, for a time at least. Three years after the boy was born, Alice went looking for her former partner, the father of her son. She couldn't make ends meet and asked him for financial help. Initially, he didn't believe her. Maybe he thought someone else had fathered the child and she simply wanted to load him with the responsibility. Later, he believed her, I don't know why. To tell you the truth, young Robert was the spitting image of Jason, there was no room for doubt. So he offered to help, but only if they got married. Alice refused. She was in a steady relationship at the time, and her partner had accepted the child. Maybe there were other reasons too. But Jason was stubborn and refused to help at all.

"Years later, she bothered him again for the same reason. This time, however, not as politely as the first. She threatened to divulge his secret if he didn't give her a monthly allowance. It was very difficult for Jason. In the end, he agreed, maybe he'd had a change of heart and wanted to help his son, his only blood relative – except for you of course – but you had disappeared.

"In the beginning, he gave Alice money with no obligations, but later he persuaded her to let him see the child and give the money directly to him. When father and son met one time, Robert revealed that the money wasn't spent on him or domestic needs, but on his mother's drinking habit. She didn't buy him clothes or feed him well but beat him and took the money from him. Jason was furious. He took Robert in and gave him everything he needed. But Alice wasn't prepared to leave it at that. She accused him of kidnapping a child, but without saying it was his son, and for that reason, she received a significant amount of money. Jason was found guilty by the courts. His reputation was ruined. His sentence was reduced due to his status as a university professor and because there was no intent to harm, and he paid a fine.

"A lot happened, and I won't bore you with the details, except for what happened in the end. Jason continued to give money to his son, until one day, he learned he had died of pneumonia, aged thirteen. It was a huge shock. And as if that wasn't enough, Alice continued to blackmail him, even though their son was dead. The situation deteriorated and however much money he gave her, it was never enough. Jason refused, but that didn't stop her.

"She appeared again on the morning of his death, continuing the blackmail. Simon confirmed it. He heard them fighting. But since he was obliged to go shopping for his master, Simon left, but not for long. When he got back, Alice was gone and Jason was dead. The scene confirmed there had been a significant fight. We assume Jason would not give in and, in a state of drunkenness, Alice murdered him. The only reasonable explanation is that it was done with a pillow. There were no external signs of injury. But on the other hand, he wasn't too weak to resist. Unless of course, she pushed him and he hit his head, and when she realised he was dead, she moved him into the armchair and left. Being drunk at the time, however, I doubt if she would have been able to think clearly enough to react in such a way. She'd have left him as he was. We're looking for her to clarify the matter, but she seems to have disappeared. Which makes us even more suspicious of her guilt."

"So who is the final suspect, Mr Lester?" Edward asked.

"Franz Herrard, a German colleague of Jason's."

"And what evidence do you have to suspect him?"

"They were both competing for promotion. Maybe because the prospects for his most recent research weren't as good and Jason's. Everyone believed it would shock the scientific world. I must admit, for the end of the nineteenth century, it's a pioneering and revolutionary piece of work."

"But if that's the case," Edward questioned, "how did he kill him? No one saw him at the time of his death."

Inspector Lester smiled.

"Mr Marlow, you seem to have forgotten it's scientists we're talking about."

Edward looked at him questioningly.

"I don't understand what that has to do with it," he said.

"It's all related and I'll explain why. These people all have their differences, professional or otherwise. It's perfectly normal for psychologists to know lawyers or physicists, or doctors. They mix in the same social circles! So our friend Mr Herrard, according to our investigations, is a close friend of Dr Walter, known for his unorthodox ways and methods in his sector. Rumour has it he knows a lot more than he lets on. Friends of his were heard talking about a poison he discovered, strong enough to kill. According to Herrard, the poison is untraceable and cannot be located in the victim's body, making the cause of death impossible to certify. And very probably capable of killing someone several hours after being taken. In this case, your cousin could have been given the poison by Herrard the morning before, or even that afternoon and the delayed reaction took effect on the morning of his death."

Edward couldn't believe his ears. He sat motionless in his chair with his eyes fixed on the inspector.

"If that is true," he said, "Herrard's guilt could never be proved."

"I admit, there is one serious problem," said the inspector. "But without meaning to boast, we are very good at the job we do. We, too, have our methods of getting the guilty individual to confess, however hard it is. Don't you worry about that!"

(A FEW DAYS LATER AGAIN)

Meanwhile, Edward was living in Jason's house and lawfully managing his estate, as settled by the courts. The inspector hadn't visited for a few days and Edward wondered about the outcome of the investigation.

Dusk had fallen. He was standing at the window, tortured by his thoughts, when he heard the sound of horses' hooves on the cobblestoned drive. He cleared his mind and focussed his attention on the carriage that was approaching. The light was failing. Before long, the butler would light the lamps, one by one. The carriage stopped at the main entrance to the house. A familiar silhouette appeared at the door. He realised right away it was that of the inspector.

"Please come in, Mr Lester," said Edward.

The inspector took off his gloves, hat and coat and handed them to the butler, who turned and left.

"How are you, Mr Marlow?" the inspector asked.

"Very well, thank you. I was just thinking about the outcome of the post-mortem, the investigation and the questions you left me with after your last visit."

"Indeed, we haven't met in the last few days, but believe me, it wasn't due to negligence or indifference." The inspector was quite serious. "I understand why you might have questions, and I wanted to reveal my conclusion to you in person. Besides, it hasn't been that long."

"Are you saying you have caught the perpetrator? And at this moment he is in your custody?"

He looked the inspector in the eye. Little did he know that all would soon be revealed!

"Oh, I didn't ask you what you would like to drink. Impatience made me forget my manners."

He pulled the chord and the butler soon appeared.

"Christopher, would you be so kind as to fix me a drink, and whatever Mr Lester would like, too, please?"

The inspector requested a cup of tea and Christopher left.

"So," said Edward, "who is the perpetrator?"

"Please be patient, Mr Marlow!" The inspector tried to reassure him. He took his pipe from his pocket and prepared to light it. "I said I was in a position to reveal information about the conclusion of the case," he continued. "But that doesn't necessarily mean the perpetrator has been found."

Edward fidgeted awkwardly and reached for the cigar box to calm his nerves. He opened it and took one. He bit off the end and spat it out.

"What does that mean, exactly?" he asked, lighting the cigar.

"Let me explain, please be patient. There's plenty of time, unless of course, you have things to do."

For a while there was silence, convincing the inspector that Edward agreed.

"Let's take it from the beginning." The inspector began his analysis. "First, the post-mortem, which was rather extraordinary. Not a single trace of poison was detectable in the professor's fateful last meal, according, of course, to the current resources at our disposal. On the other hand, all the tests regarding the victim's health were clean. He didn't appear to have died from suffocation or strangulation, either. So if it wasn't a natural death or a violent death, what kind of death was it?"

"Precisely!" said Edward. "It's all very strange indeed."

"Furthermore," the inspector continued, "all the suspects have credible alibis. Simon claims that when he returned from his errands, he found his master dead. And he wasn't alone. The grocer's son helped him bring the goods inside. A fact that was confirmed. Also, all food and drinks on the breakfast table were thoroughly tested revealing nothing sinister whatsoever. The complete innocence of it all drove us to extreme conclusions. What if the methods at our disposal were incapable of tracing an unknown poison responsible for the death of your cousin? To confirm our suspicions, we tested each content of the breakfast meal on different animals. All the results were negative, leading us to conclude that Simon is innocent.

"Next… you. You left the house much earlier than the time of death. There is no way, as far as I can think, not even in the most unconventional circumstances, that you could have committed the murder from a distance. So that proves you innocent too.

"What about Alice? Whatever they say, whatever might have happened, she did not kill him, for the simple reason, that if she did it out of anger, rage or for revenge – and I can't think of any other reason – there would be external signs of injury. Alice claims that at some point during the fight between them, he turned pale, as if he suddenly felt unwell, and died almost immediately after. First, she thought he'd fainted. But when she realised he was dead, she was scared and ran off, fearing the blame would fall on her. She hid for twenty-four hours and gave herself in the following day. It seems she was telling the truth. The sheer horror on her face and the fear in her soul were impossible to disguise. So she's innocent too.

"Finally, Mr Herrard. We knew he couldn't have acted alone. Unless, of course, he was assisted by Dr Walter and his infamous undetectable poison. But while we were interrogating Walter and explained why he might be considered a suspect, he gave his complete cooperation. He disclosed he had also discovered a strange method where the alleged undetectable poison could be traced in the liver. Since he made the discovery within a few days of his initial achievement, he was determined it should not be annulled. He allowed time to pass and kept it secret from his colleagues. Incredibly, he revealed it much later, at the next medical conference, introducing it as progress in his topic of research. The truth of the matter is, the tests were first carried out on laboratory animals, and the same method was adopted in the test on Jason's liver. The result was negative. I have come to the conclusion therefore, that no one is guilty."

The door opened and Christopher entered, carrying a tray. Their drinks were served. The inspector extinguished his pipe and placed it on the table. Then, he put a spoonfull of sugar into his cup, added a little milk and stirred. He raised it to his lips and slowly took a sip.

"But I'm certain the case was a murder," he said suddenly.

"What makes you believe that?" asked Edward.

"Everything appears to be normal, but it certainly isn't," he replied.

He was determined his opinion was correct, not merely an assumption. He was as sure about it as his name was Lester.

"Unfortunately, however," he added, "I can't prove anything or even suspect anyone."

"So what do you intend to do?" inquired Edward.

"I have several cases to be getting on with and am forced to bring this one to a close. It will have to remain on file. This is my first ever case that remains open. Who knows? Maybe in a few years' time, some new evidence will show up and lead me to the perpetrator. But then again, maybe not."

"You look unhappy, Inspector." Edward was able to tell.

"I am unhappy," he admitted. It means I am burdened with a case that hasn't been solved. It's nothing to be proud of."

The inspector stayed long enough to finish his tea, then bade Edward goodnight and left.

(SEVERAL WEEKS LATER)

Before reaching the entrance to the house, he turned and looked behind. He was right. He caught sight of someone who knew he'd been seen and was in a hurry to disappear. But it was too late.

This has been going on for a month,' though Edward out loud. *It's so annoying. The inspector must have assigned someone to follow me. I wonder what he has in mind.*

He took the key from his pocket and tried to unlock the door but failed. The door stubbornly wouldn't open. He looked at the key. Nervously apprehensive, he had chosen the wrong key from the large bunch on a chain. He tried again, this time with the right key, and the door opened.

'Damn it!' he said to himself. *This whole business is driving me mad. Fortunately, in a couple of days, I'll have sold the estate*

and be able to get away from this blasted town, and be rid of it all forever.'

He went inside, closed the door behind him and locked it securely. He took off his coat and then, confused by his frustration, his hat, and hung them on the coat stand. Christopher was absent due to a family affair so he would have to see to himself. First, he urgently needed a drink. With trembling hands and some difficulty, he poured himself a drink, spilling most of it and making a mess.

"Good morning, Philip!" a voice behind him said.

Startled, he turned around. The glass slipped from his hand and fell to the floor with a hollow crash. With a face as pale as a ghost and lips trembling, he tried desperately to speak, but couldn't utter a word. He broke out in a sweat.

"It appears you're sorry to see me," the voice continued. "I couldn't be more thrilled!"

"But, how come…" he mumbled. "It's impossible, it can't be true. I must have gone mad. That's it; there's no other explanation!"

"That's not the case, I can assure you," he said, grinning with satisfaction. "This is a time vacuum. All that frustration, those thoughts, those worries transported you from the comfort of your material and spiritual world to the source of those troubles."

"That's just a theory, how can it possibly be true?"

"This moment is the very proof of it!"

"Very well. Assuming I understand why I'm here, what about you? How did you get here?"

"If I remember rightly, before I was murdered, I was researching the very subject. It was an integral part of me for many years and my death didn't change that. And it's still very much a part of me, if somewhat obscure. Under the circumstances, it was the only way we could meet again. I'm here to bring justice to two cases of murder."

"If that is the truth," he said after a moment's thought, then, realising he had been taken by the hand, "you can't do anything to me, ghosts are intangible! You might be able to walk through walls and howl like a wolf, but you can't touch me. You can't kill me. You're just a pocket of air and I'm not afraid of you!"

"You've been deceived by all accounts, and anyway, I'm not a ghost. I'm a living being, complete with flesh and bones. When you travel in time the tangible and the intangible are intertwined, the body and soul are one."

"I don't believe you!" he shouted.

"I don't care. And anyway, you'll soon discover it's true," he replied.

"But if I am not in the present, then where am I?" he asked with a look of despair.

"Certainly not in the future," he said sarcastically, "because if that was the case, I wouldn't be here. It's quite simple, you have travelled into the past, and if you had your wits about you, you'd have noticed the house looks quite different. Was this your choice of décor after my death?"

He looked around and was amazed to see what he said was true. Even the hearth beside Jason was lit. There was no one home, so how could that be possible? He certainly hadn't been near it since his return.

"I have come from the land of the dead," he continued, "where I bumped into Edward and discovered the truth. You took advantage of your friendship and murdered him, thinking he was wealthy, but you were wrong. Then you remembered the stories he'd told you and hatched the perfect plan. You knew as much about him as you did about me.

"There was no reason to be suspected, or for your plan to go wrong along the way. You got rid of his body and spread the word he had left for America to look for his only relative, in other words, me. You were well aware that we hadn't seen each other for many years and that I would hardly remember him. You disguised yourself as Edward intending to steal my fortune. When I died, it would legally belong to you.

"Who was to know we weren't related? For I was your host, providing you with the proof required. Philip Elliot," he shouted angrily, "you're a bastard! You didn't even appreciate my hospitality. The desire to swiftly deliver your evil plan, inherit my wealth and take possession of my estate drove you to murder me within hours of our acquaintance. And to give yourself the best possible alibi, you made sure you left before I woke."

"I must admit it all went off without a hitch," Philip confessed. "No one suspected a thing. Of course, the inspector had his doubts but was missing all the evidence. It's not easy to leave a person alive and murder him from a distance!"

"I have to admit you are fiendishly clever," Jason added. "Before making an appearance, you stayed in town for a few days, were informed, to your great advantage, that I had no family, and tracked my movements and daily routine. You discovered the most innocent way to serve your murderous intentions, without stirring the slightest suspicion. You foresaw every move the police would make. Where they would look and what would they would try to trace. And then you acted.

"The cyanide you poured onto the mouthpiece of my pipe, both inside and out, was of the weakest possible strength, enough to poison me but not enough to be traced, either on the pipe or anywhere in my body. How could Inspector Lester ever have imagined that? After two or three puffs, the entire amount had been absorbed and destiny claimed its victim! But now," he said, raising his voice, "it's time for our souls to rest in peace. There is no one to carry on my name and you are responsible for that."

Philip began to tremble. He realised how determined his opponent was. He racked his brain for a method of escape. The first thing that came to mind was to throw bottles from the bar beside him, one by one until one of them injured him or distracted his attention. Then he would seize some heavy object and hurl it in his direction and manage to escape or even kill him for a second time.

He snatched the first bottle he set eyes on. But Jason was quicker off the mark, having foreseen his next move. He grabbed the handle of the iron poker, the tip of which had been resting in the red-hot coals. It was glowing. Before Philip could manage to fling the first bottle, the poker struck him hard on the head.

Dazed, he collapsed, paralysed with pain. He instinctively grabbed his wound and looked Jason in the eye, unable to react. Then, he felt the tip of the red-hot poker pierce his stomach like a sword, dissolving his flesh, and burying itself within his core. He screeched like a beast being torn apart by a pack of hyenas. A river of redness trickled to the floor as his body folded in two, disabled and lifeless.

(ONE HOUR LATER)

"It's bound to be murder," he said, rationalising the scene. "But who committed it? Ted, are you sure nothing has escaped you?"

"Certain, Inspector, sir," replied Ted, without any hint of a doubt. "I came running as soon as I heard the victim's piercing scream. It was the most terrifying sound I have ever heard." He continued to describe the scene to the senior officer. "The door was locked from the inside. I tried to force my way in but it couldn't be done. Look how solid it is! Luckily, another two police officers appeared. They were on the beat at the time and were alerted by the excruciating scream.

"Together, we broke down the door and one of them stayed outside to guard the entrance. The other officer and I combed the house from top to bottom. There was no one to be found. The only exit was through the main door or a window, but they were all locked from the inside as well as facing the road within the other police officer's view. It's inconceivable that someone was inside and managed to get away. And there are no secret hideaways either."

Inspector Lester paced the floor, deep in thought, muttering to himself.

"It's certainly not a case of suicide. But on the other hand, if it was murder, and since we have a victim, logically speaking, there must be a perpetrator. And if there is, what happened? How did he get away? Was it a ghost?"

"What are you going to do, Inspector, sir?" Ted interrupted his thoughts. "Will the case be closed?"

"I'm afraid so. It defies all logical reasoning. According to the evidence I have, Jason Marlow was murdered by his cousin, who is now dead too. That means we will never learn how Jason was killed, or who killed his cousin, and how it all came about."

He looked again at the dead body, sunk his hands deep into the pockets of his overcoat and made his way to the door, shaking his head and muttering to himself as he left.

"Not a single trace of logic. Inexplicable, to say the least."

«*Let me explain. There are two worlds, the world at your fingertips — the world in which you live — and the world you indirectly perceive*»

6. BEHIND THE MIRROR

*"Beyond Human understanding
is a dimension.
A dividing line between the
Rational and the Absurd,
Light and Dark,
Intellect and Ignorance,
the pinnacle of Wisdom
and the depths of primal Fear.
It is the Dimension of Fantasy."*

The clock on the wall struck eight. Eight slow, prolonged chimes of increasing volume. The first three he heard faintly but from the fourth onwards, his drowsy indifference came to an end. He listlessly opened his eyes and looked to where he knew the clock was hanging. It was too dark to see the hands.

The surroundings were a neutral witness, sober and aloof to the game of light or dark. The flames in the fireplace vigorously lit up the room, then weakly surrendered to the darkness. Erratic explosions from the burning logs gave an encore of cheers for the dominance of light, then a surge of shadows frightened it off. For hours, the scene was unchanged; the logs in the fireplace were now red-hot coals and traces of cellulose would soon disappear, leaving a hearth of glowing cinders.

He threw off the woollen blanket and sat up. The wicker rocking chair tipped forward. Eventually, he flicked the light switch and the darkness disappeared. Ample light filled the room, celebrating its victory. He had been asleep for hours and hadn't slept so peacefully and deeply for ages. He'd been extremely edgy for the past few months and was probably right to have abandoned the noisy turbulence of the city for his solitary cottage.

He washed his face to awaken his senses, thinking about what he had to do next. First, he would have to fetch firewood to maintain the heat, then he would make some coffee and enjoy it beside the hearth. He might even go for a walk later. *'The fresh air will do you good,'* he often said to himself. A walk helps to clear your mind when you have important decisions to make, or so they say. Who knows! Maybe he would finally find some inspiration; for the past seven months, he hadn't written a single word. There was much to divulge and write about but he had failed to come up with a particular theme. *'I've got the words, but no theme,'* he found himself repeating. But now, maybe all that would change.

If he hadn't needed firewood, he wouldn't have bothered to leave the house. It was bitterly cold. The wind howled like a rabid dog, tugging at his unkempt, jet-black hair as if it was trying to pull it out. It blew against him, slapping him in the face, taking his breath away. There was moisture in the air and he could hear the gigantic waves mercilessly crashing onto the shore. He quickly and mechanically gathered as many logs as he could carry and dashed back inside at a pace a wild cat would envy. The sudden change in the weather had taken him by surprise. It had been an amiably warm winter's day before he went to sleep.

He raked the ashes in the grate and threw on a log. It was voraciously devoured by the flames in no time. He warmed his hands in front of the fire and went into the kitchen to make some coffee. There were no clean cups – hardly surprising since he hadn't washed any dishes in days. Crockery, cutlery and glasses were piled high in the sink putting New York skyscrapers to shame. He would have to wash one of the cups to drink the coffee he craved. It was a stupid idea to break up with Rosie, he thought. She always did the washing up. His precious time was better spent waiting for inspiration to come than on mundane and ridiculous tasks.

He found himself reminiscing. Rosie was patient, friendly and cheerful and when his quirks and peculiarities got the better of him, she would make him feel better. She boosted his confidence and self-esteem. She was quite a bit younger than him – ten years to be precise, which was hardly a huge difference, and was relatively mature and astute for her twenty-five years. She loved and respected him and he trusted her but one day, unable to contain his anger, he lashed out at her with words the most stone-hearted woman would have found difficult to stomach. It was the stupidest thing he had done in his life. And his inspiration or lack of it was to blame.

He watched the flames playfully jumping over the logs. He sipped his coffee, taking the cup in both hands, and leaned back into the comfort of the wicker rocking chair. Looking back, it had been seven months since he had left the place. He was on a frantic downhill course and had never reached these depths before. From a man who hated the smell of cigarette smoke, he had turned into a heavy smoker. Once a strict teetotaler, he was getting through bottles of hard liquor at a time. On the advice of friends in similar circles, he had even tried pills, marijuana and for a while, cocaine, to bring on inspiration, all to no effect. Not a single word, let alone a sentence.

He dabbled in other stuff at the same time. There was the time he'd taken off for a while without a penny to his name. He hitchhiked his way around, getting lifts in all kinds of vehicles. Trucks, caravans, tractors, jeeps, limousines, heavy goods vehicles, choppers, even a police car. For a while, he hung out with a band of bikers, who terrorised their way through towns, making a living out of looting terrified shopkeepers. His drug addiction grew in their company, where he got a lot more practise.

It was a life of debauchery and temporary highs, toil and tiredness, crime and pursuit, squalor and luxury. He worked at a gas station to get by. One night, he was robbed, his boss didn't believe him and he was fired. In town after town, he washed dishes, sold newspapers and books, and collected scrap from bins. A variety of jobs he hoped would bring him inspiration. *'I've got the words but no theme.'*

He spent time on the Greek islands, in the south of Italy, Morocco, India and Egypt. When he returned, he realised he had failed on a grand scale and his attitude changed. He was abrupt, anxious, irritable and irrational. It was then he lashed out at Rosie and threw her out, decided to give it all up and moved to his cottage for a change of scenery. There, he would have to take care of himself, do the cleaning and the shopping, cook meals and tend to the garden. True enough, the routine distracted his attention but he still hadn't found what he was desperately looking for. But maybe the scary secret would soon be revealed and inspiration would finally come.

He didn't know how long he'd be staying at the cottage and he didn't like to set limits in life. He could spend the winter there or leave much sooner. The nearest village, where he did his grocery shopping, was fifteen kilometres away. His car came in handy for this and other such necessities. His nearest neighbour was a kilometer away, which was fine by him since he was not keen on unexpected guests.

He went over to the window. It had started to rain. The water streamed down the windowpane and random flashes of lightning were followed by claps of thunder. He noticed something weird. Normally, he should have been able to see his reflection in the window but it was not the case. Perhaps it was the brightness of the light, but he didn't dwell on it.

The following morning, while he was combing his hair in front of the mirror, he thought he saw a move he hadn't made. Absorbed in a myriad of thoughts, he continued to mechanically comb his hair. He could see his reflection in the mirror but didn't pay it much attention. He was looking without seeing. At some point, he saw – or he thought he saw – himself pulling the comb through his hair. The comb was in his hand but lost in his thoughts, he had stopped combing a while ago. Nevertheless, he couldn't be sure whether it was actually the case or if he had imagined it. He stared harder at his reflection for a moment and then moved away from the mirror.

'The time has come to give it all up,' he thought to himself. *'The drink AND the drugs.'*

He spent the whole morning cleaning and tidying the house. It was Saturday and if he didn't want to go hungry the next day, he would have to nip to the village and buy food. He hurriedly got dressed in his thickest, warmest clothes and when he passed the mirror in the hall, his reflection wasn't there, or so he thought. He took two steps back and looked again. There it was, staring him in the face.

"That's it! I'm packing it in from today," he mumbled, "I'm starting to hallucinate."

His trip to the village went off without event. He was somewhat anxious, but not overwhelmingly so. On the way home, about halfway along the route, he looked in the rear-view mirror to see if he was being followed. It was then – and this time he was absolutely sure of it – that he saw his reflection wink at him. He stared in the mirror again, lost control of the car and skidded off the road. He came to his senses, and thanks to his fast reflexes, slammed his foot on the brake and saved the car from landing in a ditch. The car screeched to a halt, thrusting him against the windscreen, slightly injuring his forehead. It bled a little, but it was nothing serious.

"I can't be hallucinating all the time," he said to himself. "Who do I keep seeing things? Am I going mad? Is the isolation is to blame?" They were rhetorical questions.

He returned to the cottage in a more reflective mood. He had promised himself to cut out the alcohol but was in desperate need of a drink. He poured a generous shot of whiskey into a glass and knocked it back. He took off his coat and scarf and hung them up. He stood in front of the mirror in the hall with courage and perseverance. No! Everything was normal. The *man in the mirror* had the same scowl on his face. His hairstyle and stance were identical and he was wearing the same fluorescent blue sweater, the same trousers and the same shoes. How stupid he had been! How could he possibly have taken what he'd seen for real? But… wait! He briefly took his eyes off the mirror and looked at the sweater he was wearing. It was burgundy! In a panic, he looked back in the mirror. The sweater he was wearing was neon blue. He froze.

"What the hell is going on?" he yelled.

This time, *the man in the mirror* smiled. And it wasn't his smile, that was for sure. He was as pale as a ghost and had no inclination to smile whatsoever.

"Don't be afraid," said the man in the mirror. "You haven't gone mad."

"You can speak! How did you do that?" he mumbled.

"It's somewhat difficult" he replied, "but it is possible. Let me explain. There are two worlds, the world at your fingertips – the world in which you live – and the world you indirectly perceive. You, for example, are in the former, and I am in the latter. These two worlds look similar but are entirely different, just like positive and negative, night and day, tears and laughter, life and death, the beginning and the end, the subject and its reflection. At first glance, they all seem like opposites. In reality, however, there is a space, a thin line, where opposites harmoniously coexist. They are so interconnected they are inseparable.

"When the day ends and the night begins, it is impossible to say at exactly which point day becomes night. At the end of life and the beginning of death, you can't distinguish between the time one ends and the other begins. It is a space that few people in your world are aware of, and fewer still are able to communicate – to a certain degree – with our world. We decide whether you will be made aware of us and to which degree. We loyally follow the laws of our land and do not reveal its secrets. But sometimes, people escape and try to share the secret of our existence, destroying the border between us and eradicating the space where opposites merge, if only for a moment in time."

"And you are one of them, I suppose," said the writer, sarcastically.

"Yes," replied *the man in the mirror*, smiling. "But until now, no one in your world has ever been able to prove it, so both worlds continue to exist without much confrontation."

"And those in our world, who have tried to make contact with those in your world, what kind of people are they?"

"People with restless spirits, – writers, musicians, artists, composers, poets. Normal people with supernatural powers and a highly developed sense of perception. People you might consider to be mentally unstable, *simple-minded* or mad. But there aren't very many of them and their attempts to approach us have been extremely rare."

"So can I assume this communication of ours is a significant personal achievement?"

"No. Because it took a lot of effort on my part to get this far. The fact that you have no inspiration to write and have run out of ideas is exclusively down to me. And the same applies to everyone else in your position. When a person's other *self* tries to communicate with him, it saps his inspiration and drives him out of his mind. He seeks to develop his imagination to the full and eventually makes his presence felt through the Dimension of Fantasy. As far as we are concerned, any attempt by our other self to come closer to the source of his existence is quite normal. It is a relationship far superior to that perceived to be the greatest of all – the relationship between a mother and her child. But unfortunately, very few manage to achieve their goal. With no regard for our painful effort, most of those in your world, while overwhelmed and disappointed in themselves, inadvertently lead their other *self* to defeat or suicide."

"And what effect does that have on you?"

"We automatically die. We become lost in a world of non-existence, where it's possible we co-exist in an, as yet, inconceivable situation. As you see, we pay a price. If we want to break free and enter your world we have to drive you to insanity. At the same time, however, our own existence is threatened, because if you die, we die with you."

"Do we always have to lose our inspiration for communication between us to take place?"

"Yes. It's not ideal, but that's the way it is. You could even say we thrive on it. Draining you of your inspiration is the only way to make you aware of our existence."

"Let's assume for a moment, that we do come into contact with each other. What happens next? What is your goal? Why all the effort? What are your expectations? What do you seek from us? What will you actually gain?"

"Don't expect there to be a logical explanation because as I mentioned before, our worlds might look the same but they are entirely different. What seems rational to you is irrational to me. And vice versa, of course. What destroys you keeps me alive. The fact that we have reached this stage of communication is quite amazing. A man and his *alter ego* have never come this far before. I don't intend to flatter you, but you are the only person in your world with such a wild imagination and as a result of that, I have evolved sufficiently to be able to talk to you. But your sorrow is still my joy. So it gives me great pleasure to inform you, and you will undoubtedly be displeased to discover that my goal is to drain you of every single particle of your *self*, your mind, and your imagination. Of course, it is imperative that you stay alive. So don't worry, I won't be leading you to the point of self-destruction."

"Just a moment. Isn't it possible for us to co-exist without you destroying me, and me causing you harm?"

"No, it's impossible."

"But you just said there is always a place where opposites co-exist. Maybe we could achieve it if we tried hard enough," he begged.

"It's not worth it." He was quite categorical. "Your interest in my welfare will automatically work against you, and vice versa."

"But if…"

"Listen," he blurted. "Contradictory intentions never lead to viable solutions. It is impossible for us to co-exist, even for a millionth of a second."

The writer felt he was sinking into an abyss with dizzying speed. His mind smashed into a million pieces. Was the end really upon him? Had the countdown already begun?

"Besides," *the man in the mirror* continued, "we will not come into contact with each other very often any more. Maybe one or two more times. After that, only one of us will survive."

"And if you are the one who survives, what will happen?"

"I will gradually enter your body and once I have taken control of your mind, I will take over your life. I will enter your world and you will enter mine. I will be you and you will be me. I'll be free."

The writer smiled.

"Why are you smiling?" His reflection was criticising him. "What's so funny? Let me tell you this – your world is a free world, however oppressed, restricted or coerced you may feel. Our world, on the other hand, is the most oppressive world that exists. Think about it. We are entirely dependent on you – how you move, how you function, how you react. We only exist when you want us to. We will forever be your eternal slaves because we exist behind a mirror – any kind of mirror, as long as a reflection is there. You comb our hair, shave our faces, dress us, take care of us, and allow us to make love if that's what takes your fancy… Honestly, has it ever occurred to you how many people make love in front of the mirror? You are our masters, our rulers. And none of us like you. Indeed, it would give me great pleasure to have you carry out *my* orders, and be present only when *I* want you to be. That will be my revenge. For the time being though, you still have time to write. You've got the words, and now I'm giving you the theme."

He quickly pulled himself away from the mirror. He would hear no more of it. What difference did it make whether he was writing or not? All he wanted to do now was escape from *him*. If that was possible. He had been made to believe there was no point in trying. He'd either have to commit suicide to kill him or he'd forever be his slave. But for all he knew, when he and the man in the mirror exchanged places, he could live forever. Maybe there was no such thing as death in the other world, maybe time didn't work against you.

There had to be a way out of this. If he was thriving on his inspiration, he would have to stop thinking and writing at once. But it was the only thing he knew how to do. For how long could he do anything else? He would always come back to it eventually. Could he survive without reading books or fail to keep up to date, electronically at least, with his sphere of interest? Could he let himself become inspirationally dead? On the other hand, if he was going to die anyway, he might as well die with his head held high. That was it! He would write about his current predicament. No one would ever believe it was true – it was purely a figment of his imagination. It would be the book of the year. The year? The decade, more like. Or even the century, and that was no exaggeration. At least he would die with a timeless piece of work to his name. He'd be among the titans of global literature! He was famous already, of course, having won several prizes and written many best-sellers. But this would be the gateway to eternal glory. Yes, he had to end it this way, not to make a fool of himself. Otherwise, his work would be lost forever and so would he.

He worked all day and all night. He hardly ate or drank, and smoked and slept very little. He hadn't seen *him* since then and avoided looking in the mirror. It would only cause upset. Now he knew what to write about he was full of inspiration. The cure for his sickness had been found. Not that he wasn't still suffering. He was, and his days were numbered. It was like taking medication despite it being useless. And the faster he finished the book, the sooner he would die; he was aware of that, too. But it didn't bother him anymore. The end was coming, so what did it matter whether it was sooner or later?

Before long, despair set in. Obviously, something was wrong and it dampened the mood of the previous days. He sat and slowly drank his coffee, contemplating and puffing away at his French cigarettes. It was weird. He wanted to relax and enjoy the moment but felt a pull towards the mirror. He tried hard to resist but to no avail. His brain had lost control of his feet, or at best, was being ignored. It was like trying to stop a car with no brakes. It was true what they said about the soul being trapped by the body; he was experiencing it for himself at that very moment. It panicked him to find he was being drawn towards the mirror in the hall. When he got there, he was waiting with a stern look on his face.

"What is it now?" he asked, angrily.

"I called you over so we could talk," said *the man in the mirror*. "I'd like to ask you the same thing. What is the matter with you? You haven't written anything for days and I'm in a hurry to get this over and done with. You must have noticed I'm taking over your body and before long, I'll take over your mind, too. But the hold up with the book is ruining my plans. Do you think a delay will allow you to get away with it?"

"It's not that at all," he brashly replied. "I've just got writer's block. I can't come up with an ending to my story. There has to be an ending, but I haven't experienced it yet, so I don't know how it will turn out. And maybe I'm too young to come up with an appropriate ending to this life I'm living and writing about. Look at it from my point of view. If you've been sentenced to death, you know the end is coming, you know you are going to die, but I don't know how it will happen and neither can I imagine what it will be like when I get there. However much I try, I reject it straight away. Strange as it seems, I am in as much of a hurry as you are to get this over and done with. I can't wait to get to know the world you live in. My appetite for new experiences is greater than my desire to avoid immortality. If you really want my story to come to an end, why don't you give me the ending? You tell me how to bring the book to a close!"

The man in the mirror looked at him in surprise. He didn't expect that. He had it all worked out, down to the very last detail, or so he thought. One thing had escaped him, however. Where there's a beginning, there has to be an end.

"Write that the hero commits suicide or eventually becomes enslaved by his *alter ego*. Or something to that effect."

"But that's much too common, much too simple, it's so clichéd, it'll ruin the whole story," he complained. "It needs a distinctive ending. Something totally unexpected, just like the story itself. The finale is the requiem of any piece of work. All great composers have a requiem of some description, either in their works or their lives. I need one in my work and my life. I'll be going down in history and it has to meet my satisfaction. Do you understand? I don't care how much of a hurry you are in. I would prefer not to finish the book rather than give it a soppy ending."

"Whether you like it or not, you are dependent on me," his reflection angrily reminded him. "The countdown has already begun. It won't be long before your clock stops ticking and we swap places. And then you'll disappear. Believe me, your insolence will cost you dearly. I will torture you incessantly. I'm going now, but remember, the next time we meet will be the last. After that, our roles will be reversed."

Suddenly, the weight was lifted from his shoulders and before he had a chance to react, he dropped to the floor. He was himself again. He had to come up with something now he knew time was short. He had to do something to rescue his *ego*. To hell with the ending and to hell with the book! Besides, humanity had nothing to lose. Even if he did finish the book, how many people would actually read it? There'd be places where they'd never even heard of the title, let alone the author. How many people had actually been affected by a book, a song, a painting and had their lives transformed? Humanity can't wait for so-called artists to provide the solutions. On the other hand, who or what else could save the dereliction of mankind? It was all pointless.

Divine Inspiration? What a joke! *Divine Inspiration* is a concept invented by publishers to encourage non-conforming losers to write stories about the secret remnants of their lives or the lives they would never live, or to pressurise *respectable* people into buying books and make them enormous profits. Come to think of it, publishers and go-betweens were bigger losers than people like him who came up with the stories in the first place. However big or small, publishers were parasites. And if that was the case, what was the point of writing?

It was an awkward truth. He, who had never given a damn about others, he who had only ever been interested in satisfying his own arcane desires – whatever the cost – was suddenly concerned about humanity! It was awkward because now, he had a personal problem to face: it was a matter of Life and Death. But now, more than ever, he didn't need to get emotional about anyone apart from himself. Was guilt to blame? He had often heard that just before you die, your life flashes before you like a film. You realise your mistakes and ask for forgiveness. He didn't believe in all that, of course, because the people who said it were still in the land of the living. Who knows if it was true! And why should he believe them? But what if it was true, after all?

"To hell with eternity," he shouted hysterically. "I want to live and life is all I'm interested in. Surely there's a way, there has to be a way to be rid of him. All I need to do is calm down and think it through from the beginning."

He went to the bar, half-filled a glass with whisky, threw in a couple of ice cubes and sat in his chair. He lit up a Gauloises and inhaled deeply. So deeply, the bitterness of the nicotine stung his lungs. He reflected on what *he* had said.

'Two worlds that look the same but are entirely different. Different…What destroys you keeps me alive. However much you try to please me, it will automatically have the opposite effect on you, and vice versa… The opposite…Just a moment! What's the opposite? However much you try to displease me, it will be good for you… What's bad for me will be good for you… Bad for me… good for you…'

"That's it!" This time he shouted for joy. "Yes, that's it!"

But the joy was soon over. He had found the solution but was too scared to contemplate it, even in his mind. He didn't want *him* to find out and ruin his plans. He got the impression his mind and his mind were still one. He was still in his possession. He'd better not take any chances. He was better off waiting for their next encounter when he had already begun to take over his brain.

At least he had come up with his much-desired ending, or so he believed. Of course, he could be plain wrong or have made a mistake along the way. But it was worth a try. There was every possibility it would work out just as he had imagined. He had nothing to lose, and on the other hand, if it didn't go well, there would still be a lot to gain. He wouldn't get his book finished but if the final outcome was positive, he would be able to finish it under much better circumstances, calmer and more attentively.

A previous incident suddenly came to mind. He didn't know why. Back then, an admirer had approached him for his autograph.

'I'm a fanatic reader of your books. I've read them all. I'm fascinated by how your words paint pictures. You have an artful way with words which is very impressive. There is so much hidden meaning in your words and the things you write,' she had said.

Ugh! What a load of crap! Stupid girl! She would have slept with him if he'd offered, but he had no need for women like that. He had a different outlook on women as partners. He remembered he had smiled at her politely and written an ordinary, cold, clichéd dedication. *'Season's greetings,'* or something equally as bland. But if she was standing in front of him now, he knew exactly what he'd say.

"You are wrong, young lady. My words, the things I write, do not hide anything. They say exactly what they mean. The hidden messages, the ones I want to be heard but remain secret, are in my silence."

He attributed the flashback to the unprecedented situation he found himself in. Perhaps it was because he was at death's door. He had cut himself off before but had never felt this lonely, this silent. He had come to realise that only in isolation do thoughts reveal their true magnitude, like noises in the silence of the night. Silence was the most expressive language of life.

Days went by without meaning, like at the beginning. He was edgy, like at the beginning. But now he was under greater pressure and was more anxious about the final outcome. And the moment he had been waiting for, the moment that had been spinning round in his head, trying to find flaws with finally came. There was an invincible certainty about him and he felt rest assured that nothing was missing.

Initially, the pain penetrated his head. Then his feet began to move in the same, familiar direction, just like last time. The pain was excruciating. He hadn't expected that. He assumed his mind would be clear. What now? How would he be able to think under such pressure? As he walked towards the mirror, he made a huge effort to concentrate. It would be best to relax and as soon as he thought he had control of him, he would carry out his plan. His image caught sight of him and grinned with satisfaction.

"You see," he said, "the big moment has come, just as I promised. You will already have noticed that time in both our worlds is almost on the same scale. I am grateful for your discretion, by which I mean you have understood there is no escape, and haven't shown any spontaneous signs of despair. Believe me, I can honestly say how proud I am to have been given the opportunity to be your *alter ego*."

"How can you be so sure?" He interrupted half-way. "How do you know I will obey you until the end? How can you be sure I won't run away from the mirror and make you disappear, or that I won't close my eyes and you'll be gone?"

"Ha! I have no such doubts," he calmly reassured him. "It seems you have forgotten that I am in control of the bulk of your brain. It is me who orders your feet to walk, and your eyes to open or close. In which case, any such attempt would be futile."

"I was stupid not to have committed suicide much earlier," the writer mumbled to himself, loud enough to be heard. "Or at least not to have a knife handy to stab myself in the heart. I know it wouldn't do me any harm, because I would automatically become you. This body is almost exclusively yours, not mine. So if I do you any harm, I automatically do myself no harm. It was you who told me that, remember? What's bad for you is good for me, if I'm not mistaken."

"You continue to impress me," he admitted with surprise. "You have won my admiration and to be honest, it is a pity I have to destroy you. You are extremely clever. It's true, that would indeed be the case, but you're forgetting I have control over your hands as well."

"You speak with such conviction; it's as if I don't exist. The fact that I am answering you and am thinking means I am still in control of part of my brain. How can you be sure I won't tell my hands, my feet, and my eyes what to do? It would mean the end of you. Look at it from another perspective: we are two masters with one slave. The slave has an old master and a new one. Right up until the new master takes control, the slave will surely carry out the orders given to him by his old master, even if the new master has given him a different order. Maybe he'd be neutral for a moment, while he thinks about what to do, but surely, in the end, he'd realise it would be better to obey his old master."

Now it was *his* turn to feel uneasy. He hadn't foreseen that, either. Two opposing commands from two different people. Which would his body carry out? Which of the two would he obey? His real self or that of his *alter ego?* He couldn't be sure. And the uncertainty was written all over his face, giving away that everything his Real Self had said was true, and his Real Self was anxiously waiting for his *alter ego* to confirm it. Now his Real Self knew. The time had come to carry out his plan.

He had got him where he wanted him. He appeared relaxed, pensive, and was creating confusion. But it was not over yet. He must lead him to believe in the opposite of what he intended to do. His *Real Self* pretended he was going to escape, by urging his feet to do so. His *alter ego* felt the vibes he was giving off, thought he was trying to escape and gave an order with the part of his brain he had begun to take control of for his feet to stand still. His *Real Self*, milliseconds before, had commanded his left hand to grab the weapon that had been lying there on the unit for the last few days. His hand was to obey one command only and did so without delay. By the time *he* became aware of the trick his opponent had played on him, it was much too late to react. With horror, he watched the barrel of the revolver pointing in the direction of his heart.

"Farewell," his *Real Self* said, as the sweat dripped down his face. He smiled a victorious smile.

"No, don't do it!" *He* screamed, aghast.

Under enormous pressure, and using all the energy he possessed, he finally pulled the trigger. As he fell to the floor, he watched *him* drop dead. The blood gushed from his heart. Then, everything went dark.

Persistent knocking and the erratic ringing of the doorbell made him realise that someone was desperately trying to be let in. He got up from the floor and with slow but heavy movements, opened the door.

"Good evening." It was a female figure he could not clearly see. There was another woman with her, more beautiful than the one that had spoken, and younger too. It looked like a mother and her daughter.

"Good evening," he replied, rubbing his face with his hands, trying to pull himself together.

"We are neighbours," the woman continued. "We live three kilometres down the road."

"And?" he asked, trying to convince them he wanted to be left alone.

"We're having a party tonight and we thought we'd invite you, if you'd like to come, of course. It would be a great opportunity to get to know each other, at last."

"Look out, Mum! He's got a gun in his hand," the younger woman shrieked.

"Good Lord!" the mother exclaimed, taking a step back. "Is there something wrong?"

Then, it all came flooding back. He had forgotten what had gone before. He thought he had been asleep and it was all a dream. He was clearly astonished.

"Am I alive?" he mumbled.

"Were you going to commit suicide?" asked the younger woman.

"You're drunk," her mother added. "Anyone could tell it a mile off. From the smell of you!"

"So I'm not dead, after all?" he mumbled to himself. "Have I done it? Has he gone? Was I right in the end?"

"What on earth are you talking about? Is there anyone else in there?" said the mother. "You live alone, don't you?"

"I think he's *stoned*, mother," the daughter replied. "Let's get out of here," she urged. "I'm scared."

"Goodnight!" Mother and daughter spoke in one breath, jumped into the car and sped off.

He closed the door and looked around. It all looked normal. There was no indication of what had gone before. He hurried over to the mirror. His reflection was identical. He made some sudden moves and pulled stupid faces. His reflection mirrored him to the tee.

"So did it really happen or was it just my imagination?" he asked himself. "Was it the drink, the cocaine? Was it all a dream?"

What did it matter? He was alive, hungrier for life than ever, and had found the inspiration that had tortured him for so long… The first thing he promised himself was that he would get rid of all the mirrors in the house. He never wanted to look at himself in the mirror again.

Oddly, Rosie came to mind. He had hurt her and regretted it. He wanted to make amends. He dialled her number. He talked to her calmly without being invasive or making excuses. He won her over. She was going to come to the cottage the next day. They'd stay there for a while and then return to the city.

He got rid of all the mirrors. He left the one next to the unit in the hall until last. As he was unscrewing it, he noticed some spots of blood below it. At first, he thought they were on the floor and were reflected in the mirror. He didn't remember cutting or bumping himself. He looked for the blood on the floor but there was no sign of it anywhere. He looked in the mirror again.

'It must be on the mirror somewhere,' he thought.

He took a cloth and wiped it. The blood did not go away. He discreetly took a closer look and a shiver ran down his spine. He froze. Now, it made sense. The blood stains ware in a place without a status, in another Dimension, beyond the realms of Logic. He opened the door and ran out into the cold, screaming and writhing with pain. He was frantic. It was absurd! The blood was behind the mirror!

«*The shore, the mountain at the centre of the island
and its enormous caves formed the shape of a skull,*

7. ATLANTIC PRINCESS

The port was heaving. The end of World War II had been declared just months earlier and ecstatic crowds piled into the streets to celebrate but even then, it wasn't as busy as today. It was bedlam, people were swarming like wild bees and having to shout at the top of their voices to be heard by the person standing next to them. Porters walked up and down the gangplank of the ocean liner *Atlantic Princess* doing their best to cater for as many passengers as possible and guarantee a decent day's wages.

Despite an abundance of porters, Mrs Jones couldn't find anyone to assist her. The taxi driver had dropped her off, leaving her standing with her suitcases and had driven off with another customer.

"Allow me to help you, if I may!" It was a voice she didn't recognise of a man standing behind her.

She turned around to find a kind-looking gentleman of medium build wearing a tweed jacket and a trilby.

"You don't look much like a porter," she said.

"Oh, I'm not a porter," he said with a smile. "I happen to be travelling on this ship, too. I noticed you were desperately looking for help but hadn't had any luck. Realising how difficult it must be to carry both your luggage and the baby, offering my assistance seemed the decent thing to do."

"I'm sorry if I offended you," said Mrs Jones, blushing. "Any assistance would be wonderful."

"Allow me to introduce myself. Thomas Lloyd, Architect and Interior Designer," said the man, giving her his card.

"Pleased to meet you. Sally Jones," said the woman, holding out her hand to greet him. They shook hands, smiling.

"Is it a boy or a girl?" asked Thomas right away, pointing to the baby.

"A little boy. His name if Timothy."

"How old is he?"

"Eleven months."

"He's very handsome!"

"Thank you," she smiled, looking at the child.

Thomas took the suitcases and headed towards the ship. The luggage was not heavy but making his way up the metallic steps through the crowds was troublesome and took quite an effort.

"What's your cabin number?" he asked, out of breath.

"408."

"Okay, come this way."

Sally was taken aback by his undeniable certainty.

"How do you know which way to go?" she asked.

"I got here much earlier than you," he replied. "You might have noticed I didn't have any luggage with me. I settled into my cabin and came down to the port again to buy a carton of American cigarettes. I won't be able to get them in Europe. That's when we met."

"But it's almost an hour until departure, if I'm not mistaken. Why did you get here so early?"

"Well, I've dreamt about going on this journey since the war," he continued. "The Europe I knew then was a terrible place, transformed into a giant battlefield by the hostilities. I always thought it would be wonderful to have the opportunity to get to know her from another perspective once it was all over, and now I'm eager to find out. That's why I arrived early. I couldn't wait to get here."

"I hope you won't be disappointed."

"So, do I. Well, here we are. 406… 407… 408. Settle yourselves in and maybe you'd like to join me for dinner afterwards. What do you say?" He opened the door of her cabin.

"Very well," she agreed. "I'll just put the little one to sleep and I'll meet you there."

"Should I reserve a table for two?"

"Yes, somewhere quiet, if you don't mind."

"Not at all. Going on past experience, I hate noise so I'm glad we agree on that. If plans changes and you need to contact me, I'm in 212. Ask one of the crew for directions. Otherwise, I'll see you later. Goodbye for now." He pushed her luggage into the cabin.

"Goodbye, and thank you for everything."

A short while later, the Captain's voice came over the loudspeaker informing visitors for the final time to leave the ship since they would be departing in five minutes. Some would be saying sad farewells because of the uncertainty of their return, and many would be hoping to see their loved ones again soon. Others were coldly indifferent. A drawn-out, hoarse and thundering blast of the ship's horn heralded the beginning of the end.

The passengers squeezed against the ship's railings looking for their loved ones among the crowds on the quayside. It was difficult to make out faces. Hands held high were waving back and forth, some with white handkerchiefs, and some without, for the final farewell. The second blast of the horn sounded as the enormous iron mass set off; the anchor had been raised as the engines started up to set sail.

After settling comfortably into her cabin, Sally prepared to go for a walk with Timothy to find her way about on board but also for the child to get some fresh air. As she opened her door, the door of the cabin opposite opened almost simultaneously. A couple of about fifty years of age appeared. The man was wearing a formal, dark blue suit and a white silk shirt, a light blue silk tie, and black crocodile skin shoes. He had thick, black hair, greying at the temples. He stepped out first and was followed by a woman of the same age wearing a crimson, linen suit, fitted at the waist and carrying a red patent clutch bag with heels to match. She had grey-green eyes and brown hair.

The man saw Sally first and smiled. She smiled back, closing her cabin door behind her.

"Hello," said the man. "As we're neighbours, we might as well to get to know each other from the start. Sooner or later, we'd have bumped into each other on this long journey, anyway. Now is as good a time as any. We're the Rutherfords. I'm James and this is my wife, Ellen."

"Pleased to meet you," she said, shaking hands with him. "I'm Sally. Sally Jones and the little one here is called Timothy."

"What a lovely little boy!" said Ellen, charmed. "Very handsome too!"

"You're right," added James. "But judging by the look of him, there's something amiss, if I'm not mistaken."

"However did you know that?" asked the mother, surprised.

"I'm a paediatrician, it's as simple as that!"

"Oh, so…"

"Walk with us, and we'll discuss it if you like," suggested Ellen. "James is one of the finest paediatricians in New York."

"Please don't exaggerate, my dear," her husband modestly replied. He turned to the mother.

"Don't listen to her, Mrs Jones, I'm simply good at my job and respect the profession. We have no offspring of our own, so I heap my affection on other people's children."

"It would be very interesting to discuss Timothy's problem with you," the mother confessed. "You may be better informed than some of your colleagues. Besides, I was just about to go for a walk myself."

"Wonderful," said James.

The four set off for the deck. It was a beautiful day. The sun's rays shone playfully on the water and it glistened every once in a while.

"Tell me, what, exactly, did they tell you?" said the doctor, returning to the subject of their conversation.

"It's a very rare medical condition," Sally explained. "It's something to do with a lack of nutrients found in meat. I've been advised to feed him meat every day without fail."

"Did they give you any hope of a cure?" asked Ellen, this time.

"If he continues on this diet until he's ten years old," continued Sally, "the problem will be solved. As long as he gets the nourishment he needs while he is still growing."

"Do you mind if I ask a question? It's rather indiscreet," said Ellen again.

"Go ahead," the woman urged.

"I notice you are alone. Are you shouldering this responsibility by yourself? Isn't your husband involved? Why isn't he with you?"

"It's a very sad story," said Sally. Her voice was gloomy and her face looked grim. She looked at the Rutherfords and went on.

"My husband was killed just before the end of the war. He never met his son."

"I'm very sorry to hear that, Mrs Jones," replied Ellen, biting her lip. "Please forgive my ignorance."

"Oh, please, it's not your fault."

"My husband and I would very much like to help you," she said kindly. "Whenever you think you need us, please don't hesitate to say. We realise how difficult it must be for a woman travelling with a baby, alone and unprotected."

"Thank you."

"Tell me this," said James, "what is the reason for your journey? What led you to make such a bold decision?"

"In America," she began, "I was in terrible financial straits. It wasn't easy to find work, and when I did, there was no one to look after the child. I was all alone, without friends or relatives to help and forced to live in awful conditions. One day, I wrote to my sister who lives in England, in a place near Newcastle, and she invited me to stay with her for as long as necessary. At least she'll be able to take care of Timothy while I am at work."

"I have another rather awkward question," said James. "Please forgive my indiscretion over the matter. How did you find enough money for this trip to Europe? It's certainly not easy to come by."

"With God's help," Sally explained again. "The only thing I haven't lost is my faith in God. I used to go to church every evening, despite my misfortune and hardship, and endlessly prayed to God for courage and strength to bear the burden of it all. Mostly, for Timothy's sake. The church priest noticed I was always sad and tearful, and one evening, he asked me what was wrong. I told him everything I have told you and, touched by my plight, he promised to help. He raised the money which paid for our tickets. If it wasn't for him, I don't know what would have become of me." Her face beamed with gratitude.

"Good for him!" Ellen was touched by her story. "A true representative of God!"

"I promised to write him a letter as soon as I arrive at my sister's and get myself sorted out," added Sally.

Suddenly, young Timothy sneezed.

"I think he's getting cold," said the mother, "so I'll leave you for the time being. I'll try to get him to sleep and then go and get myself some dinner. What if I meet you there and we continue our conversation?"

"We'd be delighted," they replied.

She returned to her cabin and the Rutherfords stayed on deck for a while, discussing what had gone before.

"How terrible it must be for her," said Ellen finally, showing concern.

"Misfortunate indeed, but a brave young woman, nevertheless," added James, admiringly.

Thomas Lloyd was drinking a brandy when Sally arrived in the dining hall. He was dazzled by her presence. She looked nothing like the Sally he had met a few hours earlier – a troubled, dishevelled woman. She had smartened herself up, combed her hair and put on some rouge and light coloured lipstick, though her outfit was not particularly striking. She had simply freshened up, but it was sufficient to highlight her natural beauty. She was a brunette with large, brown, almond-shaped eyes. Her skin was slightly dark; she was probably of mixed race. She was the epitome of femininity, but modest about it. She could easily have rich, handsome men falling at her feet and enjoy the material things they had to offer if she so desired. By contrast, her modesty would not allow her to look a man in the eye for more than a moment while speaking to him. She hastily lowered her glance or looked the other way.

She greeted him with a smile. He rose from his chair and went to the other side of the table, pulled out the chair and helped her to her seat.

"I'm so glad you came," said Thomas, beaming with delight.

"I promised you I would, how could I not?" replied Sally, charmingly sincere. "I admire your patience; I think I'm rather late. I had difficulty getting Timothy to sleep."

She looked lovingly at her little one wrapped up in a wicker basket. She carefully put it down on the chair next to her, ensuring that Timothy wasn't in the slightest disturbed by the change of environment.

"Think nothing of it! I haven't been waiting long. Would you like something to drink first or shall we order our meal straight away?"

"I'd prefer to order; I'm terribly hungry. I haven't eaten a thing since this morning."

"As you wish."

He attracted the attention of the waiter who was standing nearby. He came to their table at once.

"Yes sir, what would you like to order?" he asked, looking politely at the woman with a broad smile.

"Something we can eat straight away. I can't wait much longer."

He looked at Thomas.

"I have no particular preferences. I'll leave it to you."

Thomas paid special attention to the order so as not to disappoint her. From the dozens of meals available, and after consultation with the waiter, he decided on duck in Havana sauce for himself and the ship's speciality dish, *Atlantic Princess*, for Sally. Both dishes would be accompanied by French rosé wine.

During the meal, the Captain's voice sounded over the megaphone, warning passengers that the weather was forecast to deteriorate. Meanwhile, the crew had taken up their positions in accordance with safety procedures and were in constant contact with the port authority. The news – as expected – put a dampener on most people's moods. They certainly wouldn't be able to dance. With no exceptions, they ate up quickly to avoid unpleasant surprises and dinner plates sliding to and fro as the ship ploughed through the waves.

Thomas and Sally did the same. Thomas cursed under his breath through gritted teeth about his fate. The idyllic setting they found themselves in was disappearing like fog in sunlight. Sally was extremely worried about her child. It monopolised her thoughts and attention, setting everything else aside. After all, she was a woman alone, weak and unprotected from imminent danger. And it was for that reason that Thomas offered his generous assistance. All three hurriedly set off for her cabin to retrieve some of her personal belongings.

They weren't far from cabin number 408 when a heavy shudder and a loud explosion occurred simultaneously. Losing their balance, they fell to the ground in the corridor and Thomas hit his head. Fortunately, it wasn't serious. Panic-stricken passengers rushed to the deck. Suddenly, they heard the deafening screech of sirens and the Captain's voice, anxiously informing them that the ship had struck a mine – one that hadn't exploded during the war was the most probable explanation. Everyone was to stay calm. Then, he gave the order to abandon ship, for everyone to be kitted out with a life jacket and for the lifeboats to be launched into the water. Priority was to be given to women, children and the elderly. Naturally, his recommendations were ignored. Panic ensued among the passengers as water filled the cabins on the lower decks, one after another. The crowds ran screaming towards the lifeboats disregarding their belongings, with the single intention of saving their backs, ignoring the Captain's orders and priority request.

Thomas was constantly at Sally's side. With Timothy in one arm and shoving the seething crowds aside with the other, he cleared the way to the deck. As soon as they got there, they put on their lifejackets. Mother and child managed to secure a place in one of the lifeboats ready to launch. The ship was filling with water and sinking fast. There was another explosion, and another not long afterwards. In his mind, and through no desire of his own, he was taken back to wartime – bombs, fire, explosions, bullets, corpses, the terrified innocent…

And to cap it all, there was a torrential downpour. Rain, sea spray and gusts of wind whipped the survivor's faces. Desperation and fear grew as the first bodies began to appear on the surface of the waves. Would they survive, or was a similar fate in store for them? They were in the middle of the ocean. As a matter of course, each lifeboat was equipped with a basic supply of food and water. But how long would it last? At best, and if luck was on their side, a ship would coming sailing by. But when? Would they still be alive?

Meanwhile, the ferocious waves were doing their utmost to engulf them. Their sodden clothes clung to their bodies but the worst was yet to come. Dark, triangular fins appeared. Even the youngest child could tell they were being attacked by sharks.

First, they devoured the bodies of those who'd drowned. The waves carried the blood further afield, attracting other sea creatures. Passengers who had failed to secure themselves a place on the lifeboats were bobbing up and down in their life-jackets, terrified out of their wits. Then the battle began. A battle of life and death. The floating survivors tried frantically to clamber onto the lifeboats to save their souls. Those on board tried desperately to cast them off, beating them mercilessly over the head with the oars. Eventually, they lost consciousness and became prey for flesh-eating ocean wildlife. Amid the confusion, several lifeboats capsized tossing dozens of passengers into the ice-cold water.

They closed their eyes and ears to the unbearable sound of a screaming five-year-old being ripped to pieces by a shark. Their hearts froze as his desperate mother shrieked, then instinctively dived into the water in a brave attempt to rescue her child. Attempts to overturn the capsized boats proved unsuccessful. It was clear that the frenzy of sharks had been hungry for days.

The only lifeboat to survive, complete with crew, was the one that Sally, James and Ellen had boarded. They wondered if the man-eating sharks had satisfied their appetites after their enormous feast or if they were still hungry. It soon transpired that after devouring everything that moved in the water around them, they abandoned their prey – not all of them dead – and made off. The cries of pain and calls for help had no impact whatsoever on the survivors. No one was willing to forfeit his seat for an injured person when it was obvious that even the most basic medical assistance was impossible to give and the soon lifeless bodies would be drifting in the bottomless depths of the ocean.

Thomas was lucky. While clinging in the water to a remnant of the sunken ship, the flesh-eating creatures had passed him by. As soon as the sharks disappeared, satisfied by their unexpected meal, he swam over, clambered onto the lifeboat and joined the other survivors. There were twelve of them in all, not including Timothy. One of them – Stevenson, a former mariner, gave makeshift instructions. No one doubted the captain's role he had adopted for himself. In such situations, taking responsibility for the lives of others is not an easy decision to make. Besides, most would prefer to have someone to moan and complain to and relieve themselves of their anguish. That became clear very quickly.

The former mariner suggested they throw the belongings they didn't need overboard, keeping only the absolute essentials. The rain had soaked everything, adding extra weight, and they were already in danger of sinking. There were some immediate reactions. It wasn't long before they divided into two groups, both claiming to be right. Neither, however, had a majority, because there were six in each group. It was then that the mariner took command. If they didn't agree with him, he insisted he would be forced to toss a portion of the food and drinking water into the ocean so the boat wouldn't sink. They would have to choose. Meanwhile, the boat was steadily filling up with water. The zealots gave way, realising it was in their interest and began to empty out the water. They were surrounded by a horrific sight. The severed limbs of the victims were floating in the sea around them and it reminded them how lucky they were to be alive.

Five days of drifting in a desert of waves passed by. The lifeboat had no sails to speed it along. And even if it did, which way would they go? They had no compass. Their only flicker of hope was for a ship to appear on the horizon. The dense fog that besieged the location was a significant disadvantage, however. Search parties were bound to be looking for them, but how would they detect them in the fog? The twelve-man crew had already been reduced in size. Three died of the cold, rain and general hardship. In addition to that, a fat woman who had begun to hallucinate because food was rationed to essential amounts only, threw herself overboard, where she swore she could see tables piled high with delicious treats. Attempts to hold her back failed; it was a powerful illusion. The boat had almost capsized. So now there were eight of them. Eight and a dog, the fat woman's dog.

Every now and then Sally would swap her rations for canned meat to feed Timothy. The others took advantage of her situation, driving a hard bargain for a tiny portion of meat. Usually, Thomas would offer her some of his. What's more, the sharks were still making eyes at them.

Meanwhile, the weather had radically changed. The powerful heat of the sun relentlessly beat down on them and the air was still. As good as naked, all they could think about was quenching their thirst. They were parched. They begged Stevenson for a sip of water, but fitting of a mariner, he was rigid and uncompromising and only relaxed the rules for Timothy. Naturally, tensions brewed quickly.

A man of about thirty-five, clearly a crew member of the *Princess*, tried to grab hold of the water barrel to satisfy his thirst. Stevenson and Thomas jumped on him and held him back. As quick as a flash, he took a flare gun from his pocket, ordering them to back off. The two men, powerless to resist, let him go. The crewman grabbed the ladle and sunk it into the barrel. The crystal clear sound of the metal scoop as it plunged into the water stirred basic instincts in the remaining survivors. All eyes fell on him. Someone made a move against him but backed off when the pistol was pointed in his direction. The thirsty crewman slowly lifted the ladle, took a long sip of water and groaned with satisfaction. He dipped the ladle into the barrel again. His mind was made up; he would fully quench his thirst. He filled his mouth with water again, momentarily closing his eyes to make the most of his crime. It was a dreadful mistake.

Where the penknife came from, how swiftly the doctor got hold of it, raised his hand and stabbed it with alarming accuracy into the heart of the offender, no one was able to tell. It was over in tenths of a second. The victim's basic instinct was to shoot. A green beam of light escaped from the barrel of his gun. The flare travelled a short distance and lodged itself between the terrified eyes of an elderly man, who, sadly, was sitting opposite the perpetrator. An agonising scream slowly poured from his throat; he'd been taken completely by surprise. Smoke escaped from his skull.

The women screamed hysterically, then burst into fits of mournful tears. The men threw the body into the water. Thomas took it upon himself to calm Sally and James did the same for his wife. Now, they were seven. Stevenson, Thomas, James, his wife Ellen, Sally, Timothy and a bald-headed man, who for the past five days had been relatively calm and collected and hardly ever spoke. They barely knew he was there. And, of course, the fat woman's dog.

Addressing James, the bald-headed man broke his silence. "That was murder!"

"What on earth do you mean? You can't be serious, sir," he responded. "Can't you see what might have happened?"

"It was rather reckless of him, I must confess, but I don't think he should have been punished like that." The bald-headed man was adamant.

"Are you mad?" yelled James. "It was our only hope of survival, don't you realise that?"

"God is great and would have helped us." He seemed confident.

"If He is as great as you make him out to be, He'd have seen us by now and sent help," argued Stevenson.

"God moves in mysterious ways. These things are sent to try us."

"Look here, Mister!" Stevenson was fuming. "Whose side are you on, anyway? God's, – and it's doubtful if he exits, by the way, and He certainly hasn't helped us until now – or ours?"

"On God's side, of course, my son. I speak as His dedicated servant. Allow me to introduce myself. I'm Father Cornelius."

"They stared at him in amazement. He certainly didn't look like a priest. He noticed they were curious.

"Please, don't look at me like that! I was asleep when the ship started to sink. I managed to pull these clothes on at the last minute."

"To hell with you," muttered Stevenson. "That's all we need now. Okay, so what next?" he said, raising his voice. "If you've got connections to God, we're bound to survive, I suppose!"

Thomas smiled. Father Cornelius remained calm.

"That, my son, is an insult. Not against me, but the name of God."

"Listen, Father," interrupted Stevenson, infuriated, "why don't you just leave us to our sins and let us come up with a method of salvation of our own. In the meantime, you can pray to your God for help as soon as possible. Otherwise, he'll lose seven of His very own creations."

"I've been doing nothing but praying all along."

"In that case, it looks as if He's too busy to hear you. Or maybe we should all pray out loud because He's old and going deaf," he said, sarcastically.

"Rest assured," replied the cleric, peacefully. "He *will* help the rest of us. You, on the other hand, will be punished for blasphemy."

"You and your God can go to hell!" The mariner was losing his temper.

"Anyway," shouted Sally, "why don't you just leave him alone? We're all annoyed but it's not right to pick on each other, especially on someone so harmless."

"But…" Stevenson wanted to retaliate but wasn't allowed to finish.

"Land! Land!" yelled Ellen, ecstatically.

The group turned around and looked to where she was pointing. Yes, she was right. It was neither a hallucination nor a fatigue-induced optical illusion. Six people, excluding Timothy, who wasn't aware of the circumstances, couldn't all be witnessing a mirage!

"I told you so, didn't I?" said the priest with an air of satisfaction.

Stevenson smiled.

"If it's true, Father, I promise I'll start going to church," he replied, cheered by the unexpected development.

Using all the strength they had left, they steered the boat in the direction of dry land. They were overjoyed. Stevenson, still in charge, set out their priorities from the start.

"First of all, we don't know if this is an island or part of the American mainland. The sun is setting and it will soon be dark so we'll find that out tomorrow. One of us will need to go up to the highest point and figure out if we are surrounded by land or sea. What's more, we have no idea if this place is inhabited or not, and if people do live here, what kind of people are they? Friends? Enemies? Cannibals? A group of us will need to find out what kind of food is available – both plant and animal – and if there is a supply of water. For the time being, we'd better find some kind of shelter for the night. We can think about the rest in the morning. And since we're still unsure of the possible risks, I suggest we keep watch."

Everyone agreed. They unloaded the useful items from the boat and dragged it far enough back onto the shore to prevent it from being washed away by the waves while they slept.

Four months passed and not a single ship had appeared. Yet they were stronger and more creative than they could ever have imagined. They had discovered they were on an island – not a very big one – which didn't seem to be surrounded by other islands or close to the mainland. It was impossible to orientate.

Two kilometres from their makeshift camp, they had discovered a well which provided them with water but, at first, they had no water carriers or cups. They made basic utensils out of wood carved with stones. It was a primitive means of existence.

Dr Rutherford was a great help with sources of food. He knew which plants and trees were safe, how to sterilise and preserve foods – animal sources were mostly cured – and he showed them which poisonous plants to avoid and those which shouldn't even be touched. Stevenson taught them to hunt and fish and how to study the sun and stars in the sky, which enabled them to calculate the time and changes in the weather. Thomas taught them to build shelters, makeshift ovens to cook their food and how to make various appliances. Father Cornelius taught them to light fires by rubbing wood or stones together and encouraged them to have hope and faith that the day they left the island would soon come. He laboured the same as everyone else and took part in all chores and missions, no matter how hard they were.

The two women helped with a variety of domestic chores, making the men's lives easier. They made a cradle for young Timothy and a small area where he could play without bothering his mother and the fear of him wandering off. He had learned to say some words, started crawling and had made a few attempts to walk. The doctor assisted with his health. There were no vaccines or medications of course, so he made alternatives from plants. As far as his special diet was concerned, they all agreed to provide him with double rations of meat, which was essential to his health. The dog wandered off within days of reaching dry land.

Initially, they built two shelters. They chose a spot near the shore – a kilometre or so from the sea – so they would be able to see any passing ships. The Rutherfords lived in one shelter and the rest of them in the other; Sally and her son slept behind a partition.

Once they had learned the basics of survival and their lives had become routine, another matter arose. It was of a sexual nature. Not, of course, where James and Ellen were concerned. Sally, on the other hand, was alone and very attractive.

As much as the men tried to ignore it – and the hard labour helped – it wouldn't leave their minds. A former mariner, Stevenson was used to being at sea for months and was able to restrain himself. But Thomas was used to a different style of life and he mentioned it on several occasions – discreetly, of course, – to Sally. At first indirectly, by being evasive but when he saw it wasn't working, he spoke up. He asked her outright to be his partner. Sally refused. A few days later, he asked her to marry him. There was even a priest to bless the marriage.

Sally refused again. She wasn't convinced he'd asked her because he really wanted to marry her. It was more a biological need caused by their current situation. If circumstances had been different he probably wouldn't even have considered it. The more uncompromising Sally became, the more passionately Thomas behaved.

One day, something quite unexpected took place. The three men set out on a gruelling mission and Ellen went off to gather plants. Sally was alone with Father Cornelius. She noticed the priest was praying more than usual. *"Lead us not into temptation,"* and *"deliver us from evil,"* she overheard him say. She looked hard at him. He seemed troubled.

As soon as their eyes met, he pounced on her, overcome with passion and desire. Sally tried to avoid him and rushed out of the shelter but he chased after her. Sally ran like mad, like prey within breathing distance of its predator. The man, who was faster, caught up with her and threw her to the ground. He flipped her onto her back and ripped open her dress. Her pert, round breasts were exposed to the sun's rays. They were more beautiful than he could ever have imagined! Sally was ashamed and tried to fight him off.

Taken by surprise, the predator ripped off her dress with increasing passion, leaving her naked. Neither her tears, screams nor pleading could hold him back. He started to kiss her, first her breasts, then her neck, before seeking her lips. She stubbornly turned her head left and right. Losing his temper, he grabbed her long hair and held her down. When he found her lips, she bit him until he bled.

Passion was mixed with pain. Primitive instincts awoke within him. He was hungry for more force. He kissed her breasts again, groping them with lust. He quickly pulled down his trousers, seeking her loins. Sally turned into a beast. She shifted from side to side and up and down, constantly changing position. He slapped her hard, twice, to force her to stay still, but it didn't work. She resisted him even more. His overwhelming desire drove him in search of redemption, satisfaction, and sexual delight. He grabbed her by the throat with both hands. Now she was immobilised. It was impossible to fight him off and difficult to breathe. He fumbled awkwardly for her vagina with his genital organ. All he had to do was push. She stared at him, expressionless, unable to hold back the tears. His lust had reached its climax. It had been an unbearable strain but her beautiful, bitter, tear-stained eyes pierced his conscience and he loosened his grip on her.

Only then did he realise what he had attempted to do. He kissed her forehead and pulled himself off her abruptly. *"Forgive me, if you can,"* he mumbled and disappeared into the dense vegetation. They searched high and low, albeit with a sense of understanding and goodwill, and when, after five days, they had given him up for dead or assumed he had committed suicide, he appeared out of nowhere, full of disgrace. Sally had no hard feelings. He, on the other hand, wouldn't speak to anyone and bowed his head in shame. When not at work or busy with collective chores, he shied away from the rest of them. He slept alone outside the shelter in order to punish himself, though they all tried to persuade him to forget the unfortunate event. Guilt was more powerful. Eventually, they decided to build a third shelter – for better or for worse – for Sally and her son.

One day, when the weather was particularly bad and tumultuous waves churned the sea, remnants of a shipwreck washed up on the shore. They included a compass and a first aid box, some clothes and blankets, emergency flares and tools, as well as some canned food and other similar objects. These useful items helped to improve their living conditions and everyday lives.

The island turned out to be uninhabited. It provided mainly plant-based food since there weren't very many wild animals. Recently, there had been a lack of prey and hence no meat, which was deeply concerning for Sally as far as Timothy's diet was concerned. The weather was gradually getting worse and it was dangerous to take the boat out fishing. Winter had begun. They had made an important discovery, however – a cave close to the shore, which was always cool due to the breeze. They decided to use it as a refrigerator. As yet, they had come across no other human beings on the island.

Dawn broke with a penetrating chill when a piercing shriek was heard. Everyone rushed outside to find Ellen running into the arms of her husband with tears in her eyes. Father Cornelius, who was still sleeping outside, was dead. They had all forgiven him for his misdoings, but that was irrelevant. He hadn't forgiven himself and begged for mercy and redemption while punishing his sinful *self* at every given opportunity.

They came to the overwhelming conclusion that his soul was finally at rest. He was probably better off that way. What really mattered was that they had lost an ally, a pair of strong, labouring hands, particularly useful now winter had begun. The weather was atrocious so they decided to bury him once it improved. Until then, his body would remain in the cave, in cold storage, where it wouldn't decompose. Stevenson heaved him onto his back and carried him there.

Seven days passed and, finally, the weather was showing signs of improvement. Meanwhile, the survivors hadn't left their quarters without good reason. Luckily, they had planned ahead and stored supplies and, once again, Stevenson's expertise had come in useful. On the eighth day, they decided to bury the body, so the three men made their way to the cave to fetch it.

When they got there, they were startled to discover that the corpse had been almost entirely torn to pieces and some of its limbs were missing. As far as they knew, they were the only people who lived on the island. It suddenly became clear they were sharing it with indigenous cannibals. What other explanation could there be? If a wild animal was to blame, there would be bite marks and other visible clues in the surrounding area. The corpse had been dismembered using a sharp instrument.

What kind of abominable creature could have carried out such a gruesome act?

The questions remained unanswered. They buried what was left of the body and returned to their shelters. They decided it was best not to tell the women about the unpleasant and disturbing event so as not to frighten them. But they would certainly have to be more cautious and keep their wits about them.

Three weeks later, it was James's turn to look for roots, shoots, and fruits, or whatever else was edible. Or animals, if he came across any. That would be even better. It had been a while since they had eaten meat. It didn't matter what kind of animal it was, either. Once roasted, it would be equally as tasty. Night fell early, so James set out at sunrise so any food he returned with would be ready to eat by the afternoon. Two to three hours usually sufficed to find the necessary amount of food.

Five hours passed and James had not returned. They assumed he was hunting for a better catch and had a pleasant surprise in store. Meat, maybe! Ellen was the only one to worry and her anxiety grew when, looking at the sky, she realised it was almost midday. It gradually dawned on the others too. Stevenson and Thomas decided to go and look for him.

It wasn't an easy task. There were so many places he could have been. And they couldn't just guess either, because a random search would have gone on into the night. They looked for clues – trodden grass, snapped branches or footprints in the mud. The ground was soft from the previous day's rain. Before long, they found a trace and followed it to a footpath which led to the mountain. They assumed their friend had chased after an animal which had tried to take cover in one of the many natural habitats on the mountain. They carried on in earnest, assuming James would have stopped to rest somewhere. The higher they climbed, the colder it became, so they stopped in crevices here and there to shelter from the wind. It was in one such crevice that they discovered James. He was dead, his body untouched. They wondered what had happened to him.

They didn't have to think for long. As they moved his body, a spider crawled over his neck, exposed inside his fastened overcoat. Thomas stamped on it with hate and aversion as it moved along the ground. Apart from everything else, poor James had sat down to rest and obviously hadn't noticed the *black widow* – a spider more poisonous that the tarantula – that crawled onto him and killed him with a single bite. Later that evening, they returned, carrying his body.

It was a terrible shock for Ellen. She could hardly believe it. She blamed herself; she had been the reason for their voyage to Europe. If she hadn't insisted, they wouldn't have been shipwrecked, would not be on the island and James would still be alive. The unfortunate doctor's burial would take place the following day. His corpse was already giving off an unpleasant smell, so they left it outside the shelter. The widow remained by her husband's side until late into the night and, exhausted, with the chill biting into her bones, she went inside to bed.

Relentless crying, heartbreak and weariness bring on the deepest sleep, though she was not the only one who slept soundly. The others probably had nightmares. But for Ellen, there was no bigger nightmare than the one she awoke to – relatively calm under the circumstances – when Sally called by in the morning to see how she was doing. As she clapped eyes on her husband's mutilated body, she froze to the bone. Some of its limbs were missing. She was horrified. The others were woken by her screaming. The men could no longer keep their secret. After consoling the women, they revealed what had happened to Father Cornelius's body. Sorrow took the place of fear and the question returned to their minds. What kind of abominable creature could have carried out such a gruesome act?

After the burial and some serious consideration, Stevenson summoned them all to share his thoughts. Now they were five, including young Timothy. Two men and two women. It would be difficult to protect the women if they lived in separate quarters, so they decided to divide up into pairs. Stevenson with Ellen and Thomas with Sally. To overcome any fear of suspicious behaviour, they promised there would be no sexual contact between them. The fear for survival, or rather the need for constant protection that only a man can provide, quickly convinced both women and they accepted the proposal.

Their everyday life had become routine. But the questions still remained: *how had the bodies been dismembered t? What kind of abominable creature had carried out such a gruesome act?* Safety measures were urgently stepped up. Besides, not a single ship had appeared on the horizon since they had been there. Somewhere in the back of their minds, they were beginning to accept they'd be stranded on the island forever. Was the island completely isolated from the rest of the world or were its coordinates just a long way off from the routes the passenger boats followed? They couldn't figure it out. Their only hope was for a ship to deviate from its course due to the thick fog that prevailed in the area. Maybe then, their presence would be somehow be detected.

But that seemed like a miracle. It had taken a miracle for them to discover the island in the first place; they knew there wouldn't be any more, especially if man was entitled to a certain number of miracles and they had reached their limit already. Were their hopes of a miracle disappearing or was the fact that they had stopped praying for one to happen to blame?

Often, they would sit around the fire reminiscing about their former civilised lives. Each would describe what they'd done before the voyage or how they imagined they would spend their time in Europe, had they arrived at their destination. What was the world like now, after such a long time? How much would things have changed? What were they missing out on? It seemed as if destiny had other plans. Reminiscing gave way to nostalgia and finally led to despair.

Another month went by. For the past few days, Stevenson had been trying to convince them to make a brave decision. If they were to carry on as they had done until now, they could be there forever. So if they were going to die passive and defeated anyway, why not try to make a raft with sails and venture out to sea? Maybe they would be lucky and catch sight of a ship.

Significant amounts of food and water would need to be gathered to last them for as long as possible. And if they didn't make it, at least they would die fighting for their lives and freedom. There was nothing to lose by trying. Spurred on by the despair that had overcome all four, they feverishly began to prepare. The woman sewed rags together for sails and the men cut down trees. Stevenson demonstrated his nautical skills, along with several others.

They had almost finished building the raft when an accident happened. Stevenson and Sally were testing the sails that day. Stevenson hoisted them to see if they worked but they were much too heavy for the mast. It fell on top of him, instantly crushing him to death. Sally panicked and rushed to tell the others. By the time they arrived on the scene, only the raft remained. Stevenson's body had disappeared.

Disheartened, they returned to their quarters. Ellen's nerves were in tatters. They had lost a strong and clever man, skilled and knowledgeable as far as their escape was concerned. Despite the loss, they would have to continue the effort. Fortunately, they were almost ready. The damage would be repaired and very soon they would be setting off on their life or death expedition. It was better and more dignified than slowly dying, day after day, on a fantasy island the civilised world had never seen or heard of. Ellen had lost her partner for the second time and was overcome with fear. Her nightmares were so bizarre that Sally begged Thomas to stay with her at night until she got over it. Sally felt strong enough in herself, and besides, she had Timothy for company.

A few weeks later, the life raft was ready. Stevenson had left them with the perfect plan. Now they would just have to wait for the weather to improve. They prepared the maximum amount of supplies they thought the raft could carry – including their own weight – and waited day in, day out for the right time to come.

Thomas left the women in their quarters and went hunting for food. Their stock of food steadily dwindled from dome-like piles to tufts of cotton wool. They reflected brightly in the sunlight and were as white as snow. But when the weather turned, they looked more like grey cumulonimbus, mountains or tower blocks. Suddenly, a torrential rainstorm and giant hailstones forced Thomas to return with all but empty hands. The shelter was deserted. He searched high and low shouting loudly as he went but there was no reply. What had happened to Ellen and Sally? Had they fallen into the hands of the mystery abominable creature? On the other hand, Timothy was fast asleep in his bed.

What was he supposed to do? Minute by minute, the storm raged harder. An enormous wet blanket of rain was being chased by almighty wind. Sporadic lightning flashed across the sky and the thunder roared, swiftly followed by fiercer and more frequent bolts of bright, electrical discharge. Already soaked to the bone, Thomas decided it would be best to change into dry clothes and wait a while to see if they returned. After all, they had left the little one alone. Surely they hadn't gone far and would be back soon.

Less than half an hour later, he heard the sound of footsteps on the doorstep. He cautiously turned to the door. He expected it to open but it didn't. Could he have imagined it? Was the sound caused by the thunder and the rain? He'd better go and look. But what if it was a native tribesman or a hungry wild animal? It was probably better to arm and be able to defend himself, if necessary. He picked up an axe and moved towards the door. Suddenly, there was a muffled thud. With the weapon grasped tightly in his hand, he slowly opened the door. To his surprise — and relief — he discovered Sally had collapsed before him, rain-drenched and covered in mud. He picked her up, sat her beside the fire, changed her out of her wet clothes and wrapped her in a blanket. He was rubbing her hands and feet when she began to respond.

"Whatever happened?" he asked, anxiously.

"It's tragic, Thomas. There was nothing I could do," she mumbled weakly.

"Where's Ellen?"

"Listen. I'll tell you all about it."

She took a deep breath, a sip of water and went on.

"Just after you left, it began to rain. Ellen had had enough. *'It rains every day,'* she said, *'and it's never going to stop. When will the weather improve so we can leave this cursed island? We're condemned to death here.'* I tried to give her some hope, and spring isn't far away. She was desperately anxious and acting strangely. There was a vacant look on her face, she was staring into space. Suddenly, she got up and rushed to the door. I tried to call her back. *'I'm leaving,'* she said. *'I can't wait any longer. I'm taking the boat.'*

I insisted it wasn't right to leave without you and that the weather wasn't suitable to hoist the sails. It's impossible to venture out to sea like this. I tried my best to change her mind, to convince her. When she hesitated for a moment, I thought I'd succeeded. But she opened the door and ran like mad to the shore. I chased after her but couldn't catch up with her. I watched her dive into the water, battle with the waves and disappear out to sea. There was nothing I could do to help. She must have drowned." Sally burst into tears.

"She was right, Thomas," she sobbed. "This island is cursed. We'll never survive. It'll be the end of us, as well."

"Come now, calm down," he said, putting his arms around her. "That's nonsense. The weather will improve in a few days' time and we'll get out of this place, I promise. There's more than enough food in store for the three of us and now we have a better chance of surviving for longer. Don't worry. We'll find a ship and be rescued. Come now," he said, wiping the tears from her cheeks, "don't cry. We'll get by, you'll see."

God must have taken mercy on them. Maybe he was giving them one last chance. The very next day, an enormous rainbow appeared in the sky, its colours strong and vibrant. It was a good omen if nothing else. With a spring in their stride and without further delay, they carried the essentials to the raft, checked they had left nothing behind and looked back at their set up for the last time.

The whole adventure, from beginning to end, flashed before their eyes. The fight for survival, the fear and insecurity caused by the unknown, how desperately worrying their unexpected situation had been, the false hopes that cropped up all the time, the tears over the needless loss of their companions, so many of them dead! Would their minds ever be free of the tragic events they had witnessed? Who would believe them when they told their story? It was a chilling thought. Now they were finally leaving, would it be forever or would they fail in their attempt to escape and be forced to return? Thomas grabbed hold of Sally's hand and squeezed it tightly, reminding her they were in this together and he would keep his promise.

"We'll be alright," he whispered, "you'll see."

They heaved the life raft into the water, rowed a short way and once a good distance from the shore, they opened the sails. Now, they were at the mercy of the wind which had abated after toiling for days. A sleepy, breath-like breeze wafted them gently along. They looked at the island in wonder as they drifted further out to sea. Their hearts trembled with fear. It was the first time they had seen the island from a distance and from that particular view. When they landed, it had been from the other side. The shore, the mountain at the centre of the island and its enormous caves formed the shape of a skull, crushed on one side. It had to be seen to be believed. They'd been living on the misshapen island all along. It looked so hostile. Sally buried herself in Thomas's arms. He glanced at the supply of food. According to his calculations, they would last for about nine days. After that…

On the thirteenth day, a ship appeared on the horizon. Sally started screaming and waving her arms hysterically with all the strength she had left. But the ship was some distance away. No one saw or heard her. Then, she remembered the emergency flares. They were surely the most useful items they had rescued when the remnants of that shipwreck washed ashore. She caught hold of the gun and fired. Thomas had shown her how. Her signal was seen by the ship's crewmen. She watched as the ship turned around and sailed in their direction. It was a luxury cruise liner. The Captain and crew stared at them in wonder as they climbed on board. Shivers ran down their spines.

They both looked gaunt, almost skeletal, but young Timothy's face, in particular, chilled their souls. The sockets of his eyeballs were sunken like dark caves and there was something intangibly brutal about his penetrating glare. He had the face of a wild animal and his body was similar to that of a feline predator watching its prey. His mother's eyes, on the other hand, were filled with kindness and tranquillity. She was obviously a patient, stoic woman and displayed the genuine characteristics of a conqueror who had won the unrelenting battle of survival. Sally told the Captain her story in detail. He listened in amazement.

"I must admit, dear lady, you are extremely brave," he said admiringly. "To have survived for so long, in such hardship, to have plotted your escape and finally made it with your son! You are quite remarkable. The most capable of men couldn't have done better."

"Two things gave me strength – maternal instinct as far as Timothy's survival was concerned and despair," she added. "I was all alone and forced to battle with all my might."

"You'll be famous, Mrs Jones. You'll be on the front page of all the newspapers. I can already see the headlines: *'Mother and child: the only survivors of the Atlantic Princess Ocean Liner. Missing for eighteen months.'* You'll be a hero. Your luck will most certainly change."

"I want nothing more than to find a decent job for myself. But now, all I want is to get something to eat and go to sleep. I'm exhausted. As you see, I managed it all alone."

"I understand. But I'm afraid you will have to be quarantined because you might be carrying diseases from the island. It's nothing to worry about. In three days' time, it'll all be over. Our doctor will take care of you; he's an excellent physician. There is absolutely nothing to fear. I remain at your disposal for anything you might require. I hope you understand."

"That's fine by me. Besides, three more days of adventure, especially in these luxurious surroundings, is nothing compared to what I have been through already. But," she implored, "I would like there to be meat on the menu for Timothy every day. He has a rare disease and meat is an essential part of his diet."

"Don't worry, madam. I will see to it at once."

Their cabin accommodation was quite luxurious. The Captain insisted on detailed daily updates on the health of his guests. He was surprised that Timothy, despite his mother's insistence, was not eating his meat, while the opposite was true of his other food, fruit and vegetables in particular. After discussing it with Sally, the doctor came to the conclusion that the prolonged deficiency of the particular food had caused the child to subconsciously forget what it tasted like. Patience and determination would be required for him to get used to it again and accept it as part of his diet.

By the evening of the third and final day of isolation, the tests proved negative and general clinical observation was good. The following morning, it would all be over. Sally would finally come into contact with people again and be allowed to freely wander amongst the crowds. At last, she would be able to see what the wealthy women were wearing, the latest fashions, what kind of hairstyles they had…She thought about how the passengers might react as she passed them by. Surely, she'd be the talk of the town. Her thoughts were suddenly interrupted by a knock on the door. It was the steward, bringing their meal. Sally thanked him and set the tray down on the table.

"Don't bother coming to collect it later," she said. "We're going to take a hot bath and go to bed early tonight. We want to wake up fresh and relaxed in the morning."

"Actually, Madam," the young man said with a sigh, "the regulations say that I must trouble you again for the dishes."

"Please," she said politely, "I've been awake all night worrying about the results of the tests for the past three nights. Can you possibly imagine what it's like to have been shipwrecked for a year, enduring so much hardship and danger and then being diagnosed with some disease for which there is probably no cure?"

The young man stared awkwardly.

"I was more worried about my son," she continued. "What if he'd caught a disease? What would they have done with him? Where would they have taken him? His health is compromised enough as it is. We mothers can be a little overprotective at times, you know. When they informed me today that we are both in perfect health, I felt very relieved but also very exhausted. I don't even know if I have the energy to eat. So, please, do me a favour, if you would. It can't be that important." The steward scratched his head indecisively.

"If there is a problem you could inform the Captain. I'm sure he'll understand and turn a blind eye to the regulation."

The man looked out into the corridor, nervously playing with a button on his uniform.

"To hell with it," he thought, *"surely it's not that bad if the dishes aren't washed for one night. There's no way I'm going to bother the Captain for the sake of a few plates, a knife and two forks! He'll only shout at me."*

"Very good, Madam." He finally agreed. "There's no need to blow such simple matters out of proportion, is there? I'll call by tomorrow and pick them up. Good night."

After thanking him and saying good night, Sally ate some of the food, fed her little one and made the most of the hot running water. Her muscles were so relaxed she could hardly feel her feet and her eyelids gave way to the pull of gravity. She took Timothy in her arms and fell asleep. Safely in the hands of the Sandman, she basked in a cradle of delight, a secret smile written all over her face.

The following morning, the Captain and the doctor went to Sally's cabin to officially announce the end of their isolation. The Captain intended to invite her to have breakfast with him and later he would take her on a tour of the cruise ship. But the scene they witnessed would never be extinguished from their memories for as long as they lived. Their blood froze. The sheets, the bed, the floor, the wall and the whole of the room were covered in blood. Timothy had stabbed his mother in the stomach, disembowelled her and greedily devoured her internal organs.

The two men opened the door to witness Timothy with his mother's eye in his left hand, having stabbed a fork in the other with his right. When he heard the door open, the child turned towards them and stared at them playfully. The doctor threw up on the spot. Timothy shoved his mother's eye into his mouth with his little hand. Chewing on it, he smiled at the men and licked his fingers.

"Yummy mummy!" he said casually. That was all he could say

*«…it gave me a unique, relentless feeling of tranquility
when I lay on the graves of the deceased,
bare of emotion»*

8. SOUL SANCTUARY

*'Death bedevils broken dreams
and destroys all traces of bliss…'*

1950s provincial Greece.

When a certain place comes up in conversation – you'll soon find out its name – people pull frantic, fearful faces and fidget nervously. *'Touch wood,'* they say, reaching for the nearest wooden object. *'Be careful what you wish for…'*

In this place – its name escapes me – there are marble slabs and crosses inscribed with names and dates, often decorated with flowers. Oil lamps or candles burn in secluded nooks so the wind doesn't blow them out. Often, there are photographs.

Likewise in this location – it's on the tip of my tongue – the marble slabs are surrounded by slender, solemn cypress trees that echo the eerie and monotonous whistling wind as the sun sets in a shadowy embrace.

Outside the place in question – it'll come to me in a moment – the riff-raff gather. Beggars with yowling voices selling flowers and candles, others peddling icons of the saints and visitors buying Christian keepsakes, donating their small change to the down-and-outs ever-present at the entrance.

Oh yes! Now I remember. It's called the *SOUL SANCTUARY*. Walk through the entrance, follow the third path on the left, go straight ahead, then take a sharp right onto the last path but one, and at the third headstone, sculpted from the finest Pendeli marble and meticulously engraved with vague, mystic symbols (I have strange taste) you'll be standing right in front of me!

Beneath the tombstone – you can't help but notice its glistening shades, especially at dusk, in the fading light of the setting sun – is the bed I have occupied for a number of years. Its black, wooden case is made of the finest oak with a hand-carved rim, embossed with a cross and lined with black cloth. The choice of oak for my final resting place was a twofold decision: the Will-o'-the-wisp fairies dwelled in the oak forests in ancient times (the sacred oak was the holy tree of Zeus), and Christ was crucified on that cursed oaken cross…

It's easy to find because it's the only grave that differs from the rest. There are no flowers or candles, nor a photograph. It doesn't even bear my name. Just weeds and bugs and shrivelled pine needles. They decided it should remain anonymous, as if I had never existed, so I would be remembered as a myth rather than a reality. Mostly out of fear that some poor person in the distant future would, after hearing the stories about me, relive my life in full, or at least part of it. Fear and trepidation would return.

The inside of the grave is equally as distinctive from those of my companions. If it were ever unearthed, the lid of the coffin would appear slightly ajar and careful observation would reveal the fingers of my right hand just visible between the lid and the walls of the casket.

I'd best tell the story myself, however; an untold story, not written in any book − whether old or new, or anywhere else in the world, a story missing from the myths and legends of any country, race or people or indeed, the boldest imagination.

It may seem absurd, or that my imagination has run wild, or that I am taking advantage of artistic expression, but the horror of the living souls who attended my burial, the horror that remained locked in their memories and never dared to mention, is the only true witness to this terrifying tale and it would be selfish to silence the awe I hold in its memory, albeit after so many years.

It was towards the end of the eighteenth century when destiny uncovered its plan for my bizarre demise. The circumstances pertaining to my birth were so perverse it was considered a *miracle*. They assumed I'd be stillborn or would die as soon as I took my first breath. Lack of medical expertise prohibits me from explaining further and even my parents couldn't remember what the doctors said.

I came from a middle-class family with moral and religious pride, and was particularly averse to their principles from the beginning, often coming into conflict with my parents and social environment. From early childhood, I never believed what I was told was true unless I'd confirmed it through personal experience.

Very often, the knowledge I acquired led me to ask myself bizarre and perverse questions. When I talked to people of my own age or somewhat older, they became defensive when I shared my beliefs or described my experiences. As a result, arguments were unavoidable and I wasn't always welcome. I would even say I was undesirable in certain company. Rumours spread that I was a secular, sacrilegious and contradictory person. The parents of my peers were very clear, and in the most abhorrent ways, that I should cease to keep company with them.

It all took place during a period of inner speculation and spiritual unrest as far as the supernatural and the dead were concerned. *'Hell'* and *'Heaven'* stimulated my imagination. Lucifer, the king of the *'Underworld'* and a host of other absurd, in my opinion, social norms grabbed my attention. I never understood family ties or human relationships in general. I believed that reform was necessary, based on personal freedom rather than perceived reality, which denied it in terms of social advantage.

As a consequence of losing my friends, I turned to books. They were my only true companions. I would lock myself away in my room and read. Hours went by without my realising. I avidly devoured my books, aiming to digest their contents rather than learn sentences or conclusions parrot-fashion, or sayings that sounded good in conversation and made a good impression.

The rumours probably originated because, in my youth, my father tended to punish me by locking me in my room for a week at a time, chained at the hands and feet. I was about twenty-two years of age if I remember rightly.

I was possessed by an inexplicable and, at the same time, terrifying obsession which − I am no longer afraid to admit − I revelled in. I hung around in graveyards from midnight until dawn. The attraction is hard to explain and would require theoretical and philosophical analysis of the views significant elders, as well as detailed reference to my own personal reflections and the conclusions I came to during my lifetime.

All I can say is that it gave me a unique, relentless feeling of tranquillity when I lay on the graves of the deceased, bare of emotion, listening to the gentle rustling of the cypress trees and the discordant call of the owl. The starry sky was often illuminated by the pale light of the moon. When the moon was full, a powerful, primitive delight gushed within me and the rising sun, welcoming the new day with the ritual that normally inspires poets to write delicate dithyrambs (choral hymns), was purely mundane, as far as I was concerned.

I felt particularly inspired and there, I was able to think logically, calmly and profoundly, irrational as it may seem. But my deliberate, unjustifiable absence did not escape my father's attention. He woke one night to discover I was not in my room, though I had made as little noise as possible on the way out, or so I thought. Maybe it was destined to be that way. He said nothing the next day but secretly followed me the same evening.

My state of glorified ecstasy was interrupted by a voice, livid and desperate at the same time, yelling my name. My father's beady, frantic eyes and furious face sent shivers down my spine. Before I had the chance to recover from the shock of his sudden appearance, he grabbed me with both hands and beat me with unbridled wrath.

Residents in the local neighbourhood were alarmed by our screaming voices and came running out of their homes. They probably saved my life. Otherwise, he'd have killed me. Graveyards, in those days, were located some distance from the nearest houses, I hasten to add. Evidently, we were yelling at the tops of our voices.

By the following day, everyone knew about it, and my name was freely bandied about, monopolising every conversation. The story, passed on from person to person, became quite distorted. People were horrified by what they heard.

I have no idea why my father locked me away the way he did. It was impossible to know what took place within the confines of his heart. Was it purely to force me to comply or because he was too ashamed to let me out? The bruises on my body were, after all, evidence of the violent, inhumane beatings he was guilty of.

It's true to say that afterwards, I realised how different I was spiritually to the people around me. Even the most basic form of communication with them was unlikely, impossible, dare I say unachievable. I did not get on with them and they did not get on with me. Relationships between us had come to a dead-end and I avoided contact with them, even in the most typical situations. It didn't take long to come up with a crazy idea to renounce the world with which I had absolutely no connection.

Everyone thought I was dead. Lying face-up on the bed I usually slept in, I stretched out and closed my eyes, neither eating, listening nor responding. I also refused to speak, even for essentials. I was massively disappointed that my soul was being suffocated by a world that had become horrific and unbearable.

One day, someone, who described himself as a doctor, certified me dead. He shared his diagnosis with the others

– the ordinary, simple people, who believed what the *learned* said. They accepted it at once and without a hint of a doubt because they wanted it to be true. Mourning and burning of incense began, wreaths and purple bands were chosen, my final, wooden resting place was ordered and the priest summoned to read me the last rites.

Their priorities were somehow ironic. Before my *'death'*, their exchanges were fleeting and superficial, I noticed. They gave nothing away about their lives and cemented every crack that threatened to reveal their true identities. They were isolated in their own little worlds, vulnerable and insecure, and reeked of self-obsession. Selfishness was their main pursuit, their souls were reluctant to empathise and clenched by suspicion and cleansed while they were still alive. I was already dead so there was no need for redemption.

I was lost in my thoughts. The carriage, drawn by two black horses and onto which my body would be loaded had already been summoned, however. They followed on foot, dressed in black. During the procession, I could hear them crying and reminiscing about my life. I had been a good, sensitive, popular person. There were other generalisations of a positive nature, too. Were they were talking about someone else? Not a single good word had been said about me while I was alive.

Though surprised by their comments, I managed to distinguish *Her* sobbing voice among them. Her inarticulate, unruly ramblings were easy to identify. There was some remorse, at least. She was asking me to forgive her for the times she had made me feel bitter and even rejected me. People are so stupid! They live under the same roof but argue, hurt each other and bicker away precious time. It always flies back in their faces, though. It's only when they break up that they realise their mistakes and revert to making ambitious, yet unrealistic promises.

The tragedy of the situation suddenly dawned on me with the chilling sound of earth being thrown onto the lid of my coffin. Determined to put an end to my refusal to associate with them and explain my mistake, I rose from the grave.

Upright, eyes wide-open and ready to speak, I was greeted by the sound of terrified voices – howling, screaming, crying, and faces as pale as the moonlit sky. The mourners were numbed to the bone, gazing at each other in horror and desperately waiting for it all to end. Some passed out, and one old man had a heart attack.

Others kept their cool, shouting *'but the dead don't move'*, while the doctor who had certified my death claimed the reason for my vertical position was a posthumous nervous muscle spasm and hit me hard with a heavy, iron spade to calm my squirming body. Dazed, I fell unconscious, full-square into the coffin, deader this time than before. The gravedigger was stiffly ordered to drive extra, stronger nails into the lid of the coffin. As their

«Along the way, the riverbank sloped gradually downwards.
A massive, craggy, granite rock dominated above the rapids»

sharp ends pleasurably penetrated the black, oak casket, faint, surreptitious smiles appeared on the faces of the assembled, who refused to leave until they were certain they had finally seen the back of me.

I don't remember what happened next. Once they had left the graveyard, I recovered from the violent beating and noticed a distinct lack of air. I thumped and kicked the lid of the coffin with all my might, gasping for air. As mentioned before, my life had been devoted to exercising my brain rather than my body, and it was obvious that battling against the resistance of the wooden lid would be useless.

As luck would have it, a couple of nails were less erotically entwined with the wooden box than others, and I managed to force the lid slightly to one side. The desperate attempt cost me my final haggard but rewarding breath, as I squeezed the fingers of my right hand between the lid and the walls of the coffin. Since then, I have remained in the same position, having accomplished little more than providing an easy way in for the worms that slowly devoured my scrawny body, exposing my weak and feeble misshapen bones.

And when the time comes to exhume them, my mouth will still be open, but not to rip you apart and eat you. I'm simply trying to breathe. It's all we have in common!

9. THE FREAK OF NATURE

(or A Tale of Diversity)

Great Britain at the end of the 1800s. The Romantic Era characterised by the evocation of powerful emotions through the medium of Art and expressed as Sentiment rather than Logic...

He had a strange attraction to the element of water in all its forms, whether it was the enormous, dark waves of the stormy seas, a cascading waterfall, a silent, serene lake or a gushing river, where he found himself now. Magnetised, he walked along the riverbank in the direction of flow with his eyes transfixed on the water. He was amazed by the moving water, by movement in general, having always hated stagnation. Whenever he was called upon to make an important decision, needed to think clearly or be inspired, he would walk or move about. And that was the case today.

To the right of the footpath just above the ground, a forest of burly-torsoed trees towered imposingly into the sky. Random traces of thick, rotten bark were exposed on the saturated tree trunks, while dense, inflated, verticle grooves like erupting, wooden veins branched into narrow capillaries and wider arteries. Between them, on the body of the tree, cracks betrayed damage from the passage of time. A sticky, dark liquid spurted from the cracks here and there like pus from an abscess.

Dense foliage made it difficult to pass, even where the sun shone through, while shadows in the undergrowth gave a haunted feel to the forest. Dankness chilled the bones of those foolish enough to attempt their way through. The heart-shaped bases of the tree trunks were sheathed in various shades of green slime. Vile, insipid roots randomly emerged from the soil beneath, invading the space of neighbouring trees.

The ground was covered with verdant moss and lichens that greedily shrouded the burly trunks of thriving, aged and storm-felled trees, voraciously coating the branches with floating, green, arachnid veils. The wind whistled through the trees like a gruesome death-bed groan, terrifying casual explorers and impeding their entrance to the lush forest pathways. Urban myths of occult worship by the light of the full moon add to the erratic nature of the scene.

Along the way, the riverbank sloped gradually downwards. A massive, craggy, granite rock dominated above the rapids. Two areas of sparse foliage in the depths of the forest were visible from the granite peak. Rumour had it that one stormy night, the incessant, raging wind and merciless, lashing rain terrified the locals into the confinement of their homes, convinced that a vicious beast had enthroned itself in the forest. A dozen bolts of lightning set fire to the branches of the trees and neither tree nor flora grew there ever again. Here, the door of darkness opens and allows the sun to penetrate, drawing the attention of the rambler. A pair of eyes appear to be staring at him; the eyes of the forest. A chill runs down his spine, he trembles from head to foot and his heart pounds. The illusion haunts his soul.

"Help!" a begging voice called out.

Had he imagined it or was it for real? He was soon to find out. A short distance behind him, an ugly Creature was struggling in the water. It did not resemble a human being. The Creature was pleading for help, eyes full of despair. The man was stirred with compassion. The powerful roar of the river reminded him there was a waterfall ahead. If he didn't act now, the ugly, repulsive Creature with the human voice he nevertheless felt sorry for, would be swept away to its death.

There and then, he looked around for something to help. It would be foolish to dive into the water, he thought, because then they would both drown. He tore a long branch from a nearby tree and cast it into the river in the stranger's direction, keeping tightly hold of one end. The Creature grabbed hold of it at first, but it soon slipped through his fingers and he drifted away. The man picked up the branch, dashed along the river bank and threw it back into the water. This time, the ugly Creature managed to keep hold of it and was slowly dragged ashore.

As he pulled him out, the man was able to get a better look at the strange individual. He had a human face but the body of a reptile. Each limb had four outward-facing digits with sharp claws. His spine was deformed – a hunchback tilting slightly to the left, making it difficult to breathe. When the Creature finally regained his breath, he lifted his hairless head and stared gratefully at his saviour. A tear rolled down his face as he attempted to speak.

"Thank you… you saved my life. If it weren't for you, I'd be dead."

"I think anyone in my position would have done the same," humbly replied the man.

"No one has ever treated me that kindly before," sighed the Creature, shaking off the water. "Most people would have been too shocked by my strange features to help. I've suffered a great deal because of my appearance, you know."

"Diversity is a game nature plays," replied the man, "where no one has any choice. Not many people admire or pursue diversity. Most simply reject it. Poets, painters, writers, actors – artists in general, those driven by inspiration, let's say, and sensitive people, too, are not afraid to do so. On the contrary, they readily accept it because being different is not a disadvantage as far as they're concerned. Every living creature is unique and important in their own right. The majority of artists recognise inequality, injustice and prejudice and even try to express it in their work. It's a way of exorcising it.

"Cultivation of values, a spirit of solidarity and toleration are also necessary so that *different* people do not become introverted victims. People – and artists in particular – should broaden their spiritual and cultural horizons and respect disparity by showing solidarity and empathy. It is our duty to destroy stereotypes. We are all different but essentially, we are equal."

"That's all well and good, but it's simply not true," replied the deformed creature. "And you know it! People expect others to feel, think and behave the same as they do. If they don't, it's considered wrong. Will that ever change?"

"I'm not saying it's easy and it will take a lot of effort. People are different. That's the plain truth of it but to build meaningful relationships, we have to believe in it. Why try to change people? Respect and understanding, acceptance and care, appreciation and trust are what we need. True love does not set limits or make demands. It simply acknowledges and affirms. Only by recognising and acknowledging our differences can we unleash our repressed emotions, reject our obsession with perfection, and appreciate the value of diversity. Only then will we be able to confront our misconceptions, accept the power of diversity and recognise the uniqueness of every individual."

A tear rolled down the Creature's cheek.

"Have I offended you with something I've said? That was not my intention," said the man.

"No, quite the opposite. Your very kind words reminded me how terribly life has treated me," said the Creature, hanging his head in shame.

"Would you like to tell me about it?" asked the man.

His strange companion took a deep breath and began to tell his story.

"I came into this world as a result of a genetic quirk. Naturally, my parents were shocked when they first set eyes on me. They were ashamed, they shut me away inside the house, locked down the shutters and never opened them again, afraid their curious neighbours would catch a glimpse of me. I never saw the light of day or met any other people. My parents had neither friends nor companions. Every day, they reminded me how ugly I was, how I would terrify anyone who set eyes on me, that I would never make any friends, and how lucky I was that they loved me and were protecting me from harm.

"It was cruel but I loved them nevertheless! And I believed what they said. All I wanted was their love and affection. But every time I reached out to touch them, they pushed me away as if I had an infectious disease. I realise now that they were forced into isolation because of me. They hated what I was, they were ashamed of me. That's why they didn't have any friends. Shame... shame... shame... is all I felt. That's all I could see in my parents' troubled eyes. My whole life. Shame and never-ending solitude!"

"And how did you come to be here?" asked the man.

"When my mother died, my father, saddened by the loss, became silent and withdrawn but he also realised the mistakes they had made and decided to make amends. He eventually came to love the ugly creature that I was and regretted locking me away for so long. One day, he opened the door. *'Go away, go wherever you want,'* he said. But where was I to go? I had never been out of the house before and had no idea what was out there. Freedom called but my experience of it made me want to lock myself away again and hide.

"I had no idea how bright the sun was. As I said, I had never seen it before. When I opened the door, I was blinded by its powerful, golden rays. I put my hand in front of my eyes but I was still dazzled by it. I closed the door and sat down, sad and frightened. *'Don't be afraid,'* my father said, without looking at me, as usual. *'It's always like that the first time. You'll soon get used to it and see how beautiful it is out there.'* Then, he returned to his world of silence. I curled up with fear.

"When night fell, he came up to me and looked me in the eye for the very first time. *'Come on, let's go,'* he said. I had no idea where we were going and didn't ask. I walked free for the first time in my life. My father led me down dark, secluded streets to minimise the risk of meeting people. We walked without incident until we came to the banks of this river where we stopped for a while to rest. Howling screams and rasping voices rang from the forest nearby. I was very frightened. Hungry, exhausted and delirious, I leaned on my father's shoulder. I still remember his fingertips tracing the outline of my face for the very first time. Then, I fell into a sweet and peaceful sleep.

"Naturally, I was awoken by the dawn. My eyes were too sensitive to withstand even the faintest light of the sun. I looked across at my father thinking he was still asleep. I kissed him gently on the forehead but it felt cold. I was gripped with fear like a victim in a boa constrictor's grasp. I shook him repeatedly but he did not respond. The sound of voices came from further along the riverbank. I panicked and ran into the woods to hide. When they saw my father, they went up to him and I heard them say he was dead. *'The forest has devoured his soul,'* they said, seeing no indication of attack or murder.

"I had nowhere to go and was not used to being in the company of humans. They scared me even from a distance so I stayed in the forest. Growing up and coming to terms with who I was, I chose to remain in isolation but that doesn't mean being alone was bearable. Loneliness drives you mad.   Animals don't live alone either and whoever says they aren't bothered by loneliness is telling lies. If you live alone and go out for a walk in a crowd, you feel better. I would never dare to do that. People would scream and run away, collapse with fear or even chase after me and try to kill me. I've suffered enough from the hate, revulsion and contempt of my parents; I need no more of that.

"On the other hand, due to my mysterious combination of features, I was accepted by the animal kingdom but I couldn't get along with them either. There was some communication between us but they knew I was not one of their kind. It's unbearable not to belong anywhere, not to have any friends. It's insufferable knowing how ugly you are. It's intolerable being a freak of nature. I'm nothing but a revolting reptile, I know. And if it weren't for you, I'd be dead. Maybe, that would have been better. At least I'd have escaped this life of torture."

The forest was quiet and still.

"Forgive me," the Creature said, breaking the silence, "if I've bored you by rambling on. You see, this is the first opportunity I've had to talk to someone or at least have someone listen to me. I've never had any friends or been offered any sympathy. I know, I don't deserve it. But that doesn't mean I wouldn't like it to be otherwise. In fact, this is the happiest moment of my miserable life. I often wondered if I'd ever feel grateful for anything. Now, my life is complete. I couldn't care less about death anymore. Thank you!"

"How did you come to be in the water?" he asked, knitting his brows. After hearing the Creature's story, what more could he do or say?

"I was watching you," replied the Creature, bowing his head in shame. "I wanted to share your solitude, without disturbing you, of course, but I slipped and fell," he whispered sadly.

He stared at the Creature and smiled, stretched out his hand and tapped him amicably on the shoulder.

"Don't worry I'm not angry with you." Rather, he felt sorry for him.

"Thank you for everything," he said, shedding a tear.

"My friend," he said with a smile, "if you will allow me to call you that," – the Creature nodded – "we are one and the same. The only difference between us is that you are terrifyingly ugly on the outside and I am that on the inside. Don't confuse your *appearance* with your *personality*. If you knew what I am capable of, you wouldn't even speak to me."

The disfigured Creature was taken by surprise. How could anyone feel worse than he did?

"But that's impossible," he stammered.

"I am here today," the man continued, "and happened to save your life because I was looking for solitude. Life is hard at the moment. I've done some things I am not particularly proud of and it's troubling my conscience. You may consider yourself ugly but to me, you are as radiant as fresh, spring water whereas I am a murky, forest swamp."

"Whatever have you done?" The Creature was curious. "Why are you tortured by guilt?"

"No human would want to hear about the things I've done, I can assure you. Even the Devil would abandon his kingdom in shame because I am much worse than he is. The bright, blue sky would cloud over and disgorge its macabre secrets. The most despicable human blasphemy is divine by comparison. No prayer can save my soul, no god can forgive me. If there is a single person alive on earth today who knows the meaning of retribution, that person is me. The sacred gates of Hell avidly await me."

"Tell me what's on your mind," said the Creature, determined to satisfy his curiosity.

"Betrayal," he said, turning away. "I betrayed the purest living soul on earth. A golden beam of goodness, honesty and warmth. She was born to smile and I caused her so much anguish. She was mine, and instead of being grateful for her, I treated her horrendously, putting the human race to shame. I'm ashamed of who I am. I don't deserve to think about her. I am a monster, a living nightmare. Even Death can't bring itself to take me. I will never be forgiven. I am worthy of the most harrowing archaic torture. I thank you for hearing me. Dear God! Why was I ever allowed to be born?"

The Creature looked at him sadly but for a moment, rejoiced with all his heart. Finally, someone felt worse than he did. But he soon regretted it and felt sorry for his unusual friend.

"Is it *love* you're talking about?" he asked with empathy.

"Yes, it was love back then. At least that's what I thought. But what is the definition of love? Everyone perceives it from a personal point of view. But do you know what I think? Love is based on internal spontaneity. It's a perpetual confrontation between two equal but opposing forces, a centrifugal force that is the simple, primordial fear of solitude and freedom. It thrives on hope, like the universe thrives on interstellar matter, and results in the gradual conquest of selfishness. But mostly, it's nothing but a mirage. A mirage, I created myself."

"Do you know something?" said the Creature after a pause. "Your humility proves you have a conscience. It takes strength, a kind heart and courage to be humble. A rare virtue for the human species. I can also disclose a secret. As you see, Nature played a very nasty game on me. I must be the worst freak it has ever created and ashamed of the misery it had caused, it generously bestowed a gift on me. I have been given the power to grant two wishes to the person who calls out my name and begs for their wish to come true.

"My name is Thing, and because I appreciate your kindness, I shall offer you this gift. First and foremost, because you saved my life but also because it's the first time I've met someone in a more miserable state of mind, or is falling apart, should I say? I don't know the reasons for your current situation but I respect your pain. I do not expect you to explain and granting you two wishes is the least I can do. I hope this will make you feel better. You will be the only recipient of this favour. But be careful! Make one wish at a time. Do not wish for two things at once. That would indicate greed and you'd be severely punished."

He took a deep breath, stood up, and as soon as he'd regathered his strength, he turned to leave.

"Before I go, I would like to thank you once again for rescuing me. I hope you use my gift wisely. Goodbye."

The man thanked him in turn and bid farewell.

"I promise to do what's right," he added.

The hero watched the Creature disappear into the forest undergrowth. He'd been given an exceptional gift. Two wishes would be fulfilled. But what should he wish for? How would he decide between the hundreds that came to mind? He would have to consider wisely so he moved on to collect his thoughts.

He continued along the riverbank until he came to the waterfall. He watched the water plunging over the edge. It was phenomenal charging like a gang of angry buffalo but lower down, it was as calm and as quiet as a sleeping baby. The contrast played on his mind. Thoughts spun around inside his head, echoed throughout his mind until they finally came to rest. That was it! The *Before* and the *After*. It was the best thing he could wish for. He knew what had gone *Before* but what would happen *After?* He had to find out what his future held, what her future held. Guilt would get him nowhere and how would he be rid of it otherwise?

"Thing," he yelled at the top of his voice, "I wish to see what happens *After*."

Moments later, his surroundings changed like a scene change in a movie. He found himself in a dark, dusty, cluttered room with filthy, dank walls that stank of decay, mould and damp. It hadn't seen the light of day in months. Cracks in the door and windows were the only way in for fresh air.

A human silhouette was barely visible in the dim lamplight, though the image wasn't clear. A mythological figure, skeletal, weak, with deep, sunken eye-sockets and a pallid face. It vividly reminded him of someone but he wasn't sure who. He was horrified to discover it was an older version of himself and it looked as if every last drop of life had been sucked out of him.

Suddenly, there was a knock on the door. His alter ego did not look up. He was engrossed in a big, thick book. There was another knock on the door, this time louder. But again, he did not answer.

"Andrew, let me in. I know you're in there," said a woman's voice. "Please, Andrew, you have to let me in."

When she called out his name, his suspicions were confirmed. He was indeed that man and the female voice was not unfamiliar though he couldn't put a name to it.

"Andrew," she called again, more desperate this time. "You must open the door. Please!"

The sound of faint, slow breathing filled the room.

"Andrew, why are you doing this to me?" said the woman.

She began to sob.

"I've been begging you to open the door and listen to me for days and you've simply ignored me. Why do you hate me so much? What have I done to deserve this?"

Andrew, who had aged considerably, almost shed a tear but managed to hold it back. This was no time for cruelty. He heaved himself out of his chair, dragging his feet along the floor. Haggard and frail, he unlocked and opened the door. For an instant, he was blinded by the light and shielded his eyes with his hand. When he saw the woman's tear-stained face, he reached out and caressed her long, brown hair. She was as beautiful as ever, though her face had aged a little. It didn't make much difference; her skin was still smooth. She wrapped her porcelain-white arms around him.

"Why, Andrew, why?" she sighed.

He led her inside the house. Looking around the room, she was filled with bitterness. Why take care of the place when he couldn't take care of himself? She threw open the windows to let in some fresh air.

"Why have you been avoiding me?" she asked.

"It seemed the right thing to do. I didn't mean you any harm," he replied.

"We haven't spoken in years. It was impossible to get through to you, however hard I tried. I think you owe me an explanation."

"Isn't it obvious? There's nothing to explain."

"We were in love. We were going to be married. And then one day, you disappeared without saying a word."

"It's pointless, Eleonora. Why dig up the past?"

"I had no idea what went wrong. What did I do? Why did you just disappear like that?"

She stared so hard at him that he couldn't stay silent.

"You might remember I had a passion for painting." Bowing his head in shame, he began to explain. "One day, without telling you, I wrote a letter to Caspar David Friedrich, the leader of our movement and much admired by the young romantic artists of the day. I asked him to take me on as his apprentice. I never imagined he'd reply, let alone accept me! That's why I didn't mention it."

"Months later, having almost forgotten about it, I received a handwritten reply saying I had been accepted but would have to respond as soon as possible. He needed an assistant there and then. It was a huge dilemma. I was afraid to admit what I'd done. I desperately wanted to take up the position but thought you wouldn't allow me to. So I chose to go quietly. After a while, I realised how badly I'd behaved. I bitterly regretted it and felt extremely guilty about the way I'd treated you. You can imagine why I didn't want to see you again."

He paused for a moment.

"I heard you got married," he said curtly, changing the subject.

"Yes, many years ago. You had disappeared. I hadn't heard from you. I didn't even know if you were alive," she said. "I was looking for the perfect relationship but it was a utopian thing to do. No one could ever compare to you. Our relationship was perfect, I realised that afterwards. If only you knew how much I thought about you, I wanted you... how I cried when you left me. Eventually, I got used to it. Then, I found someone else. He adored me, I was alone... if you hadn't disappeared, it would never have happened."

"So why have you come looking for me, now?"

"One day, I saw you across the street by chance. I hardly recognised you. I felt sorry for you. I followed you from a distance and found out where you lived. I promised myself to discover the truth. I know we can't go back to the way we were but I beg you, let's at least be friends! That's all I need. Surely it's not too much to ask!"

"Aren't you afraid your husband will find out?" he said bluntly.

"He left me some years later for a much younger woman, after spending all our money first, of course."

Andrew smiled sarcastically.

"Life is cruel, Eleonora. But now it's too late, there's nothing I can do. I have something to confess but I'm afraid of hurting you again."

"What is it?" She was anxious to know.

"I have but a few weeks left to live. I'm suffering from tuberculosis. Soon it will all be over. But I'd hate for your beautiful face to be pained with sadness again because of me. I'm not worth it. I never deserved you. It's the good things you do in life that count, and mine was bereft of those."

She sobbed her heart out. It echoed around the room.

"In that case, I'm staying here with you," she gasped.

«The thought process is the powerful combination of ideas and the birth of new ones aided by judgement, imagination, memory and all the elements of intellect»

"Eleonora, please understand. Divine justice awaits me. You were a beautiful flower and I the thorns that choked you. The time has come to pay the price for what I did to you," he stoically replied.

"Why are you treating me like this? Haven't I suffered enough?" She wrapped her arms around him.

"You shouldn't have had to suffer because of an unworthy creature like me. My time is almost up and I thank you for coming back but please, let me live the rest of my life as I deserve. Alone and scorned. *No heroes, idols or perfection, just guilt, conscience and regret'*. Do you remember how I used to say that? I was right, wasn't I?"

"No, Andrew," she protested. "This time, I'm staying with you until the end. I'm determined to do so, whatever you think."

"Are you a fool?" he shouted. "Who am I to deserve such meaningless, ridiculous behaviour?"

"That's enough! I'm staying with you whatever you say. Until the end. This time, I won't let you get away. I'll follow you wherever you go."

Hiding in the shadows, Andrew was visibly shaken. He couldn't bear to watch anymore. He raced back to the riverbank, burdened with pain. He sat down on a flat stone, rested his elbows on his knees and sank his head into his hands. Guilt filled his head. If he was to become the haggard wreck he had seen in the *After*, he had to do something about it now. It was wrong to keep on hurting her. She should never have become trapped in his personal pain. He had to change the course of events, but how? And how could he be sure the situation would improve? Maybe wishing to see the *After* had been a bad idea. Would it help or plunge him into deeper pain?

He had one wish left. His final wish. What could he wish for to rid him of this permanent nightmare? He was confused. How would he untie this Gordian Knot? He desperately needed a solution. His head began to ache. His temples throbbed. His blood boiled. He had never in his life felt worse. He was losing control. His head was about to explode.

"Why did I ever meet her?" he yelled. "If only that moment would vanish into the abyss of time. Why did I do it? Why did I hurt her? If only we'd never met. I should never have rescued you, Thing, and been rewarded with your gift. I wish with all my heart that I had never set foot on this earth..."

He stopped short, realising what he had done. Recalling his final words, he was horrified to discover that his final wish had been granted. Trembling, he broke out in a cold sweat that drowned every fibre of his being. *"I wish I had never set foot on this earth."*

The forest hummed eerily as if from the depths of the Underworld. The wind rose in the trees and the branches swayed in a pagan ritual. A gust of icy wind thrashed against his body. Malicious pair of eyes, the eyes of the forest, was staring at him. A powerful force uprooted his soul. Instantly, his body began to shrivel, disintegrate and finally decompose until all that remained on the flat stone was a friendly fleck in the shape of a smiling face. The wind died down and the river babbled away on its eternal, monotonous course.

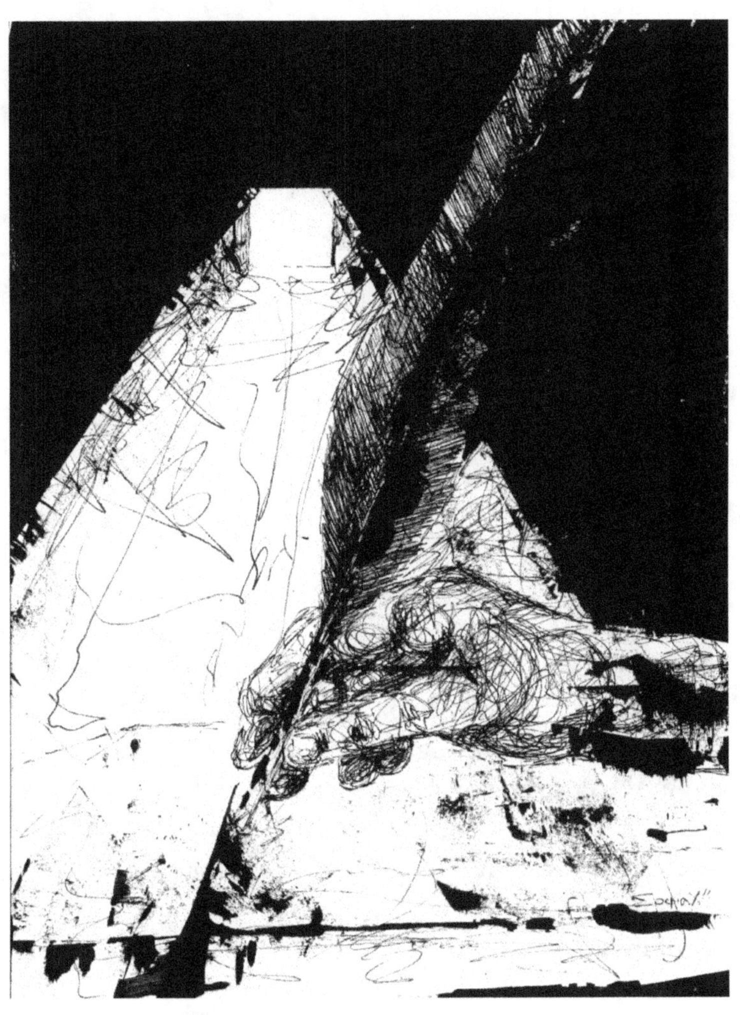

10. THE CONQUEROR WORM

*"Now faith is the substance of things hoped for,
the evidence of things not seen."*
HEBREWS 11:1

It was a cold, damp winter's night. An enormous, thin, white carpet of frost glistened on the ground. The monotonous whistling of the wind was interspersed by a myriad of arrhythmic steps that indicated the pedestrian was in no hurry. Making sure no one was watching me, I hid in the entrance of the first apartment block I came to and let him pass me by. Luckily, I wasn't lighting a cigarette at the time. Judging by the amount of alcohol coursing through his veins, one stray spark would have sent him up in a ball of flames.

I proceeded a little further along the secluded road and turned onto the main avenue. It was swarming with people, lights and cars buzzing around like mad. I stopped at the pedestrian crossing and waited. The traffic lights, unmoved and indifferent to the feverish pace of the city traffic, changed colour at strictly determined intervals regulating its flow.

I crossed the road and walked down the steps to my destination – the subway station. I bought a ticket and made my way to the platform. Among the crowd on the opposite side of the platform stood the person I was about to meet. He was lean, of medium height and had short, brown hair. He was wearing a grey trench coat. I zoomed in on him like a movie lens on the leading role. He was staring into space. He hadn't noticed me or anyone else, as far as I could tell. He bumped into a couple of people as he walked along, clearly preoccupied.

Reaching the end of the platform, he stopped in front of a little girl with blond hair. He watched her playing with her curls for a few moments. I watched him sink his hand into the right-hand pocket of his trench coat and was horrified to see him pull out a pistol. A train came roaring around the corner blasting its horn, floodlights blaring like beady eyes dazzled by the view. A passive victim of an ugly scene, it was too late to react.

The first two carriages blocked my view when a shot was fired. I waited eagerly for the monster machine to come to a halt, and when the doors finally opened, I jumped through to the other side. What on earth had driven him to shoot the random little girl?

It was a shocking scene. The person I was supposed to be meeting was lying on the ground with his head blown to pieces. I walked back to the office with the image inside my head and the questions began to multiply like shadows at sunset. The person, who'd have solved my latest case, explained everything in detail – as promised on the phone– revealed the name of the culprit and confirmed my allegations with his powerful evidence, had shot himself in the head. The answers I was looking for had disappeared into thin air.

I sat in the oak revolving chair I'd inherited from my step-father – I had never known my real father – and removed from the second drawer of my walnut-coloured desk the transparent calibrator of cognitive equilibrium – a bottle of Jack Daniels. It was less than half-full and almost ready for the bin. Two swigs were enough to cool my throat and burn my vocal cords at the same time, and cause a coughing fit.

The ***thought process*** is the powerful combination of ideas and the birth of new ones aided by judgement, imagination, memory and all the elements of intellect. It was time for military-precision brainstorming to discern whether the information I had gathered was securely ring-fenced in my conscious mind or if any of it had managed to escape.

It all began about a month ago. It was two in the afternoon when my shapely secretary called out in her familiar, stringy voice.

"I'm leaving now, Mr Einstein. Is there anything I can do for you before I go?"

I signalled there wasn't. She closed the door, said *goodbye* and left. I followed her shadow as it disappeared behind the opaque glass of my office door.

'She's pretty enough, I must admit,' I thought to myself, *'but as soon as she opens her mouth, you want to run a mile. She's got a voice like a laughing magpie.'*

She was good at her job, however, and dedicated too, and for that reason, I was reluctant to let her go. What was the point? A useless secretary with a cute voice would get me nowhere. Anyway, it would go against my rules. Rule number one: never get into relationships with clients, and rule number two: never become romantically involved with secretaries.

I made a 180° turn and looked out of the window. There was a lot of traffic on the road – normal for the afternoon – and the sky was overcast. It was an unusually warm winter's day and a smog alert was surely imminent. Suddenly, there was a knock on the door.

"Who's there?" I said, staring smugly at the view.

By the sound of her footsteps, it was a woman. How did I know? From the clacking of her heels, of course. It was a game I often played. I hear a sound and try to imagine who or what is making it. A cough, for instance. I can tell by its depth, emphasis and volume whether it's a man or a woman, and how fat, thin, tall or short they are. From the footsteps of the unknown visitor, I concluded she was a large but poor woman because her heels were relatively worn.

I turned around and looked. I was spot on! One thing I hadn't foreseen, however, was how ugly she was.

"Are you Mr Albert Einstein?" she asked. Her voice trembled.

"I am indeed," I replied, thinking how different it was in movies, where the detective's clients were always tall, thin, sexy women with velvety voices. I'd never been lucky with women and nothing was about to change.

"Please, sit down."

"Thank you," she said, and without beating about the bush, began to tell her story. "I was walking along minding my own business when suddenly, I noticed your sign. You're just the person I need, I said to myself, and without any more thought, I decided to pay you a visit."

"Would you like to tell me what this is about?" I was extremely curious.

"My child..."

She hadn't even finished her sentence and was already in tears.

"He disappeared a few days ago. Something's not right," she sobbed.

"Have you been to the police?" I asked. It was the obvious next question in my profession.

"Yes, but so far, they haven't come up with anything." She looked at me in despair. "That's why I turned to you," she added.

I got up and walked over to the coat stand where my black, woollen overcoat was hanging. I took a tin of eucalyptus-flavoured lozenges out of the left inside pocket and popped one into my mouth.

"They're great for the throat," I said, lightening up the atmosphere. "The climate is dreadful; it causes such dryness. These lozenges are soothing and refreshing. Would you like one?" I offered her the tin.

"No, thank you," she politely replied, wiping her tears.

"I put the lid on the tin, placed it on my desk and sat down again in my wooden armchair.

"Is it a boy or a girl?" I asked, getting back to business.

"A boy, eleven years old," she replied.

"Do you happen to have a photograph of him? It would be extremely useful if you did," I explained.

"Here you are."

She took a photograph out of her handbag and handed it to me. It was fairly recent. He was a cute, happy, cheerful-looking boy.

"What's his name?" I asked, staring at the picture.

"Leonardo. Leonardo Da Vinci," she replied. There was a sweetness in her voice.

Next, I asked her what she knew about the case.

"Nothing," she said. She was quite categorical. "He left for school that morning, the same as he always did. But afterwards, he didn't come home." Unable to say more, she burst into tears.

"Did he usually get home on time?" I asked.

"He was never late."

"Did anyone see him that day? Does he walk home with friends, maybe?"

"Yes," she replied, "but on that particular day, one of their fathers picked them up in his car. They didn't all fit in so Leonardo walked home alone. He hasn't been seen since."

"Have you received any threatening telephone calls or letters?" It crossed my mind that he might have been abducted.

"No, nothing. Besides, we're poor people, Mr Einstein. If he's been kidnapped, where would we find the money to pay the ransom?"

She was right. Abduction was out of the question.

"In that case, had there been any conflict between you? Had you scolded him for any reason? Is it possible you overreacted and he just took off?" I stared hard at her to see whether she was telling the truth.

"No, sir," she replied at once. "Quite the opposite. He's an only child and we spoil him all the time."

"I see, madam." I was done with my questions. "I'll be in touch if there are any new developments."

"Oh, please…" she sobbed, "just find my son and I'll pay your price. We may be poor but we'll find the money somehow. Just as long as you find him."

"I'll do my best," I said, trying to console her. "You can be sure of that."

I got up and showed her to the door. Her head sank and with the weight of the world on her shoulders, she slowly made her way out, dragging her feet as she went.

'Easy enough,' I thought. 'A youngster disappears. Probably angry with his parents and they never realised. Maybe he wanted to take off with his friends but was too afraid to tell them. He might even have realised his mistake and be reluctant to return, knowing he's done wrong. Maybe I acted too quickly. I shouldn't have taken on the case. On the other hand, why not? It's easy money. There are bills to pay, after all.'

My line of work conjures up a range of emotions in people's minds. Admiration, indifference, condemnation, to name but a few. The fact remains that a detective is often seen as a **Worm**, slithering in the dirt and the mud (the underworld), digging holes when there is no way out (a dead end), hovering in the shadows (surveillance), avoiding the light (personal life), and all for the sake of a piece of information. What's more, he exposes himself to risk and gets trodden on by lowlife (personality, esteem, physical integrity). But surprisingly, you hardly ever come across a detective that begrudges the profession. Most of them adore it and wouldn't change it for the world, given the opportunity. There's great satisfaction to be had when a case is solved. Nothing compares to the sense of **Conquest**. Conquest that inspires pride. A detective may be a worm, but he is a **Conqueror Worm**.

There wasn't a moment to lose. I decided to go along to Leonardo's school, get to know his friends and meet them one by one. Nobody knew a thing. And no one in the school's vicinity had noticed anything unusual. Maybe it wasn't as simple as I'd imagined. Maybe that's why the police hadn't come up with anything either.

If you're a castaway on a desert island, you have a certain chance of being rescued, depending on the situation of course, but if you're cast away by life, you are usually doomed. One thing is certain, however. Homeless people are a lost cause. Left to the mercy and generosity of the few, they survive on the fringes of life in their own obscure, contradictory, often indifferent ways. Thousands of people pass by them by and look the other way or pretend they don't exist.

I realised this when I ran into one of them outside the school. Homeless people normally have their own pitch. There was a strong possibility he had seen something. I approached him, my mind full of possible scenarios. He was a *strategic* part of the case, though he would never realise that.

"Hello there!" I greeted him with a smile.

The scruffy, smelly, dirty-looking guy gave me a weird look. I didn't expect him to return the greeting; how stupid would that have been? Instead, I took a generous wad of notes from my pocket and gave it to him. He stared at me more vaguely than before.

"I can give you more, if you like," I said, egging him on. "In exchange for some information, that is."

I pulled out the picture of the youngster and showed it to him.

"He's been missing a couple of days. Do you remember anything unusual?"

He looked like a wild animal that had come upon unexpected prey, though his eyes revealed his internal struggle. *'Is this a trap? If I look down to eat, will I be shot?'* He was right to be suspicious.

"There's nothing to fear," I said, trying to console him. "I'm not a cop."

It seemed to calm him. He took a good look at the photograph and nodded his head.

"Yes, I do remember something," he slurred.

I hung on his every word. He half-closed his eyes, took himself back to the specific moment and deleted the junk from his mind.

"It wasn't the boy that stood out, but the person who took him," he began to tell. "He was a well-dressed man, around thirty-five years of age and he smelled of cologne. He was very rude. I remember him well. He was no *gentleman*, whatever he looked like or whatever he was trying to prove."

"What gave you that impression?" I asked.

"I held out my hand for help. He stared at me, spat on the ground next to me and looked across the road. Instinctively, I watched his movements. He crossed the road, spoke to the young boy, took him by the hand and walked off with him. I assumed he was his father."

"Would you be able to recognise him if you saw him again?"

"Sure," he said. He was absolutely certain of it.

"Would you be able to describe him to the police, if necessary?" I continued.

"The police?" He leered at me. "That would cost extra."

"Naturally, I'd make it worth your while." He needed reassuring again.

"No need to worry then. Apart from that, he looked pretty malicious; I'd be very happy to see him behind bars."

True enough, with the help of police experts and the homeless guy's description, a photofit of the abductor was put together. Almost the entire police department took to the streets in search of the perpetrator but my mind was still mercilessly plagued with questions. If this was a kidnapping, the stranger should have contacted the boy's parents by now and demanded a ransom. But who would kidnap a boy from a poor family and why? What kind of ransom could he demand? It wasn't an abduction; I had a hunch this was something else. It troubled me deeply and I feared for Leonardo's life. My blood froze at the very thought of it because unfortunately, my suspicions were usually confirmed.

Two days later, the boy was found. He couldn't speak – the dead can't speak. The coroner confirmed he had been raped and then murdered. His body was then dismembered, several of his organs removed and, despite a meticulous search carried out by the police, were never found. It was now up to them to find the perpetrator.

A week later, after promising myself for the thousandth time to fire my secretary because she still couldn't make a decent cup of coffee, there was a knock on my office door. It was Mrs Da Vinci again. The police were overwhelmed with tough and urgent cases. Dozens of murders, rapes, robberies and violent attacks were waiting to be solved. The investigation into the Da Vinci case had gone cold and been left untouched, just like my coffee. The stuff my secretary called coffee was cold before it was served but the investigation into Leonardo's death was as hot as ever.

The coroner's verdict became the focus of my investigation. It didn't add up. Sex crimes were reasonably commonplace. Dismemberment was more unusual. Internal organs' going missing was very rare. Sex crime, dismemberment and missing internal organs all at the same time was almost unheard of. Why would anyone rape his victim, dismember him, and then get rid of his organs? Had I stumbled on a case of cannibalism?

I delved into the archives of various newspapers that same day. I came to the conclusion that Leonardo wasn't the only victim of such a heinous act. In the last year, seven similar murders of people of all ages had taken place in different parts of the country, but without sexual assault. In each case, the victim's internal organs had disappeared. The perpetrator or perpetrators were still at large. I knew the killings had a common denominator, but couldn't put my finger on it.

In the **affairs of love**, women always have the last word. It's impossible to get away with anything they're not open to or against. The man is a weak, helpless victim skillfully trapped in the woman's web to be devoured as and when it suits her. REASON would have it that women are LUCKY in love. The opposite was true for me but at least as far as my profession was concerned, luck had always been on my side. I was still alive, after all.

That morning, quite by chance, an alluring opportunity came my way and I wasn't going to miss out on it. It was up to me to turn on the charm.

As usual, on the way to my office, I stopped at the end of the block to buy a newspaper. Unusually, I made another stop. I might live dangerously but this wasn't another risk I was willing to take. As I've mentioned before, I'm hounded by bad luck where passion is concerned. It's like an ugly mole on the end of my nose. But the time had come for a little cosmetic surgery. I stopped at a cafe and bought – what else – a coffee. Black – no milk, no sugar. At last, I was in for the thrill of reading my newspaper and drinking a good cup of hot coffee at the same time.

I passed the coffee machine with a roguish smile on my face as I walked into the office. As usual, it was full of the brown stuff concocted by my secretary. I sat back in my comfy wooden chair and flipped through the pages of the newspaper, one by one. But my long-anticipated thrill would have to wait. My luck had failed again.

A piece of news grabbed my attention and a thought flashed through my mind like a bolt of lightning. Taking a sip of coffee, I jumped to my feet and cried with joy, spilling it all over me in the process. At last, I had found the first piece of the puzzle!

It was one of those news items that make you feel sad at first, or admire a fellow human being for his courage and strength. Sooner or later, you forget about it. A little girl had been hit by a car and died instantaneously. Her parents bravely donated her organs to the hospital and four people's lives were saved.

Intelligence is described as a person's ability to solve or suitably deal with problems as they occur through logical reasoning and effective use of insight. In practice, it is the ability to adapt to the demands of everyday life with the right attitude depending on the current situation. Thanks to my intelligence, once again, I was on very good form.

The magic word was _organs_. The ones that were missing from the victims I was investigating. It was highly likely that the killings were neither cannibalistic nor satanic, but linked to human organ trafficking. As gruesome as it sounded, it was probably the most credible explanation.

Ignoring the spilt coffee, which by now had soaked my favourite desktop items, I jumped into the first available taxi, did a deal with the driver and told him to take me to the headquarters of the organ donation agency. I asked for the person in charge and requested information about the number of members who had died in an accident or been killed in the last two years. A quick search on the computer sufficed. The number he came up with was horrific! Next, I followed up on the people the organs were donated to. There was a huge demand (and a thriving black market). The second critical piece of the puzzle was equally as impressive as the first. All the organs had been bought by a single institution, ironically called LIFE, and came from Iran and the Balkans. All I had to do now was find tangible evidence about this institution of death and the case was solved.

Personality can be described as a combination of an individual's mental and spiritual characteristics and behaviours that contribute to their uniqueness. They include mental and intellectual factors, emotional status, behavioural tendencies, character and temperament. Personality is shaped by a mixture of hereditary and environmental factors, particularly in early childhood.

Few of the characteristics of human personality are present at birth. Most develop according to the mental and social experiences of the individual. Complex genetic, environmental, social, and emotional factors determine whether an individual's personality develops normally and harmoniously or deviates from the norm and turns hostile.

I admit without doubt that I have several personality disorders as far as   social settings are concerned. I have been described by many as anti-social. In short, I'm at the bottom of the scale in terms of social prestige, but it doesn't bother me in the slightest. I couldn't give a damn. On the other hand, I stand out in my working environment and can hold my head high thanks to certain characteristics. I have learned to be responsible, discreet, methodical, headstrong and efficient. In a word: *professional.*

I took the sketch of Leonardo's killer. He still hadn't been found because, according to the police, the guy had no criminal record. I decided to try and gain access to the members of the Institute for LIFE. Some of them were bound to be suspicious. I didn't have a car so I rented a black Cadillac and set up camp outside the Institute. Day and night for a whole week, I photographed everyone who entered or left the building. After much effort, long nights and very little to eat, I got lucky once again.

Among the dozens of people who went in and out, no one fitted the profile, but I had no trouble recognising the infamous Dr Anne Bancroft, better known as Mrs Robinson. I knew she'd be able to provide me with information. It was as certain as death and taxes.

Memory is the mental process by which experiences from the past are revived and come to life. A certain movie came to mind when I saw Anne Bancroft's face and I was also reminded she owed me a big favour. Many years ago, she was involved in a case of child rape. Initially, she was blackmailed by the accusers, who tried to get her to pay a significant amount of money. She didn't succumb, however, and the dispute was taken to court. We all have our weaknesses, however big or small. *Mrs Robinson's* was fifteen-year-old boys. Aware of her weakness, it was easy to build a conspiracy around it. But in this particular case, she was innocent. That's when she came to me and asked for help. And I managed to bail her out without damaging her reputation.

I visited her at her villa.

"What a wonderful surprise!" she said, as soon as she set eyes on me.

"I'm not so sure about wonderful," I replied, "but a surprise, nevertheless."

Realising this was probably no ordinary visit, she suggested we retreat to the privacy of her office.

"What's this about?" she asked, getting swiftly down to business.

"I saw you going into the LIFE Institute," I bluntly replied.

"Since when has that been an offence?" she asked with an air of sarcasm.

"You're acting as if you don't know what's going on, so I'll help you out. I've discovered that LIFE is linked to the murders of various organ donors."

Her silence betrayed her guilt.

"How did you get in on a case like that?" she stammered after pausing for breath.

"It's like a ticking bomb," I explained. "A chain reaction."

"What do you mean by that?"

"I've taken on the case of an eleven-year-old boy who was raped, murdered and had his organs removed. My search for the culprit led me to the LIFE Institute, and I saw you go inside."

"Listen," she said, clearly nervous. "I have nothing to do with them whatsoever and I am not involved with any such thing. I want you to know that."

"That's good news," I said, trying to bring her round.

She insisted she was telling the truth.

"I have no reason to doubt you," I said, trying to calm her, "just tell me what you were doing there."

She walked across the room and opened the door to make sure no one was listening.

"What I'm about to tell you, you didn't hear from me, okay? And if you try to base your evidence on anything I say, I'll deny it all. I'm only doing this because I owe you a big favour."

"Go ahead!" I said, waiting with bated breath.

I couldn't have listened harder if I'd been *tapping* her phone.

"You're on the right track," she began. "It's true they did approach me and asked me to work with them. When you saw me go in there, it was to discuss the details."

I took a packet of cigarettes out of my pocket. I was about to light up when she took me by surprise.

"Smoking is forbidden here if you don't mind!"

I'd have to be patient if I wanted to hear what she had to say.

"From the start, I had no intention of working with them," she continued. I placed the cigarette back in the packet. "It seemed unavoidable at first but I came up with a good excuse and politely turned down their offer. They still threatened to *donate* my heart and kidneys to at least two people if I ever let on about the Institution, though."

It was clear she wouldn't be sharing the vital information I was looking for. I took the tin of eucalyptus-flavoured lozenges out of my pocket. The pastille slowly dissolved inside my mouth.

"They're great for the throat," I said. "The climate is awful, you know. I often get a dry mouth. These pastilles are very soothing. Would you like one?"

"No, thank you," she politely replied. "Oh, and I overheard something about your case that might be of interest to you." Again, she took me by surprise.

"Go ahead, I'm all ears." I begged her to continue.

"I was sitting outside the office, quite discreetly. I heard a couple of doctors talking about the child in your case. They didn't notice I was there. They were speaking in code. *The Messenger delivered the goods but he tried them out first.*' It stuck in my mind because it didn't add up with the reason I'd been asked to go there."

"How can you be sure we're talking about the same murder?"

She explained how it went on. *It's the first time someone seized the goods for sexual satisfaction. Remind me'* — said the other person — *'to make sure it was his last mission. Anyway, the organs will soon be frozen and safely stored in our facilities.'* I'd read about your murder case in the newspapers and when I overheard the conversation, I guessed what they were talking about."

"Did you hear any names, by any chance? Did they mention the name of the culprit?" I was anxious to find out more.

"No," she replied. I was disappointed. "They didn't mention the culprit at all. But they did say where the body went. I assumed the Messenger was to hand it over for the organs to be removed. He had to know what he was doing, whoever he was."

"A doctor, I presume?" I added.

"Spot on," she said, smiling at me.

"So, what else did you hear?"

She took a deep breath and carried on.

"*You should have seen Dr Price,'* said one of them, *'he was livid, shouting his head off at the Boss. They've gone too far this time, things are getting out of control. The killer's perverted desires have to be satisfied to keep up the supply. That's what it amounts to now. The Messenger will have to be punished,'* he said. Suddenly, the door opened, and when they turned to see who came out, they saw me sitting there. They went quiet and moved away."

"Dr Price?" I faltered, racking my brains for clues about the man in question.

"Yes. Dr Vincent Price," replied Anne Bancroft.

"How well do you know him?"

"Not very well. A good few years ago, someone died and it was his fault; that's all I know. After that, he stopped practising because they threw him out of the hospital he worked in and no one else would take him on. He was considered a genius in those days, I must admit," she enthused.

I didn't need to hear any more. I'd found another piece of the puzzle and by the look of it, it wouldn't be long before it was complete. Naturally, I didn't forget to thank her for the extremely useful information.

"So now we're quits," she said. "Remember that!"

I left her staring at me through the half-open door. I decided to visit the new member of the gang as soon as I left. I had an ace up my sleeve after all and it would be easy to prise the name of the killer out of him. I wasn't interested in anything else he'd done, anyway. The police would pick up on that. The same applied to the rest of the gang. I was being paid to find the killer. And for that alone. Nothing more, nothing less. But my luck was down. Dr Price was holding a Royal flush.

The butler answered the door and I handed him my credentials.

Albert Einstein
Private Detective
Solutions to problems of every kind
Except for the Theory of Relativity
Tough cases my speciality'

The butler showed me to the Doctor's office. I had a good look around while I waited. His wealth – but not of the opulent kind – was apparent, in both office décor and expertise. There were stacks of awards, diplomas and doctoral theses. The large, impressive bookcase was full of medical tomes but there wasn't a novel in sight.

"How can I help you?" A voice from behind distracted my attention. Captivated by my mini-investigation, I was not aware he had entered the room.

"By being honest," was my short, sharp reply. Leaving introductions aside, we got straight down to business.

"Are you saying I'm not?" He was obviously annoyed.

"I'm saying exactly what I mean," I replied, equally aggressively.

"And what makes you doubt my sincerity?" His tone was persistent.

"Intuition," I replied, walking up to him and distracting him for a moment. "I'm investigating a murder, you know." I spelt it out slowly and deliberately.

"And what makes you think I know anything about it?" he said, sarcastically.

"Reliable sources," I casually replied.

"Would you mind being more specific? I have work to be getting on with, you know."

"Have you heard about the rape and murder of an eleven-year-old boy who was subsequently dismembered?"

"Yes, I read about it in the newspapers."

"Then you will also know that some of his internal organs were removed."

"Yes, that's true. What are you implying?"

He was still aggressive.

"I would like to know the name of the killer."

"I understand it is your job to find that out," he reproached ironically, "but I am not a prophet. You are knocking on the wrong door."

He turned to leave but stiffened like a block of salt.

"My sources mentioned your name," I snapped.

A snakebite would have stunned him less. Staring at me in horror, he waited for my next move.

"It's said," I continued, in a game of cat and mouse, "that the killer worked for LIFE and they brought the body to you to remove its internal organs. And that you were angry with the *Me-ssen-ger.*"

I deliberately emphasised the last word, revealing I knew more than he imagined. He swallowed awkwardly.

"And if that was the case – although I'm sure it wasn't – what makes you think I'd admit to it?" he said, collecting himself.

"Your part in this crime is of no concern to me. All I am interested in is the supporting role played by the killer," I explained.

"Yes, but if the killer confesses to it, the investigation will lead to me."

"That's up to the police. Personally, I don't give a damn. And neither," I empathised, in an attempt to bring him round, "would it matter to me if you were to flee the country. As I said before, I have been paid to investigate a specific crime. I won't take it up with the system or the Institute for LIFE. I'm no hero and nobody's puppet, that's for sure."

He took a moment to weigh up my indirect proposal. In the end, he remained cautious.

"I'm sorry," he said, "I would like to help you, but I'm afraid I can't."

"Very well," I said as if it didn't matter, "you have my card. If you remember anything else or would like to tell me more about the case, call me. Goodbye."

"Farewell. I hope you get to the bottom of the case." What a hypocrite!

It was only a matter of time before he called me. I was certain he'd panic. He just needed time to weigh up my offer. It was to my advantage that I knew so much already and he had no idea who my sources were. But there was always the possibility he'd discussed my visit with the officials at the Institute for LIFE and it wouldn't be long before I was off the case. Against my wishes, of course.

As it happened, I wasn't far wrong. The last few days – and nights – must have been a nightmare for him, mulling it over, deciding on whether or not to call me. I was at my desk in my office when he telephoned. I had just refused my secretary's offer of a cup of coffee. She was amazed. The phone rang.

"Yes?" I said lethargically.

"May I speak to Mr Einstein?" said the voice on the end of the line. I recognised it immediately.

"Speaking, Dr Price," I replied as solemnly as I could, trying hard not to reveal my excitement.

"I have something to say that might interest you," said the Doctor, full of charm.

"I'm all ears," I replied, giving him my full attention. I popped a eucalyptus pastille inside my mouth, you know the reason why.

"But not on the telephone," he said with some urgency, "face to face."

"Say where and when and I'll be there."

"Do you know the subway station on Fourth Avenue?" he asked.

"I do," I said, though I was uncertain. Who cared? I could always look it up later.

"Be there at ten o'clock tonight. Make sure you come alone," he added, emphasising the last part.

"You can be absolutely sure of that," I assured him.

"And something else," he said before putting the phone down, "is this an amicable world we live in? And is it so by chance?"

What kind of question was that? I had no idea where that came from nor what he meant by it.

"Well, as far as I'm concerned," I loosely replied, "God probably isn't taking chances with the world."

"So what if he is?" he said, attempting to change the subject. He'd wanted to make a point but clearly regretted it. I thought he'd put down the phone but after a moment of silence, he continued.

"This hasn't been easy, you know. Refusing the job then exposing it to you like I am now."

"I understand." I wanted him to know I supported his difficult decision.

"You can't possibly understand." He was short and sharp. "And since you know more than enough already, I expect you are also aware of my unfortunate experience some time ago."

I acknowledged that I was. Dr Price went on.

"They fired me from the hospital and wouldn't take me on anywhere else so I lost my income. I had a family to take care of and bills to pay. How was I supposed to do that?"

"Do you think you made the right decision?" I asked with a dose of irony.

"You can afford to be cynical because you have no idea what it's like. I was desperate," he continued. "They knew that when they approached me. And because of it, they were easily able to persuade me. But they hid the truth from me at first, you should know that, too. They knew I'd caused that accident but still asked me to collaborate with them. They were adamant about my specific expertise and disagreed with the Authorities' verdict. They said it was ridiculous that one unfortunate mistake, which could have happened to anyone, should stand in the way of the brilliant career of an esteemed scientist. It was my Achilles Heel. And believe me, it was just what I needed to hear. On the other hand, they were cautious enough to conceal that the organs would not be procured by donation."

"When did you become aware of that?"

"A lot later, by which time it was too late to oppose. Listen, Mr Einstein, I'll give you what you need, but don't be fooled into thinking you've achieved success if the Institute for LIFE falls apart. There are dozens of other institutions all over the world, you know. Some keep patients in a *vegetative* state until specific orders come in. Others are supplied by the homeless in underdeveloped countries such as Africa, Asia, Latin America, even Europe or by kids on the streets with no next of kin. There is an inexhaustible global supply of organs covered up by legally protected, powerful people, people who wouldn't hesitate to use a significant amount of violence to remain anonymous. It's impossible to defeat them all, you know."

Though stunned by his revelation, I composed myself and returned to the conversation.

"I've already told you, I'm not trying to play the hero. I was paid to solve a specific case and I have to see it through to the end."

"Very well, you've made your point. I hope it's true and you won't turn against me after what I've told you today. As we said," he continued, referring to our arrangement, "tonight, at ten o'clock."

I still hadn't got the information I was looking for. The questions simply multiplied. But I never got to meet Dr Price, anyway. He committed suicide at the subway station as I wrote at the beginning of this tale.

Thinking it through step by step, I tried to piece together what had happened. Dr Price had probably attempted to find out who my informant was and failed. In conversation with the Boss, he casually referred to a visit from a detective but didn't mention my name. If he had, I'd be dead by now. Assuming they were keen to do away with him, he probably threatened to expose them, infuriating them even more. As a result, they threatened him with even greater brutality. Once he'd made up his mind to have nothing more to do with them, he called me, making plans to flee the country at the same time. Otherwise, he wouldn't have agreed to talk. If the police searched his pockets, I'm sure they found his getaway ticket, though no one will ever know what made him take his life.

Perhaps they were trying to silence him and he got scared. It was a Catch-22 situation and suicide, he thought, was the only way out. They might have been watching his every move and warned he'd never escape them, even if he fled the country. He was doomed from the moment he opened up to me. Finally, they might even have threatened his family – the most likely scenario, as far as I am concerned. How could they live in fear of being constantly exposed to danger?

What did it matter now anyway? He couldn't exactly tell me, could he? I was back where I started – right at the very beginning. Fortunately, I remembered my step-father's advice: *'One piece of evidence is worthier than a thousand theories.'* And this wasn't any old evidence.

Among the functions of the **Mind** are consciousness, perception, thought, judgment and memory. Mind and body are two aspects of a fundamental and inseparable entity. To me, they are diametrically opposed and evoke diametrically opposed emotions. I don't feel great about my body, but the Mind, my mind, I'm especially proud of.

Sitting comfortably in my office chair and reviewing the series of events, I was amazed by my intelligence. Many would claim this to be narcissistic but personally, I don't agree. I consider myself objective enough to distinguish my strengths from my weaknesses.

After two swigs of Jack Daniels, I took a cassette from the back of the third drawer of my desk. It looked like any other cassette on the outside. More interesting was what was recorded on it. Two voices: Dr Price's and my own. I'm of the old school, by the way, as you might have noticed. I never got on with technology and still have a phone that records conversation. Yes! I recorded our conversation. After the Doctor's death, the recording would be an invaluable piece of evidence in the case against LIFE.

I took a wooden box from the top left-hand drawer of my desk. It contained Havana cigars hermetically sealed at a constant temperature of 18-20 degrees Celsius and a humidity level of 65%. The Spanish words hecho a mano (handmade) were stamped in green on the top, confirming they were authentic. The box was decorated with coloured lithographs. Robusto cigars are my favourite – suitable for celebrations and contemplation. I insist on Havana cigars of course, for their unsurpassable, excellent taste.

I didn't smoke cigars very often. Only on rare occasions. My financial situation wouldn't allow it. Smoking cigars is the epitome of sensory satisfaction, uniting the subtle nuance of taste with the more modest, refined blissfulness of the Mind. It is a ritual that leads to ecstasy. To properly light a cigar, it must be perfectly rolled at the rounded end - not too tight and not too loose.

I took a Robusto out of the wooden box, put it in my mouth for a few seconds and then lit up, drawing on it several times. I put my feet up on the desk, exhaled the smoke and smiled. It was easy to picture what would happen next. I hand over the cassette to the prosecutor, who orders the police to conduct an in-depth inquiry. During the investigation, the underground role of the Institute for LIFE is ascertained and from then on, Leonardo's killer is easy to trace. The police arrest him and the case is closed. I get paid and... *'live happily ever after'*.

Determined to avoid any hitches should the case be closed, (if the prosecutor turned out to be one of them, for instance), I made sure a digital copy of the recorded conversation was sent to WikiLeaks, the international non-profit organisation founded by Julian Assange, bless him! The organisation is managed by *Sunshine Press* and publishes leaks and documents from anonymous sources on its website, which, under normal circumstances, would never see the light of day. It was highly likely to cause a stir and the truth would be revealed. That was certain.

The police investigation and subsequent interrogation, alongside the witness accounts and apprehension of suspects, proved that the mastermind of the criminal organization was none other than the president of the Institute for LIFE, Dr Adolf Hitler. Hitler had hired – in exchange for a hefty sum – a group of highly skilled doctors who specialised in organ transplants and the institute quickly became popular with patients in need of them. Made rich by clients from all over the world, most were famous international jet-setters – artists, politicians, heads of state, sheikhs, kings, tycoons and such.

Before long, there was a shortage of organ donations. Clients who couldn't wait turned to other institutions. Bankruptcy was inevitable. It was then that he devised his monstrous plan. Groups of people he could rely on were established worldwide to gather information about potential organ donors. Killers were recruited and provided with the details of each of their *victims*. Most of the deaths were made to look like accidents, disappearance or anything that would not arouse the suspicions of the secret services and with the assistance of a network of loyal coroners who *'covered up'* the removal of the organs.

But fate struck – they killed Leonardo and his mother hired me. Obviously, I am Adolf Hitler's new target and despite being in prison, there is one thing I know he is capable of. The organisation may have fallen apart but finding a new accomplice to do a 'deal' with will be no trouble for him, however much it costs. The final deal with the Messenger, who'll deliver the goods for the last time. In other words, me.

So I'm changing my profession. I'm going to become a writer and tell my story. A stupid story or a figment of my imagination, some might claim. Others may even admire me. Who knows? It could turn out to be a bestseller and bring me fame and fortune.

I have already changed my identity and am sure you'll never find me. After much deliberation, I decided on an ordinary name. I thank you for your kindness and patience in reading this book to its end and for that, dear Reader, the truth will be revealed. But I beg you from the bottom of my heart to respect the secrecy of my new identity. Do not reveal it to anyone. My life depends on you now.

After days and nights of scanning the globe for possible destinations and driving travel agents to distraction with never-ending questions, I eventually decided to learn the Greek language and take up residence in Greece. In Thessaloniki, to be precise. I now wish to be known as *Gianis Athanasiou Totonidis*. Please don't try and find me and thank you in advance for keeping my secret.

P.S. The famous personalities who lend their names to the fictional characters in this story have NOTHING in common with them. Any resemblance is purely coincidental.

P.P.S. The title of this short story is inspired by the title of a poem written by a great – possibly the greatest – figure of both poetry and prose – Edgar Allan Poe. A pioneering man, an authentic genius with an inconceivable mind and for whom I have the greatest admiration and respect. Every word of his allegorical verse resonates like a tolling bell in a graphic environment and discloses the derailment of the human race.

Forgive me for my disrespect, arrogance, and sacrilege. I have undoubtedly disturbed the peaceful sleep of the magnificent literary ORIGINATOR. Like him, *I do not aspire to artistic compensation or humanity's feeblest approval.* My pure and sole intention is to honour this UNIQUE GIANT OF WORDS.

About The Author

Gianis Athanasiou Totonidis lives in Thessaloniki. From an early age he loved *explosions*, and fearing he would one day blow up the family home, his parents persuaded him to study Chemistry (he graduated from the Aristotle University of Thessaloniki). His *'explosive'* mind led him to explore the Seventh Art (Cinematography).

He studied Direction and is a member of the Greek Directors Guild (E.E.S.) and the Federation of European Film Directors (F.E.R.A.). He is also a Film Critic and member of the Panhellenic Association of Film Critics (P.E.K.K.), the International Federation of Film Critics (FIPRESCI) and the Hellenic Film Academy. Since 1991, he has been writing articles for various publications and digital magazines. Former Music Producer, Radio and Television Editor of Film Review Productions, and Television Presenter of Film Review Shows.

More recently, he has taken up writing, experimenting with *'explosions' of inspiration*. In the last year he has participated in various competitions in the genre of Terror and has been distinguished in the most of them (8 awards in 9 competitions).

Finally, since September 2019, he has been studying a Master on Creative Writing (specifically in Film Screenwriting & Television).

www.ingramcontent.com/pod-product-compliance
Lightning Source LLC
Chambersburg PA
CBHW061504120726
48001CB00004B/1206